TWO SHARPE

Ryan Hunter

Published in Great Britain by Keystone Literary in 2019.

ISBN: 9781791562175

CONTENTS

This book is dedicated to John and E and our long afternoons and evenings playing spies and watching grown people play them on our TVs.

CHAPTER ONE

Shelly slams the door and wheels on Dr. Landsin, her long, fiery hair flowing as she flips it over the shoulder of her black skintight cat-suit. Her face is set, her eyes scanning the small closet for anything they can use to barricade the door.

"Well," Dr. Landsin says, "it seems you've run out of ideas."

"That's what you said in the lab AND the laundry room AND the conservatory where you tried to take us both out with that candlestick."

"I panicked. I've already apologized about that."

"Well, how about a little faith now, Doc?"

"I would love to have faith but that requires hard, empirical evidence. Frankly, all I can see is that you've trapped us in a small, enclosed room with no way out."

"No way out, eh?" a voice asks from the other side of the drywall. Shelly smiles at the wall as the sound of a rip cord causes an engine to sputter twice and die. "Hang on," the voice says. The cord is pulled again and again the engine sputters twice and dies. "Dammit."

"Did you prime it, Babe?" Shelly asks.

"Of course I primed it, I'm the tech guy. Do you think I would forget a step as simple as… oh, hang on."

"You didn't prime it, did ya?"

"No, I didn't prime it. But, to be fair, it's a silly two cycle engine, it's hardly what I would call tech."

"It's beneath you, Babe."

"Don't patronize." The cord is pulled once more and the engine springs to life this time. "I don't know if you've backed up yet but, if you haven't, now would be a good time!" Spacer, the owner of the voice behind the wall, yells over the sound of the machine. A moment later the blade of a circular saw cuts through the wall and, a few moments after that, a respectable door stands where once there was only plaster.

Spacer cuts the engine on the saw and steps through the opening. "Why, hells bells, madam," Spacer says, laying on a thick, antebellum drawl, "I just can't remember the last time I laid my eyes on you."

1

"Well, I'm right here, Honey Bunch, you just go ahead and lay those eyes on me."

"What is this?" Dr. Landsin asks. "Is this a bit that you do? Are the two of you doing a bit right now?"

"Oh," Spacer says, grimacing at him. He turns to Shelly, "Nervous fellow?"

"God, I could tell you some stories." She cuts her eyes to Dr. Landsin, "They begin with a candlestick!"

"How many times must I apologize?"

"I'll let you know when you're getting close."

"Could we please have this conversation at another place and in another time?" Dr. Landsin asks. "There are men out there trying to kill us."

"They're in here!" a guard yells as a bullet shoots through the closet door so close to Dr. Landsin's head that it fluffs his hair.

"Well, the man has a point," Spacer says, curling his arm around the back of the fainting doctor. He drags him through the opening in the wall, pulling at the crotch of his own body suit. "I hate these things."

"But they make your ass look so good," Shelly says.

"They couldn't make them a little more comfortable?"

"They aren't that bad."

"Yeah, you don't have anything crotch related to worry about."

"And you do?"

Spacer smiles at her, clips a device hanging from a cable to Landsin's belt and says, "Dr. Landsin, DR. LANDSIN!" He pats the man's cheek a time or two until the doctor is revived into semi-consciousness.

"Wha...?" the confused doctor asks. "Where are we? Is this one of the exhaust shafts?"

"Yeah," Spacer says. "It was super nice of you guys to run these all along the building. Escape routes are so rarely provided by the bad guys."

"We have them so the exhaust from the machine can escape."

"I know!" Spacer says, jumping giddily. "They all have

really big grates at the top, you may as well have put a big sign reading "Break in here, Spacer!"

"Have you thought about what might happen if the machine turns on and this space fills with noxious fumes?"

"Oh, I wouldn't worry about that. I may have trouble turning on simple machines from time to time but I never have trouble turning complex ones off for good."

"Gentlemen, have you forgotten the heavily armed guards coming for us as we speak?" Shelly asks.

"Oh right," Spacer says before turning back to the scientist. "Dr. Landsin, you're going to go up now."

"What... I am?"

"Yes," Spacer says, pressing a button on the device he'd clipped to the man's belt. It starts a motor inside the small box spinning and sends it climbing the thin cable attached to the top of the five-story shaft they are standing in. Landsin starts to protest as he is yanked upward as he is once more overcome by a faint and he disappears from sight.

"So," Shelly says, stepping through the opening, "you have a way of getting me up, I trust."

"Don't I always?" Spacer asks, broadening his grin. He holds up another device.

"There's just one."

"But it has two hooks," Spacer says, pressing a button so that a hook protrudes from either side.

"You've got me hooked," Shelly says, stepping up to him and wrapping her arms around his waist.

"Well, I've... um..."

"It's okay, you'll come up with a good one later," Shelly says, kissing him on the nose. She hooks the device onto their belts and hits the button, shooting them up to the top of the shaft where the scientist hangs limply.

Spacer nods toward Dr. Landsin, "You wanna deal with him while I get the crane?"

"Nuts to that, I've had him all evening. I'll get the crane, you take care of Mr. Dangles."

"But that means..."

"I know, just don't get used to it." She pecks him quickly on the lips and knocks a grate from the wall next to her. She hoists herself off of the hook and out through the narrow opening. Spacer watches for a moment as she climbs deftly down the arm of the crane they'd parked next to the building earlier. The leather of her form fitting suit conforms to her body so that Spacer has to take a deep breath and clear his thoughts as he watches.

She stops and looks around. Spacer looks out as well, no one has spotted her, what's she doing? She reaches carefully for her phone and presses a few buttons without looking. Spacer's phone vibrates, and he pulls it from his pocket to read her text.

STOP LOOKING AT MY ASS, PERV

Spacer chuckles and turns back to the dangling doctor. "Hey," he says, tapping Dr. Landsin. "Hey, wakey-wakey."

The tapping starts the doctor swaying and he jerks into awareness. "Wha…" he says. "Where…"

Spacer grabs the man by his collar and pulls him closer until they are both nose to nose. It's such a grotesque parody of the position he was just in with Shelly that he almost has to laugh in the man's face.

"What are you doing man?" the scientist asks.

"I need you to look into my eyes right now," Spacer says. "Look at nothing else but my eyes."

"I seem to have very little choice in the matter," Dr. Landsin says, jerking his head from side to side trying to move away from Spacer's piercing gaze. Spacer doesn't allow him, twisting the cable and bobbing his own head so that the doctor is never allowed to look at anything but his eyes.

"Doc, I seriously need you to stop that. I can make you unconscious but that means I have to carry you the rest of the way. My back has been acting up a little and I can't promise you won't be dropped."

"Well, I… dropped? What do you mean dropped?"

"All right. I'm going to say some words now and you are only going to hear some of them, believe me, I've done this before. The words I need you to hear first off are, you're going to be fine."

"Fine? Why would I think I was anything other than fine?" Dr. Landsin says, twisting more desperately trying to look at anything but Spacer.

"Stop… stop it… Doctor I need you to…" Spacer reaches up and flicks Dr. Landsin hard on the left nostril.

"Ow! My word," the doctor says, cupping a hand over his wounded nose.

"I'm sorry, but you were becoming hysterical."

"I think a slap is more traditional."

A motor cranks outside and soon a large hook appears through the opening left when Shelly knocked out the grate.

"Okay, that's our ride," Spacer says.

"Our ride, why do we need a ride from a crane? Where in blazes are we?"

"Remember when I said you're only going to hear some of the words I'm about to say?"

"Yes."

"These are those words; we're dangling five stories above concrete flooring and now we have to get on that crane hook before we're found and shot to death."

"I… wha… I…" Dr. Landsin begins to wobble and Spacer slaps him hard across the face. "No, no, I'm still with you," he says, rubbing his cheek.

"You're right, that was better."

Gunfire erupts from below and Shelly yells, "Hello, chatty boys, how about we come down now?"

Spacer grabs the crane hook and holds it out to Landsin. "Step on this."

Landsin puts a shaking foot on the hook and Spacer puts his own sure foot next to it. He wraps his left arm around the scientist and whispers, "May want to duck now," as he releases the devices from their belts and they swing outside, Dr. Landsin cracking his head smartly on the wall as they swing. "I did tell you to duck," Spacer says.

A bullet ricochets off the chain supporting them and the doctor sways. "Hey hey, stay with me, Doc. Remember my back, you are not allowed to faint," Spacer warns. He looks down to the cab of the crane where Shelly is busily kicking a guard in the face while maintaining a barrage of machinegun fire to keep the other guards at bay. "Any time you want, babe. We're sort of sitting ducks up here."

"Yeah, well if you could have wrapped up your tea party in the sky a little sooner we wouldn't be in this situation right now," she says, turning and slamming her right foot into the nose of a guard trying to climb into the cab through the window before pivoting and kicking a leaver which starts the crane turning slowly.

"Ah!" Spacer yells.

"What, what is it?" Dr. Landsin asks.

"Nothing, I just got a little shot there," Spacer says through gritted teeth, reaching into the holster at the small of his back and pulling a large pistol. "But I do think I'll return fire now."

"Where were you shot?" Dr. Landsin asks as Spacer takes aim at the guard who got him.

"Upper thigh," Spacer says, firing at the man causing him to fall and the doctor to scream and cover his ears. "Oh, yeah, this gun's pretty loud, Colt, .44 semi."

"What did you say?" Dr. Landsin says, his ears still ringing?

"I said I think I've fallen in love with you."

"Huh?"

"Hee hee."

"Are you giggling?"

Spacer aims his gun at another guard but the doctor jerks and tries to look over Spacer's shoulder, twisting them on their perch and causing the bullet meant for the man with the AK 47 to instead lodge in the cab of the crane very near Shelly's head.

"All right, you do that once more and we are not stopping for ice cream on the way home," Shelly yells as she fits a new clip into her gun before elbowing yet another guard in the throat.

"Hey, Doc, how about you not cause me to shoot my wife, at least not until she's gotten us down from the crane, huh?"

"Your upper thigh? Do you mean the posterior?"

"Yes, I was shot in the ass. Lucky thing, lot of meat, little muscle... well, not that much meat... I mean there are certainly men with a lot more meat there… take yourself for example." This time Spacer fires and takes down a man taking aim at Shelly.

"Hey, you owe me one, babe," Spacer yells.

"Yeah, I'll deduct it from the thirty I've taken out that were about to shoot you," Shelly says.

"I love you!"

"You damn well better." Shelly stops shooting long enough to pull the leaver stopping the crane's rotation and slam the button which begins the slow decent of the hook toward an awaiting pile of brush.

Another bullet ricochets off the chain above the two men, this time causing a break in one of the links.

"Uh oh," Spacer says.

"Uh oh? What is this uh oh?" the doctor asks.

"Nothing," Spacer says. He turns to the cab, "Honey Bunch?"

"Yes, my love?" Shelly asks as she works one arm around the neck of a guard which has actually made his way into the cab and is trying to wrestle her into submission.

"Any way you could speed this up just an eensey weensey bit? Our chain is about to break and cause us to plummet to our deaths." Spacer's voice is calm, almost a sing song, as if he were asking her to stop off and pick up dry cleaning on her way home.

"It's always something with you, isn't it?" Shelly asks. She kicks her leg up and wraps her thigh around the man's neck freeing her hand. She grabs a dial and begins to turn it when the man bucks and, instead of the quarter turn she'd been trying for, she turns the dial all of the way.

Spacer and Dr. Landsin free fall toward the brush. "Perhaps a little less weensey!" Spacer yells just before disappearing into the foliage.

Shelly scissors her legs, breaking the man's neck and then stares at the brush. "Come on, baby," she says to herself, her slate grey eyes staring into the now broken leaves as if she could will herself X-ray vision. "Come on, let me know you're okay."

Twelve cylinders roar to life under the leaves and a Ferrari bursts out onto the field. Shelly releases a sigh, turns and shoots three more guards in the head. "That's my guy."

Spacer pulls the car alongside the crane and Shelly jumps into Dr. Landsin's lap. "Gracious!" he yells.

"Sorry, Doc, there's just two seats. Consider yourself lucky I didn't let him work the crane."

Spacer throws the car into gear and peels away from the crane. The guards scatter toward their respective vehicles but Shelly fires a volley into each of their cars, flattening tires and destroying engines. Each burst from the gun brings a fresh tear to the eyes of Dr. Landsin.

When, at last, they are on the open road and she is certain none of the guards has followed them, Shelly turns around and collapses into the seat as if there weren't a world-renowned scientist beneath her.

"I'm certain I have suffered at least partial permanent hearing loss," Dr. Landsin says.

"Yup," Shelly says, "that'll happen." She rolls her head to look at Spacer. "So, you took long enough getting the car going."

"Couldn't find the keys."

"They're in the visor, they're always in the visor."

"Well, I remembered that eventually."

"Can we stop? I fear I'm going to vomit," Dr. Landsin asks.

"No!" Spacer yells.

"Oh yes we can, he's not blowing chunks all over me. Besides, it's my turn to drive," Shelly says.

"We'll stop, but you aren't driving," Spacer says, pulling over to the side of the road. Dr. Landsin scrambles out of the open car and crawls into the bushes retching. Shelly gets out as well and walks around to the driver's side.

"Come on, hop out. You know I'm the better driver."

"The hell you say. Besides, I reminded you when you wanted to do the crane and you said you were okay with it."

"Yes, and you got to drive, and I was okay with it, now I'm not. Seriously, hop out… is that blood?"

"Where?"

"All over the seat," Shelly says, pointing beneath him.

"Oh, yeah, I got shot."

"What? Where?"

"Back there, on the crane," Spacer says, grinning.

Shelly punches him in the arm, Spacer stops grinning and rubs his shoulder. "Seriously, where were you shot?"

"In the ass."

"Which cheek, the good one or the bad one?"

"It was the… wait, I have a good one and a bad one?"

"Yes, you didn't know?"

"No, how would I know, I don't really check out my own ass. What makes them different?"

"Just, which one, right or left?"

"Left."

"Dammit!"

"Seriously?"

"Yes! Now the good one has a hole in it. This is why we can't have nice things. Wait a minute, your left or mine?"

"Mine, it's my ass."

"Oh, okay then."

"Really? Everything's fine now?"

"Yeah, it's all good." Shelly hops back into the passenger seat. Spacer stares at her. "What? I mean we'll get you fixed up."

"Thanks, it's so good to know you care."

"I think I'm done vomit…" Dr. Landsin says before cupping his hands over his mouth and ducking back into the bushes. "Never mind," he moans.

"So," Spacer says. "Where's the vacay this time?"

"Oh, I don't know. Maybe we should just stay home. The store needs our attention. We have that new shipment of Ted & Stuff coming in and those just will not stay on the shelf."

"It's a quality book," Spacer agrees. "But it'll be there when we get back. You can't break with tradition; every time we complete a mission we go somewhere and recuperate. I've got a new hole in my ass, I really need a vacation after this one."

"Haven't you noticed how every time we go to some exotic locale we wind up getting mired in another case that's more daunting than the one from which we're recuperating?"

"Do we? I honestly hadn't noticed," Spacer shrugs. "Okay, so this time we'll stay more local. But Im'ma get me a month on a beach with rum."

Shelly sighs. "All right, but I'll pick the beach."

"Perfect, I'll pick the rum."

"I really think I'm better this time," Dr. Landsin says. He looks at Shelly and says, "Shall we get back into our former positions?"

"Mm, nope, I'm pretty comfy," Shelly says.

"But, where am I meant to sit? There are only two seats?"

Shelly and Spacer glance back at the small area behind the two seats just big enough for a largish briefcase.

"You can't be serious," Dr. Landsin says.

"I could pop the trunk for you," Spacer says. "But I think there's more room behind the seats."

"Really, I must object to…"

"Look, it's the crawl space or you're thumbing it. Now make a choice, we aren't totally out of the woods yet, Mr. E's goons could still find us."

"Very well," Dr. Landsin says, crawling behind the seats. "But I'll be lodging a complaint with your superiors."

"You're welcome to try, mine's sitting directly to my right and, to talk to hers, you kinda need a priest and an altar."

"You know, sometimes you say the sweetest things," Shelly says, leaning over and kissing Spacer hard on the mouth. She runs her hand around behind him and squeezes.

"Oh, hey, whoa, no!" Spacer yells.

"Oh, right, the bullet. Sorry," Shelly says.

CHAPTER TWO

Mystery strides across the stage, his body slicing through the machine generated fog as cleanly as his thirty blades have just sliced into his lovely assistant, Tiffany. Or so it would appear they have. He turns, abruptly raises his arms and, as she does at this point three times a week and twice on Saturday, Tiffany springs unharmed from the impaled basket.

The crowd erupts in applause. Sometimes the old chestnuts are the best. At least until they get to the grand finale, that has to be very special.

Mystery turns as the 25,000 gallon tank slides onto the stage, carrying with it, Susie, the Great White shark. Mystery turns toward the shark tank and allows himself a brief smile as the expected "Oooohhhhhh," rises from the crowd at the sight of Susie.

When he turns again the expression on his face is grim. The spotlight blinds him but his eyes, adjusted from years on the stage, beam out at them, each person thinking that he is speaking directly to him or her. Though he cannot see a single face he knows this audience; the elderly couple who have taken refuge in his theater between rounds with the slot machines, the teenage boys who were hoping to take advantage of his darkened theater to feel up their young girlfriends, the tourists who thought Vegas might be a cheap fun getaway, he knows them all, and he knows that, regardless of their reason for being there, they are all now staring in rapt attention as Susie circles in her tank, splashing water from time to time upon the dusty boards of the stage.

"For years man has striven to rule the elements," Mystery says in the same dread filled voice he has used to deliver this line for so many months. "He has conquered the land and the air and he'd like to lay claim to the sea as well." Dramatic pause as the music swells and the lights track across the stage. "But one creature still stands in his way." The music dips to a low, predatory rumble and the spotlight shifts from Mystery to the tank, giving the audience their first real glimpse of the killer in the tank. "The Great White Shark, the only creature to rival man for the top of the food chain." This is, of course, total shit. Man has no rival on the food chain and these people well know that, but Mystery's deep baritone, coupled with the sight of Susie becoming agitated by the music has them wondering.

"Today, one man is going to prove, once and for all, who is master of this world." The spot light returns to Mystery as he glares out at the audience, his blue eyes piercing to their very core. "Who is that man you ask?" He smiles, his brilliant, white, perfect smile. "Well, that… is a mystery."

The applause erupts as if the audience were cued to do so. Mystery turns dramatically and walks off stage as Tiffany and the equally distracting Veronica prance in leotards in front of the tank.

Mystery nods at Barry, his look-alike, as he passes the foot of the staircase leading to the top of the tank, the staircase strategically placed so that it starts just out of view of the audience. Mystery grimaces a bit at the idea that this bucktoothed and, honestly, way too short nerd could ever be mistaken for him, but he does have a wig very similar to Mystery's hair and Tiffany and Veronica are both out there, doing their job to draw the eye away from the man at the tank. Still, since hiring Barry, Mystery made certain that the lighting at the top of the tank was as poor as it could be and still allow the audience to see that somebody was, in fact, about to jump into the tank with the fish.

Barry smiles back at the magician and makes his way up the staircase to the tank. Mystery takes three steps away from the stage when Rachel steps forward with a bucket of water and douses him. He gasps. No matter how many times she does it, it always surprises him.

"You know, the bucket doesn't have to be kept in the fridge," he tells her.

"I like for it to be authentic," she says with a smile.

"I think you're beginning to enjoy your work a bit too much."

Rachel shrugs and nods to the microphone mounted to the back-stage wall. Mystery waits until Barry is standing at the very edge of the tank holding his arms up and says into the mic, "And now I must ask for your complete silence as I plunge into the waters and pit myself against this, the king of the sea."

Silence falls over the crowd, just as it always does. One thing he could say about his audiences, they were obedient little sheep.

Mystery flips off the mic as Barry struts along the edge of the tank. Mystery sprints toward the steps leading to the lobby. As he mounts the first step of the three flights he hears the crowd gasp and knows that Barry has jumped into the tank with Susie. Of course, the crowd does not know that Barry is actually jumping into a part of the tank safely divided from the shark by a very thick yet transparent glass divider. All they see is a man and a shark.

As he rounds the second flight, he hears the music cue that always accompanies the cut to the video showing a shark, no longer Susie, attacking a man, neither Barry nor himself, who fights back with all of his might. The video is cobbled together with a little bit of actual video and special effects that would be the envy of any blockbuster director and it is quite a gripping portrayal of man versus beast projected from an LCD screen embedded in the front of the shark tank. At first Mystery had thought about saving money on the care and keeping of the shark and only having the image on the screen but it lacked authenticity. People were willing to believe the image of the shark only after seeing the actual thing. By now Susie is on the bottom of the tank eating whatever sea creature her caretaker has released into her part of the tank and Barry is sitting on his side of the glass at the bottom with an oxygen tank and weight belt waiting patiently for the curtain to close so that he can climb out a tad pruny but, otherwise, no worse for wear.

Mystery, for his part, has reached the lobby and is sprinting to the staircase to the balcony which is always reserved for a very special patron who, for one reason or another, never seems to make it to the show.

He hears the shriek from the audience which lets him know

the screen has just gone completely red with blood and he takes the balcony steps two at a time. He reaches the top and ducks behind the first of two heavy curtains. He stops for half a moment to catch his breath and then slides past the second curtain into the balcony box in time to see Tiffany and Veronica running around in front of the tank, screaming as if they've just missed the last copter out of Saigon.

Mystery rolls his eyes remembering how, three weeks ago during a special show for the Boy Scouts of America it was at exactly this point that Tiffany's top had decided to let go and make men scouts of all of those boys. Since then he had insisted on three times the double sided tape and made sure to yank on both of their leotards until he was certain they could withstand an earthquake registering at least 6.5 on the Richter scale before allowing them to set foot on the stage.

Mystery watches as the red magically clears and the audience sees nothing but a tank of clear blue water, no man and no shark. He glances at the blue Igloo cooler at his feet and flips off the lid to reveal the head of a shark. Not a Great White, they are endangered, but one close enough to fool all but the most observant of marine biologists.

He hoists the head from its cooler and grimaces. Since he started this act he'd been through maybe two dozen heads, they go bad surprisingly quickly and, from time to time, a fan beats the stage hand to them and goes home with a unique souvenir, and each time they have to get a new one it seems twice as heavy as the last.

Probably Rachel's idea of a funny joke, Mystery thinks to himself.

Just as it seems Tiffany and Veronica are about to faint from amazement, Mystery, un-miked, yells, "DO not fret ladies," as the spotlight shines upon him. He pauses long enough for every head in the theater to turn in his direction and continues. "In the battle of man versus beast..." he hoists the sharks head above his shoulders, harder every time there's a new one, and says, "Man is victorious."

He throws the head from the balcony into the aisle and it splats with a satisfying squishing sound. Is it gratuitously gross? Absolutely. But that is the point after all. It makes the entire thing seem that much more real. It also has the appealing effect of drawing every single eye from him to the floor and, by the time the crowd puts together what they've seen and looks back to the balcony, Mystery has vanished. One last little bit of magic for them to walk away with.

Cleaning his hands with a handy wipe Mystery walks down the back staircase toward his dressing room/office. He passes Tiffany, naked save for the G-string covering only enough of her to guard against accidental pregnancy. Mystery's eyes scan over her. Unsheathed, her breasts are beginning to sag and the first signs of cellulite are appearing above the scant fabric covering her vagina. Pity that.

"You've got to do something about the shark," she says.

"I do?" Mystery asks, his tone imparting that he is already bored with this particular conversation.

Unheeding, Tiffany presses, "We are both tired of smelling like low tide after every show."

Mystery arches an eyebrow. "Both? Should I assume you are referring to yourself and your downcast bosom?"

Tiffany gasps and studies her chest for moment. "What do you mean downcast?"

"When you were hired your tits looked me straight in the eyes, now they're like a couple of orphans asking for seconds on gruel."

"They are not..." she begins, but facts are cruel and the evidence is apparent. "We're not here about my boobs, we're here about the shark!" she says.

"And you've yet to establish a 'we' either."

Tiffany looks around herself, realizing the she's all alone before her boss. "Oh, that bitch!" she blurts.

Mystery reaches a hand out and gently bounces her left breast. "I wouldn't concern myself too much about the smell, dear." he says. "I don't think you'll be putting up with it much longer."

"Oh, that is... you are..." she turns and stomps away from him, the jiggle in her ass more prominent than he'd remembered at her audition as well. "Where the fuck is Veronica?" she screams as she turns the corner and Mystery loses sight of her.

Before he can continue, Barry steps in front of him, rubbing a towel through his sodden hair. Barry too is only partially dressed, clad in only a pair of hot pink boxers and, like Tiffany, has started to let himself go. Tiffany's flaws could be hidden with the right leotard though, Barry had to appear on stage bare-chested and is meant to be a double for Mystery himself. Even with the lights and fog of the spectacle, it won't be long before people begin to suspect shenanigans when the toned abdominals of Mystery are replaced by the beer gut Barry is developing.

What the hell are we feeding these cows?" Mystery thinks to himself.

"Great show, huh boss?"

"Yes," Mystery says, unable to tear his eyes away from the bulge above Barry's straining waistband. "Why don't you see me in my office in half an hour? I've got a few ideas we need to go over."

"Ideas? You and me?" Barry asks, a goofy grin spreading over his face.

"Yes, you and I," Mystery says.

"I'll be there, half an hour, you got it," Barry says, before running off toward the large dressing room reserved for all of the lovely assistants.

Mystery steps into his dressing room and strips his sopping clothing away, tossing them in a pile in the corner for Rachel to collect.

As usual, she storms in just behind him and rolls her eyes when he turns unabashedly toward her. "Just once I'd like to write, 'Did not see Mystery's penis today,' in my diary."

"Maybe if you learned to knock."

"Really? You're actually saying that would make a difference?"

"Probably not." Mystery slips into a robe and cinches the belt around his waist.

"We need to lose the shark," Rachel says.

Mystery sighs. "Susie fills the seats," he says.

"But it takes the revenue from over half those seats to feed and house her."

"We've discussed this. Anything else?"

"Yeah, he's here."

"He?" Mystery asks but the look in her eye tells him all he needs to know. "Why is he here?"

Rachel shrugs. "I guess you'll have to ask. I'm not supposed to have anything to do with him, remember?"

"That's for your protection."

"Uh huh. Should I show him in?"

"Yes."

Rachel turns to leave but Mystery stops her as her hand touches the doorknob. "Rachel."

"Yeah?"

Mystery gestures with a tip of his head to the sopping clothes in the corner of the room. "Pants."

"Of course." Rachel scoops the pants off of the floor. "Where's the blouse?"

"Do we have to call it a blouse?"

"I call em as I see em."

"I think it's on the stairs somewhere."

"Awesome." Rachel walks out of the room without another word.

Mystery absently grabs a pack of playing cards from his desk which he allows his fingers to manipulate as he sits on the overstuffed leather couch against the wall and flips through all of the possible scenarios which might have brought him here this soon.

There is a thud on the door which Mystery knows is what passes for a knock with him and when he says, "Come in," the door opens and the doorway is filled, almost entirely by Tony Mangioni.

The large man steps into the room, flattening the jacket of his dark blue, double breasted Armani suit with the palm of his hand.

Mystery stares up at him and, for a long moment, Tony

refuses to meet his gaze. At last Tony turns and says, "Sorry Boss, I know I'm not supposed to bug you at your day job, but what I have to say couldn't be said over the phone."

CHAPTER THREE

Spacer winces as he sits on the hard plastic of the airport seat. Part of him wants to rub a hand over his wound, make sure he hasn't popped a stitch after sitting down, but a much larger part of him does not want to be seen in public with his hand down his pants fondling his own ass. Instead he tries to distract himself by watching a group of a dozen or more people stalking around the gate area looking for an available outlet.

"Forget something?"

Spacer looks to his left where Shelly stands holding up a foam rubber oval doughnut. "My ass pillow!" he says, smiling. "You do love me."

"Yeah, well..."

Shelly takes a step toward him but has to stop and dodge the throng of outlet hunters when someone yells, "There's one, over there!" and they all move, en mass, around her.

"Energy crises," Spacer says.

"They're about to find out what a real crises is," Shelly mutters. She walks over to Spacer and hands him the pillow which he slides underneath him. "You're in my seat."

Spacer arches an eyebrow at her and looks down at the hard plastic thing he is sitting on. "What makes this your seat?"

"Not that one, on the plane, you've got the window seat."

"Oh yeah, that one's all mine."

"It would be mine if you had processed the stupid scientist with the agency and let me book the tickets."

"But you're so much better at that sort of thing."

"Why would you even want the window? You know you're going to have to get up and go to the bathroom in the middle of the flight and have to crawl over me."

"It's an hour and a half flight to Atlanta, I think I can manage."

"We have never been on a flight that you didn't have to pee at least twice during."

"Hey, there's another one," someone yells and the herd migrates quickly to the newly abandoned outlet.

"Oh my God, Gary," a woman says from within the mob. "If you keep yelling every time you see one I'm never going to charge my Kindle!"

Shelly sits against her chair and taps a paperback novel against her knee.

"What's that?"

She looks down at the book. The woman on the cover stands in the middle of a prairie looking off into the distance. "Oh, just something I grabbed for the flight."

"Is it a romance?"

"I think so. I've been trying to… um… what's the word?"

"Be a girl?"

Shelly shrugs. "Not exactly what I was going for but it works."

"So… is that like Little House on the Prairie?"

"Little Whore on the Prairie from the description on the back cover. Some swooning chick waiting for her cowboy to return only to be seduced by the cowboy next door." Shelly studies that book for a moment. "I'm going to make myself read it, but I'm not terribly happy about it."

"Do the cowboys have a shootout?"

"I would imagine they do."

"I've always wanted to have a shootout."

Now it's Shelly's turn to arch her eyebrows. "You've had several. You have the ass pillow to prove it."

"No, I've been shot at and I've shot back, but I haven't been in a shootout. I haven't stepped onto a dusty road in an old west town, tossed my poncho over my shoulder to reveal my six shooter and said, 'Do you feel lucky, punk?'"

"That's Dirty Harry."

"Huh?"

"The line, 'Do you feel lucky, punk?' It's Dirty Harry, it's not a western."

"No, that can't be right."

"Actually, it isn't right, the actual line is, 'you've got to ask yourself, Do I feel lucky? Well, do you, punk?' But it's still Dirty Harry."

"None the less, in my shootout I'm going to ask them if

20

they feel lucky."

"You go right ahead."

The speakers overhead crackle and soon the disembodied voice of the gate agent says, "We're just about to begin boarding flight 1087 to Atlanta, at this time mothers with young children and anyone who may need a little extra time boarding may come to the gate."

"You know, you never see them," Spacer says.

"Who?"

"There's one, left wall!" one of the outlet hunters screams as the mob moves toward that wall.

"Oh my God, you are about to get on the plane," Shelly yells at them. "Let it go."

"The people who need extra time."

"What?"

"You never see the people who need extra time. If they're so damn slow, shouldn't there be a line of them shuffling toward the plane as the rest of us normal walkers sprint toward it in comparison?"

"Actually, yeah, there really should be. What game are these 'slow' people playing at?"

"We now ask out first class passengers to join us," the gate agent's amplified voice tells them.

Shelly jumps up and Spacer gingerly lifts himself to his feet. They scan their boarding passes and head to the jet way.

"See, not a single slow person," Spacer says.

"I guess I should have asked this before now, but why are we going to Atlanta?"

"Because that's where our commuter flight is."

"Stands to reason. And where will that take us."

"To wherever our final destination may be," Spacer says, mimicking every flight attendant ever.

"It's funny how you think I'm not going to punch you in your gunshot wound until you tell me where we're going."

"Ultimately, Bridges."

"Really? We're vacationing half an hour from home?"

"Yup." Spacer steps onto the plane and eases himself into his window seat.

"Actually, that's not a terrible idea."

"I have not terrible ideas from time to time."

Shelly opens her book and sneers at the first line. "She was like a willow in the wind, willing to bend but unable to break," she reads out loud.

"Good lord, that is terrible," Spacer says.

"You're telling me."

"What's the next line? I bet it's worse."

"No, it's just setting the scene. 'Sara stepped out of her small, one room home and stared off into the horizon, remembering the day she saw Dirk…' Yes, you heard right, Dirk, 'riding away to find his fortune.' Stupid name aside it is what it is."

"Yeah," Spacer says nodding. "How about the next line?"

"Are you trying to get me to read this thing to you?"

"I forgot to bring a book."

"Then you're just going to have to be alone with your thoughts. I'm not reading this out loud to you."

"You're no fun." Spacer watches as the last of the passengers board and the doors are shut and locked. "What's the rule about getting up after the doors are shut?"

"I think we have to be in the air before you can."

"Dammit, I really have to pee."

CHAPTER FOUR

Tony knows somewhere deep in the recesses of his mind that he has not spent his entire life watching Mystery cut this deck of cards but he can't remember a time before he had. He sits on the plush recliner and watches as Mystery shuffles the cards absent mindedly with one hand. He seems to be cutting the deck randomly but each time he reveals either the Ace of spades or the Ace of hearts; spade, heart, spade, heart. Tony can't look at anything other than the cards.

Tony doesn't remember sitting down but, the mere fact that he is sitting suggest that at one point or another he did. He does remember Mystery instructing him to tell the entire story of the spies' rescue mission without leaving out a single detail. He remembers finishing and Mystery telling him to go over it one more time, this time without the bit about the sandwich he'd eaten just prior to the attack or the number of times he had farted during the shootout. For the life of him, Tony can't remember why he'd included that in the first telling.

Now they are sitting in silence save for the crack of the stiff deck of cards as Mystery's fingers shuffle them back and forth. At last, Mystery clears his throat and says, "Two spies did all of that?"

"Yeah," Tony says. "Well, I don't know if you could call them spies. We haven't been able to find much out about them, but it seems like they're some kind of freelancers."

"Amounts to the same," Mystery says. "Though it would be a good idea to gather as much intel on them as we can. I'll put Jason on it."

The name doesn't ring a bell. Tony blinks once, then once again and then is able to tear his eyes from the shuffling cards and look Mystery in the eye. "Jason? Oh, Scooter."

"His name is Jason."
"Should have been Scooter."

"I'll let you take that up with his parents."

There's a knock on the door and Tony's hand moves toward the pistol nestled in the shoulder holster under his suit jacket. Mystery shakes his head at him and turns toward the door.

"Rachel?" he yells.

"No," a male voice says from the other side. "It's Barry. You wanted to see me?"

"Barry?" Tony asks, his voice just above a whisper.

"My double," Mystery says. "Not a good time, Barry," He yells toward the door.

The door opens a crack and the head of some guy who in no way reminds Tony of Mystery pokes inside. "Oh, it's just… You did say that you wanted to see me."

"And now I don't," Mystery tells him.

Barry frowns and looks at the floor for a moment, apparently gathering his thoughts. Tony gestures to his still holstered pistol and raises his eyebrows. Mystery shakes his head again.

"I think the problem here," Barry says, slithering inside the room and closing the door behind him, "is that you don't fully appreciate what I bring to the act."

Mystery smiles at Barry. Tony has seen that smile before and now, as always, he is very relieved not to be on the receiving end on it.

"Is that so?" Mystery asks.

"As a matter of fact, it is," Barry says, trying to match Mystery's smile and failing miserably.

Mystery stands and walks around his desk, taking a seat in his chair where he can look directly at Barry. "Perhaps you'd best explain things to me," he says.

"Well," Barry says, walking over to stare down at Mystery. "The simple fact is, without me, you have no act."

"No act? My, if that were the case then I suppose I would be at a complete disadvantage should we ever come to the negotiation table," Mystery says.

Barry smiles and sits in the seat across the desk from his boss. "Now you're beginning to speak some sense."

"Of course," Mystery says, crossing his right leg over his left and leaning back. He begins the slow one-handed shuffle again and Tony makes a point of not looking at the cards. "I suppose that, should something happen that caused me to cancel the show entirely, well that would just remove any supposed leverage you once thought you had."

"You're canceling the show?" Barry asks, his words already slowing. He does not look away from the cards.

"As it happens, I am." Mystery points to Tony and Barry moves his head mechanically in Tony's direction. His eyes fall on Tony but he doesn't see him. "My associate over there has just brought information to me that is requiring my immediate attention. As such, we will, unfortunately, be closing a little ahead of schedule."

"That's a shame," Barry says, turning back to look once again at the movement of the cards.

"It is. But, Barry, something is bothering me."

"Oh no."

"Oh yes," Mystery says, his voice never alters from his calm, soothing tone. "You've been my double for a few months now, plenty of time for you to think I can't find another fat man to draw abdominals on his gut and pretend to be me while he jumps in a tank. Yet, you haven't tried to weasel any more money out of me until today." Mystery keeps shuffling the cards but uncrosses his legs and leans over the desk toward Barry. "Do you have an ace up your sleeve, Barry?"

"Yes."

Mystery sighs and frowns at him. "I was afraid of this. What did you really come in here to tell me?"

"I've figured out all of your illusions. If you don't give me more money and take me on as your apprentice, I'm going to sell them to one of those shows that gives away magician's tricks."

Mystery slowly shakes his head. "That really is too bad, Barry. As it happens, I probably won't even be doing any of those any more so it really wouldn't have helped you."

"Damn," Barry says, his voice a monotone. For all of the emotion he put into his mild profanity he might as well have been saying shoe or lamp.

"But you had to try to blackmail me, and I'm afraid I just can't let that go."

"You can't?"

"I cannot," Mystery says, dropping the register of his voice. He arches the deck with his right hand until the deck springs, one card at a time, into his left. The sound puts Tony in mind of a machine gun with a silencer. By the time the fifty-second card comes to rest in Mystery's left-hand Barry's head hangs limply, his chin resting on his chest.

"He dead?" Tony asks calmly.

"Not yet." Mystery presses a button on his phone. "Rachel?"

"Whatever it is, it's going to have to wait. I'm still tracking down your laundry," Rachel's voice says over the loudspeaker.

"Don't worry about that. I've given what you said a lot of thought and your right."

"Come again?"

"You heard me," Mystery says, grinning. "We're losing the shark. Actually, we're closing the whole act to retool."

"Effective when?"

"Right now. Send everyone home. I'm going to stick around for a while and figure out striking the set."

"You want me to call Eddie?"

"No, I got it. Just chase everyone home and then take the rest of the night. You've earned it."

"Not sure what's happened to you, but I'm going to get out of here before you come to your senses."

"Good girl," Mystery says, pressing the end call button.

He looks at Tony. "Eddie's the shark guy. I need you to find him and tell him I'll take care of feeding Susie."

"Susie?"

"The shark."

"Makes sense."

"Tell him we're closing down and have him remove the divider. There's no sense in cooping the poor girl up when we don't need to."

"None I can think of," Tony says.

"When he's done that send him home and meet me in the auditorium. You and I get one last show." This time Mystery's smile was meant entirely for him. In his lifetime Tony had faced down a Columbian drug lord threatening to cut off his junk, a rogue cop looking to administer his own brand of justice and an honest to God Kodiak bear he'd accidentally pissed off. He'd gladly face all three together rather than stand there looking at that smile for another minute.

"You got it, Boss," he said, turning toward the door. He stopped, realizing something and turned back. He sighed in relief to find Mystery no longer smiling. "This Eddie, how do I know which one he is?"

"That shouldn't be a problem. He'll be one of the few people around here who look like they have any idea what they're doing. Also, his shirt says Eddie."

"Competence and nametag, I think I can handle that."

CHAPTER FIVE

Tony sits front row and center in the empty auditorium. It is the last place that he would voluntarily put himself under normal circumstances. When he sits in a room he likes to be in a place where he can see as much of the room as possible while being all but invisible himself.

Tonight, he wants to be seen. Mystery told him to be in the auditorium and he is not going to give him even a moment's doubt as to whether or not he is there. He's worked with the man long enough to know what to do and what not to do and what happens to the doers of the things which should not be done.

Barry is about to learn through personal experience what Tony knows through observation. Mystery could not care less about Barry's threat of giving away his tricks. What he cares about is that Barry would make himself a nuisance while they moved forward with their plan. He would inevitably become a loose thread. Loose threads get cut.

Tony will never be a loose thread.

"You'll want to come back a few rows," Mystery says from the back of the auditorium. Tony isn't surprised he didn't hear the man enter.

Tony turns to see him walking down the auditorium steps. He is wearing a black fur coat over his naked torso and leather pants; the sort of thing Tony imagines David Bowie wore in his leisure time. The one thing which stands out in glaring contrast is the white bag with red stripes in his hand. Mystery reaches his long, ring laden fingers into the bag, pulls out a single kernel and pops it into his mouth.

"I think you'll have a better view from here," he says, stepping into a center row. "Plus, I can't promise you aren't sitting in a splash section down there."

Tony shrugs and walks up the steps, finding a seat next to Mystery. Mystery holds the bag out to him. "Popcorn?"

"Where did this come from?"

"It was left over from this afternoon. It's a little stale."

Tony takes a few kernels and pops them into his mouth. He

grimaces at the flat flavor filling his mouth. "I told you it was stale," Mystery says.

"There is no way it got that stale over a few hours."

"Really?" Mystery says, examining the bag.

"God no, that's disgusting."

Mystery shrugs and continues eating. "I suppose if I were going to stay open I'd have to have a word with the concessions people. It hardly seems worth it at this point though."

"What are we going to do about the machine?" Tony asks.

"The machine is done," Mystery says, his voice perfectly level without a hint of frustration or resentment. "The entire point of the machine was surprise. Without that, it has none."

"I'm assuming we have a next step."

"We do."

Mystery looks at the stage for a moment and sighs. "It's a shame this last performance will have to have such terrible lighting." He turns to Tony. "Do you know how to operate a light board?"

Tony shrugs. "How hard can it be?"

"Never mind."

Mystery turns his attention back to the stage and whistles. The sound, surprisingly melodic, bounces off the walls of the auditorium. Tony, who has heard cries of men being flayed slowly to death while he sat calmly and read Chaucer, shivers involuntarily.

There's a sound of movement from the stage and soon Barry appears on the platform above the shark tank. He is dressed only in a speedo and under the harsh floodlights he looks nothing like Mystery. His hair lies limply on his head; his eyes stare vacantly from their sockets. He looks like nothing more than a chubby going fat middle-aged man.

His eyes find the two men without focusing.

"Hello, Barry," Mystery says.

Barry smiles at them but remains silent.

Something tucked into the waistband of Barry's small bathing suit glints in the light.

"Are you ready for your grand finale?"

Barry stands perfectly still. The shark, which has been gliding idly around her tank, flicks a little at the activity but settles once more into her lazy swim.

Mystery whistles again. Tony takes in a deep breath and rides out the feeling of his flesh trying to escape through his shirt collar.

Barry's hand goes to the glinting object in his waist band and he pulls out a dagger, slicing his leg a little as he does. He jumps a little at the cut and a drop of his blood falls into the tank. The shark does not change her course.

"That's simply not enough, Barry," Mystery says, calmly.

Barry holds up his free hand and drags the blade over it. As the metal slides into the meat of his palm his eyes at last gain focus and he screams all the while cutting deeper and deeper into his flesh.

He looks up now, directly at Mystery.

Tony starts to stand, his hand already on the Colt in the holster under his arm. Mystery places his hand on Tony's arm, stopping him. "That won't be necessary," he says.

Tony looks at the man on the stage. He is still staring at them but he has not moved from the spot. He holds his freely bleeding hand over the tank, blood showers into the water exciting the shark.

"Very good, Barry. Now you know what you must do."

Barry shakes his head. "Please, Mystery," he says. Tony had thought seeing the man as a zombie was bad but seeing him there, completely aware but powerless to stop himself, this is far more disturbing.

"Mystery, I've got a kid," Barry says, pleading.

"Really?" Mystery says. "How old?"

"Oh!" Barry says, his eyes brightening. "Um… eight! I… I think… No, yeah, eight."

"That is a great age," Mystery says. "He's probably just getting into baseball I bet."

"Yeah."

"Wait, I swear, this is the world we live in. I just assumed it was a son," Mystery says, smiling at his own unintended misogyny. "Is it a boy."

"I… I think so."

"Well, boy or girl, at that age, who doesn't love baseball?" Mystery says.

"I sure did," Barry says, tears are streaming freely from his eyes.

Mystery turns to Tony. "Did you play baseball as a lad?"

"Me? No, I was into… other things."

"Oh, you were a rascal, weren't you?"

"I did play peewee football when I was six. Got thrown off the team for giving a kid a concussion," Tony says.

"Well, that hardly seems fair," Mystery says.

"I don't know, we weren't supposed to play tackle… and the kid was on my team… and I hit him in the locker room before the game. So I think it may have been justifiable."

"My goodness, you were a rascal," Mystery says. He turns back to Barry. "All right. I think it's time."

"But what about my kid?"

"I'm sure he or she will find some way to continue living their fatherless life," Mystery says. He whistles for a third time and Barry tosses the knife off stage and jumps into the tank.

The shark, already in something of a frenzy, bolts to the disturbed water, passing Barry so closely she brushes him, her razor-sharp scales opening new cuts on his arm and side. Barry makes no attempt to swim away from his attacker. On the second pass she strikes and takes his right arm off at the shoulder. Now he does swim, haphazardly stroking with the one arm remaining to him. The shark comes around and clamps her jaws onto his thigh, twisting her head from side to side until the leg, too, is separated from the man. Barry screams once more, his voice muted by the water, his breath bubbling to the surface like water boiling on the stove. He inhales instinctively and fills his lungs with water. After a few more jerks, he is still.

Sensing that the fight has gone out of her prey, the shark takes her time with the remainder of her meal. Mystery and Tony watch in silence for a long time until at last Mystery speaks, "That looked nothing like the video we've been showing."

"Huh?"

"It's the show stopper, we show a video that looks like me being eaten by the shark," Mystery says. "It looked nothing like that."

"Oh."

"Disappointing," Mystery says. He reaches into the bag and pops another kernel in his mouth.

"I... I didn't think you could make people do things they ordinarily wouldn't, even under hypnosis," Tony says.

"You'd be surprised what people can do with the right motivation," Mystery says. "There's almost nothing one can't do when one applies himself."

"There are some things."

"Such as?"

"Um... well, one can't fall five stories and stick around to talk about it."

Mystery smiles at him, his face a serene mask. "I'll take that bet."

"What bet?"

"We've got a lot of damage control to do," Mystery says, turning in his chair and leaning in to Tony.

"You need me to clean what's left of Barry out of the tank?"

"Goodness no," Mystery says. "We need a third party to discover the tragic accident tomorrow. I'm talking about the situation with Project Pretty Lady."

"Well, if the machine is scrapped, I'm not sure where to go from here."

"That's fine, because I am. I need you to reach out to all of your contacts, I want to find these freelance spies of ours."

"All right, I can do that. You afraid they might still be a monkey wrench?"

"I highly doubt it. Because I think they may now be Project Pretty Lady." Tony chuckles. "Why is that funny?"

"Did you see the pic of the chick. She sort of already is Project Pretty Lady."

Mystery smiles at him. "Ah yes, but in a very real way, they both are."

Tony raises his eyebrows but keeps his opinions to himself.

"And if you would be so kind, reserve a seat for me on the earliest flight to Houston you can find for tomorrow. I think it's time I saw my doctor."

"Can do," Tony says. What he doesn't say is, *I wouldn't want to be THAT loose end right now.*

CHAPTER SIX

"What the hell was that thunk at the door?" Spacer asks, looking up from his eggs and sausage.

"I dunnno," Shelly says, not looking up from her crossword. "Paper boy?"

"You're reading the paper."

Shelly shrugs, "I didn't know this place had a subscription. It's a rental. Who rents a house and signs it up for paper delivery?"

"So you went out and bought a paper in your pjs?"

"I went out and GOT a paper in my pjs."

"Whose paper did you steal?"

"People across the road. I guess the paper boy does one side first and then the other. That's pretty inefficient paper boying if you ask me. If he'd just throw papers on both sides of the road as he goes by we wouldn't be in this mess."

"Uh huh," Spacer says, grabbing his cane and hoisting himself to his feet. "Well, I shall return to the people across the road their purloined periodical."

"Every time you touch that damned cane you turn into Thurston Howl the Third. I'll be so glad when you're better, you are obnoxious when you're wounded."

"I think that's probably a terrible thing you just said," Spacer says.

Shelly shrugs again. "Sometimes the truth is terrible, I can't help that."

"Well, at any rate, luvy, I'll be just a mo over there, do be a dear and don't hide my ass-pillow while I'm gone," Spacer says, jutting his chin at the pillow in question which he'd been sitting on only a moment before.

"You know I'm going to hide your ass-pillow while you're gone, right."

"Yeah, I'm aware." Spacer takes a few timid steps, his ass reminding him with each one the abuse it has suffered, and slowly makes his way to the door. He opens it to discover that, indeed, a paper has been delivered. He bends slowly and scoops it up before hobbling across the street.

He considers the two steps up to the neighbor's porch but thinks better of it. He tosses the paper onto the porch and turns to head back to the house. He hears the unmistakable click of a door opening behind him.

"Dammit," he mutters under his breath.

"Can I help you?" the man asks.

"Uh… no," Spacer says, turning. "I just… I'm, um, renting the place across the way. Thought I'd come over and introduce myself."

"But you were… you were walking away."

"Yeah, I was, I…" Spacer gestures to his cane, "the wound was acting up a bit more than I thought it would, figured I'd get off it for now and come back a bit later."

"Oh, hey, why don't ya come on in? Put your feet up in my place."

"No, I don't want to impose, I'll just…"

"I insist, you know, I just, I feel like a grade A jerk for not coming over to say 'hi' last night but, well, we've tried it before and people, particularly childless couples like yourself and your friend, well, they just don't seem to want company on their first night of vacation. Let me help you up these steps."

The man runs down and takes Spacer gently by the arm. As soon as he squeezes Spacer's bicep he lets go and steps back. "Say, those are some guns you're packing there, neighbor."

"Yeah, well, I try to get to the gym now and then," Spacer says, smiling as innocently and none threateningly as he can. He offers his hand, "Name's Spacer Sharpe."

The man whistles. "That's quite a handle to go with those guns. Why, with a name like that, you could be a movie star."

"Hey, and don't forget the good looks to go with them, huh?"

The man leans back and chuckles. "You're an all right guy, Spacer Sharpe."

"You don't seem too bad yourself, guy across the road."

"Oh, my gracious, I haven't introduced myself, have I?" The man at last grabs Spacer's hand and says, "Darren, Darren Whitman." Darren tries his best to impress Spacer with his grip on the shake but he doesn't really have the power to back it up.

"Say, now that we know each other, you just have to come in and meet Sissy and the kids."

"I do?" Spacer says. Darren stares at him smiling expectantly. Spacer grins, glances across the road to the house with his lovely wife and beloved ass-pillow and sighs. "Oh, what the hell?" he says, nodding to Daren.

"That's the spirit."

Darren tries to aide Spacer again but Spacer waves him away and climbs the two steps without a lot of difficulty. Darren hops up them quickly, smiling at the spryness of his own step, and walks in front of Spacer, kicking the paper as he does. "Say, that's the first time that paper boy has ever thrown it anywhere but my hydrangeas."

Darren pushes open the door and yells, "Sissy, kids, come on down here, we've got company, it's the guy from across the road."

Spacer steps inside to find the layout of Darren's house to be remarkably similar to that of his rental. The door leads into the living room, the kitchen is off to the left and there are stairs leading to the bedrooms on the second floor. "Are all of the houses in the neighborhood planned out this way?"

"To my knowledge, the same company did the whole housing development. Why?"

"Oh, no reason, I just find it's often handy to know things… escape routes and what not."

"I see."

"You do?"

"Sure, you're like me."

"I am?" Spacer asks. The pleasantness drains from his face and his hand slides down the shaft of his cane for a better grip. He'd been in business long enough to make enemies with long memories and ample funding. It wouldn't be the first time a killer lurked inside a tubby next door neighbor. "How so?" Spacer asks.

"You've been trapped by the most boring guy in the room at one too many cocktail parties, am I right?"

"Cocktail parties?" Spacer says, the smile instantly returning to his face. "That's it exactly."

"I knew we were two of a kind," Darren said, lightly popping Spacer on the arm.

"Brothers from another mother, that's us," Spacer says.

"Brothers from another mother? I love that. Can I steal it? I'm stealing it."

"Well, it isn't actually mine, but you're welcome to it," Spacer says.

There's a light footfall on the stairs and both men look up to see a fifteen-year-old in knee high leather boots and a matching miniskirt walking down the stairs.

"Quinn, darling, come on down and meet Mr. Sharpe."

"I already did that, Dad," Quinn says, staring at her telephone. "Oh my God, you're such a bitch," she says to whomever is on the other end of the text she just received.

"Really?" Darren asks Spacer. "You two have met?"

"Not to my knowledge, and I have a pretty photographic memory. Comes with the job."

"Oh? What do you do for a living?"

"I own a bookstore."

"Ah yes, I can see how a keen eye and memory for detail would come in handy with that."

"You'd be surprised," Spacer says.

"Anyway, I apologize for Quinn, she just stays off in her own little world these days."

Spacer takes in the girl now sprawled over the arms of a recliner, the pink highlights in her hair, the black and white striped tights, the air of disdain for humanity in general. "If you tell her I said this I'll deny it, but Shelly was just like her at that age."

"Shelly, that's your lady friend?"

"My wife, yes."

"Ah, wife, that is so refreshing. Again, you just can't assume any longer."

"Honey, is someone here?" a voice calls from the kitchen.

"It's the man from across the road, come on in and say 'Hi' Sissy," Darren yells back. "That's the wife, Sissy," he says to

Spacer.

"I put that together," Spacer says.

"Honey, I am in my dressing gown and my hair is horrible," Sissy yells back.

"Oh, I should come back at a better time," Spacer says.

"Don't be ridiculous," Darren says. "Come on in, dear, you look gorgeous," he shouts to the kitchen.

"So what's the deal with the cane, are you a cripple?" Quinn asks.

"Quinn!" Darren yells

"What? It's a question," Quin says.

"That's okay," Spacer says, shooting his most winning grin to Darren. "Actually, it's only temporary, I'll be back on my feet in no time."

"Really? Because I was going to ask you if you played tennis before I saw your, well, your.."

"My little friend?" Spacer asks, holding up the cane.

"Yes, that's a good word for it."

"As a matter of fact, I do. Pencil me in for some time around the end of the month, I should be back on my game by then."

"It's a date," Darren says.

Sissy steps out of the kitchen in a faded pink bathrobe with her hair bunched in curlers carrying a tray with a silver carafe and four mugs. "Oh, I feel so underdressed," she says.

"I'm sure Spacer has seen worse, haven't you, Sport?" Darren says.

"You look lovely," Spacer tells her.

"So what happened to you?" Quinn asks.

"Quinn, Mr. Sharpe is going to think we're all such barbarians the way you're acting," Sissy says.

"No, it's fine," Spacer says. "I... fell."

"That must have been some fall," Darren says.

"It was," Spacer says. "It was into a canyon."

"You fell into a canyon?" Quinn says.

"Yes."

"Which one?"

"Not... a, you know, famous one. Just a regular old

canyon."

"Now, what makes it a canyon? You know, as opposed to just, well, a hole," Sissy says.

"Now, Sissy, don't badger the man. He never claimed to be an expert on canyons, he just fell into one," Darren says.

"Well, yes, but he knew enough to state that it was a canyon and not just hole."

"Yes, that's point. How did you know that?" Darren asks.

"The... man told me," Spacer says.

"There was a man?" Quinn asks.

"Yes, a man saw me and asked if I was okay."

"Thank goodness the man was there," Sissy says.

"Oh my God, Mom, are you seriously buying this?" Quinn asks.

"Don't be rude, Quinn!" Sissy says.

"Now, how did the man asking if you were okay let you know that you'd fallen into a canyon?" Darren asks.

"His exact words were, 'My goodness, are you okay? You've fallen into a canyon.'."

"And what did you say when he asked," Sissy asks.

"I said, 'This is going to be difficult to explain to people."

"Well," Darren says, chuckling "that is some story."

"I'll say," Quinn mutters.

"Oh, Sissy, I haven't formally introduced you. This is Spacer Sharpe, he owns a bookstore."

"Oh, we don't have a lot of literary people here," Sissy says.

"Well, I just sell them, I don't write them."

"Still, it's quite impressive. What's the name of your store?"

"The Black Box Book Shop, over in Havenboro. We have a small theater in the back where we produce experimental shows," Spacer says.

"Yes, I've heard of it," Sissy says. "I've been meaning to stop in."

"The next time you're in town, come on in."

"I'll be sure to do that."

"What do you guys do?" Spacer asks.

"Well, I'm a homemaker," Sissy says. "But Darren is a

CPA."

"Is that so?"

"Certainly is," Darren says. "Say, who does your books? You know, the books for your books." Darren pats Spacer on the shoulder. "Get it?"

"I sure do, that's clever," Spacer says.

"Yes, I've been told I should do standup, actually. I thought about it, but who has the time?"

"And those night clubs, they're just so filthy, don't you think?" Sissy asks.

"Oh… yeah, I sure do. Hate those filthy clubs," Spacer says. "By the way, are there any good filthy clubs around here that I could hate in person?"

Darren leans back again and chuckles loudly. "That's pretty good too."

"Yes, you two should be on the television, you're a great comedy team. You're like Martin and Lewis."

"He's Lewis," Darren bellows another laugh and jabs a finger at Spacer.

"Oh… kay," Spacer says.

"If that isn't the cat's pajamas," Sissy says.

"Yeah, but, seriously, what is the night life around here?" Spacer asks.

"So, you and your, um, lady friend…"

"They're married, Sissy, you don't have to dance around anything," Darren says.

"What a relief, you just don't know any more in this day and age." Sissy sets the tray down on a coffee table and begins pouring coffee into the mugs. "So you and your wife enjoy those places?" She hands Spacer a cup. "Cream or sugar?"

"Black is fine," Spacer says. "And, yes, we've been known to cut the odd rug, though it looks like I'll be sitting out the next few dances." He holds up the cane.

"My goodness, Darren, have you not invited Mr. Sharpe to sit yet?" Sissy gestures to the sofa. "Please, help yourself."

Spacer sits gingerly on the sofa, sucking in a quick gasp as his rear takes his weight, and then graciously accepts the cup and saucer. "Thank you."

"What's going on?" a young voice asks from the stairs.

Everyone turns to see a boy of eight standing halfway down the steps, rubbing the sleep from his eyes.

"Scout," Darren says, motioning for the boy to come the rest of the way down the steps. "Come on down and say hello to our neighbor across the road for the next month." The boy obeys and walks down the steps and over to Spacer.

"Hello, I'm Scott Whitman," he says, extending his hand.

"Good to meet you," Spacer says, shaking it gently, his grip was better than his old man's. "I'm Spacer Sharpe."

"Is that a nickname?"

"Nope, it's my real name, my parents were kinda weird."

"My nickname is Scout, but please don't call me that."

"Oh, our little Scott thinks he's all grown up," Sissy says.

"I think I can handle that, Scott," Spacer says.

"You know, if you were serious about that night on the town, I'm sure Sissy and I could escort you around some evening. We've been known to cut a few rugs of our own," Darren says.

"We have?" Sissy asks.

"Yes, we have," Darren says, his voice dropping an octave.

"Darren, I just don't…"

"Could we speak in the kitchen for a moment?" Darren asks, taking Sissy by the hand and half dragging her into the other room.

Spacer looks from Quinn who is once more engrossed with her phone to Scott who is busily flipping through the channels and then back to Quinn. "So, your parents don't actually get out much, do they?" he asks.

"Nope," Quinn says.

"Yeah, I don't suppose you would know of any…"

"Look," Quinn says, dropping her phone and making eye contact. "I'm not really like them. I don't care if you like me or not. But you did make them look pretty stupid with that lame ass canyon story."

"Yeah, that sort of got away from me. I kept expecting someone to call me on it," Spacer says.

"Anyone with half a brain would have. But that means

you've got nothing to worry about with my folks. So, if you promise not to tell them where you got it, I'll drop a list of places I'm not supposed to know about in your mailbox later today."

"Deal," Spacer says. "Thanks."

"Whatever," Quinn says, looking once more at her phone.

Darren and Sissy walk out of the kitchen, Sissy looks around the room for a moment and then plucks the phone out of Quinn's hand.

"Hey!" Quinn yells.

"Well, Sport, it looks like we are a go for taking you and your wife out on the town," Darren says.

"I'm sorry, dear, but it's for the greater good," Sissy tells Quinn. She punches in a number from memory and waits a moment before saying, "Hello, Tiffany's, what is your delivery policy." She absently pulls a credit card from the pocket of her bathrobe before glancing at Spacer. "Oh, hello there, I'll be just a moment." She walks quickly back into the kitchen with the telephone.

Quinn hops out of the chair and follows after her. "Mom, this is seriously not funny."

Spacer looks at Darren. "Darren did you just bribe your wife so that the two of you could take us out?"

Darren stares at the kitchen where his wife just disappeared. "I… that is… yes. I'm sorry you had to see that. I can't tell you how sorry I am that you had to see that."

"Oh my God, you didn't have to do that. You could have just given us the names of some places. Hell, you didn't even have to do that, I have Google."

"Well, she's got the charge card now and she's going to be using it, so you might as well make it worth my while," Darren says with a shrug.

"Okay, that sounds like a plan," Spacer says, chuckling. "I weirdly feel like I should be hugging you right now."

"Hey," Darren says, opening his arms, "go with it."

Spacer glances at his cane and says, "Think you should bring it over here, actually."

"Oh right," Darren says, leaning over and embracing him in

a manly bear hug. "So, when are we going to do this?"

"Um... I don't know. Tomorrow's Saturday, is that too soon?"

"No!" Darren says, then pulling away from Spacer and straightening. "I mean, tomorrow should be fine, I don't believe I have anything planned."

"Tomorrow it is then," Spacer says, pulling himself up with effort.

"Oh, let me help..."

"No, I got it. But I should be heading back. Shelly's going to be wondering where I am," Spacer says. He doesn't say *And I've got to somehow convince her to go out with the rubes across the street so I'm going to need all the time I can get.*

"Well, I have to say it was a pleasure meeting you," Darren says, offering his hand once more.

"It was a pleasure meeting you and the whole Whitman's Sampler," Spacer says, taking it gently.

"The whole..." Darren repeats, playing it over again in his head. "Oh my gosh, that is hilarious!"

"Really? That's the first time you've heard that one?" Spacer asks.

"The very first."

"Wow, you really do need to get out, don't you?"

"I do," Darren tells him, his voice deadly serious. "I really, really do."

"All righty then, tomorrow it definitely is," Spacer says. He hobbles to the door before the poor man can make him feel any worse about his situation.

CHAPTER SEVEN

Dr. Landsin holds his breath as he pours the sodium from the container to the graduated cylinder. This is the most crucial ingredient in the experiment. A fraction of a thousandth of a gram too much or too little and the whole thing can quite literally blow up in his face. Only when he is certain that he's measured .5 milligrams, no more and no less, does he add it to the beaker mounted over the Bunsen burner and allow himself to breathe.

He smiles as he watches the mixture turn from its brownish color to… wait, it's already brown?

"Doctor, what was that you just added?"

Dr. Landsin sighs. Brandon had shown such promise when he'd brought him on as an assistant but as they worked closely together for the past week he'd found his questions to be more and more infuriating. How can he be of use in an experiment when he doesn't even know its components?

And why is the compound growing purple?

"Doctor?" Brandon asks. "Was that the sodium which you just added?"

"Yes, Brandon, I added the sodium," Dr. Landsin says, watching the bubbles grow from the surface of the violently violet compound. "Why do you keep asking me?"

"It's only that… I just added the sodium a moment ago."

Dr. Landsin turns and stares at his assistant. "Say that again."

"Doctor, I added the sodium a moment before you did."

"You?"

"Yes."

"Added   the   sodium?"
"Yes."

"To this experiment?"

"Yes!"

"The one to which I just added the sodium?"

"Doctor! We both added the sodium!"

Dr. Landsin and Brandon stare at the bubbling, volatile cocktail without speaking. Finally, Dr. Landsin says, "We should back away from this… quickly!"

Dr. Landsin and Brandon back up in lock-step until they are pressed against the far wall. "We're against the far wall," Brandon says.

"So it would seem."

"Do you think it's far enough?"

"I… can't be certain," Dr. Landsin says.

"I only ask because there's nothing here to hide behind."

"Brandon, I am a world-renowned physicist I have a Nobel prize for my work in robotics and I sit on the board of no less than three well known pharmaceutical companies for God knows what reason, you do not have to tell me that there is nothing to hide behind!"

Brandon nods at him. "It's been an honor serving with you, sir."

The mixture comes to a heated boil. Dr. Landsin holds his arm in front of his face to try to save his retinas from the oncoming…

POOF!

Dr. Landsin and Brandon freeze, both averting their eyes, for a long moment. Finally, Dr. Landsin risks a look. It's a bit smoky but otherwise the experiment is none the worse for wear. There isn't even a crack in the beaker.

He notices Brandon still cowering next to him and jabs an elbow into his ribs. "Oh," Brandon says, "we're alive!"

"Of course we're alive," Dr. Landsin says. He walks to the station to better examine the smoldering experiment.

"But… didn't you say that an incorrect amount of sodium would be extremely volatile?"

"That's what Dr. Rushmon said."

"Dr. Rushmon?"

"An old chemistry professor of mine. I think I shall have to write him a strongly worded letter." The compound bubbles up and out of the beaker. It spills onto the table instantly melting everything it touches and creating a smoldering hole in the middle of the table sending the beakers, burners and the rest of the experiment falling through first to and then through the floor. "Or perhaps not so strongly worded," Dr. Landsin says.

"What's below us?" Brandon asks.

"I think it's an insurance company," Dr. Landsin says.

"Well, that's fortunate in its own way."

A shadow falls over the two of them and Dr. Landsin looks up to see Tony, his benefactor's head goon, staring down at him. "Oh my," Dr. Landsin says.

"We need the room," Tony says.

Dr. Landsin looks around the lab. It's the size of a high school gymnasium with fifty stations manned by teams of two to four scientists each. "I'm not sure that's possible," he says.

"No, it's possible," Tony says.

The double doors open and dozens of men as large or larger than Tony enter silently and begin escorting scientists out of the lab. Dr. Conover screams "No, I cannot leave this, not now!" and the goon scoops him off of his feet and drops him over his shoulder. As they walk away there is an explosion which puts to shame the fizzle of Dr. Landsin's own experiment.

"That explosion represents the end of fifteen years of meticulous research," Dr. Landsin says.

Tony shrugs. "So, now he's got something to write on the 'reason for' line of his next grant application."

"Doctor, should I call…?" Brandon begins but is cut off when another man scoops him off of his feet and carries him away.

Tony takes in a deep breath and grimaces. "It stinks in here."

Dr. Landsin shrugs. "It's a chem lab, chemicals sometimes stink."

"What are you doing here? I thought you were a physicist."

"I dabble."

Tony looks at the smoldering hole in both the table and the floor. "Maybe you should stick with the physics."

"Noted," Dr. Landsin says.

At last the room is entirely empty save for Dr. Landsin and Tony. There is silence for a moment and Dr. Landsin says, "Did you want to say something to me in private?"

Tony grins and says, "No such luck, Doc."

Dr. Landsin nods and silently prepares himself.

The door opens and Mystery steps into the lab wearing a diamond encrusted suit with a jacket stretching down to his knees over a burgundy shirt. A young man follows him. He might be in his early twenties but the crop of acne on each cheek suggests he's yet to experience his first legal drink… possibly his first legal cigarette. His hair hangs down over his eyes and he holds a slim, leather bound book.

"Dr. Landsin," Mystery says as he strides across the cavernous room, his natural showman's voice rings out calling attention to the true emptiness of the lab. "You're looking well."

"Thank you, as are you," Dr. Landsin says, his voice filling much less space than Mystery's.

"You are kind to say," Mystery says, projecting less as he stops on the opposite side of the table next to Tony. "You've met Jason?" Mystery asks gesturing to the young man who comes to a stop on Mystery's left.

"I don't believe I've had the pleasure," Dr. Landsin says.

"Well then, this is an historic occasion," Mystery says. "Two of the greatest minds I have had the pleasure of picking coming together for the first time."

"Well, I… am flattered," Dr. Landsin says.

"Cool," Jason mutters.

Dr. Landsin takes a long, slow breath.

"I only wish the circumstances of the meeting could be different."

The breath catches in Dr. Landsin's throat.

Mystery plucks a small ring which had fallen from the beaker stand before it melted through the table and walks it over his knuckles. He smiles at Dr. Landsin who returns the smile sheepishly.

Mystery shifts so that his shoulder blocks the view of the ring from the young man. Tony clears his throat and becomes suddenly interested in something on the other side of the lab. "Yes," Mystery says, "the ring disappearing and reappearing instantly on the other side of his hand. "I'm afraid we've come to discuss the unpleasantness of the other day."

"Oh," Dr. Landsin says, "I… that is to say…" He jabs a finger at Tony, "I certainly hope he has not given you reason to believe that the blame for that lies with me."

"Doctor," Mystery says, his voice soft and even yet diamond hard and undeniable. Mystery looks down at the ring playing across his fingers and Dr. Landsin's eyes follow. It really is amazing how it moves, as if it were a strange creature running to and fro. "We aren't here to assign blame," Mystery says. "What has happened has happened. Now we are merely attempting to learn from our mistakes."

"Oh," Dr. Landsin says. He should look at Mystery, he was being very rude. He always made eye contact when he spoke with people but there was something about the movement of the ring, about the dance it performed over Mystery's knuckles, he couldn't look away. "Very well."

"I need you to tell Jason what happened the other day," Mystery says, stopping the ring between his middle fingers and tilting it to either side. "I need you to tell him about the two people who rescued you."

Dr. Landsin tears his eyes away from the ring. He looks at Mystery and then at the boy who is opening his thin book, but it isn't a book, it's a slim computer, a tablet, in a leather cover. "I don't know who they were, Mystery," he says, the boy is already typing. He turns back to Mystery, "You have to believe me, I had nothing to do…"

"Doctor," Mystery says, his voice even, solid, like a wall. Dr. Landsin can't ignore it. His eye is drawn once more to the movement of the ring over Mystery's fingers. "Very good," Mystery says. "Now, if you would be so kind, give Jason a full description of the two."

"I don't know their names," Dr. Landsin says, his voice is thick and slow.

"That's fine, tell us about them, begin at the beginning. Leave nothing out."

Dr. Landsin nods as slowly as he spoke. "I was in my lab working on the machine's lever mechanism. It had been giving me trouble since the third test which spun the arm releasing the…"

"Skip ahead to the spies," Mystery says.

Dr. Landsin nods again. He feels the heat of the blush rising in his cheeks but ignores it. "I met her first. There was an explosion outside the lab, the guards ran to check it out and then she was just there… just standing beside me."

"Describe her."

"Her hair was red, not red like any hair I've ever seen but red like the center of a flame. She wore a black body suit, one which clung to every curve of her body; her hips, her posterior, her magnificent…"

"That's sufficient description," Mystery says.

"She was very attractive," Dr Landsin says.

"Did she speak?"

"She told me that she was there to rescue me. What could I do? The world thought that I was kidnapped, I couldn't let her know otherwise."

"And then you made your escape?"

"I tried not to. I ran in the wrong direction, I ducked into rooms whithout exits, at one point I tried very hard to knock her unconscious with a candle stick…"

"She stopped you?"

"She's very good at fighting."

Mystery nods. "Continue."

"At some point she pulled me into a closet. I was certain that we'd be caught there."

"But you weren't."

"No, he was there."

"The man?"

"Yes, blond, beard, also in a body suit showing off his curves. His were not as appealing."

"He was in the closet?"

"Behind it."

"I'm sorry?"

"He was on the other side of the wall, he cut a door with a small saw."

"He had time to cut a door?" Mystery asked.

"Yes."

"Go on."

"I was in and out of consciousness after that part. At some point they hoisted me five stories up a cable and then we were dangling from a crane…"

"They brought a mechanical pulley system'?"

"That's the best description I have for it," Dr. Landsin says with a shrug. "We swung out onto the crane…"

"That's sufficient, Doctor," Mystery says. He turns to the boy. "Anything else?"

"No, that should get me started."

"They go to the beach," Dr. Landsin says.

"Come again?"

"After they have a successful mission, they always go to the beach. They mentioned that in the car."

Mystery nods. "Thank you, Doctor, that should be most helpful." He turns again to the boy and says, "I'm pushing our session to six. Work on this until then."

Jason nods and walks wordlessly out of the lab.

"What happens now?" Dr. Landsin asks. "Do we continue with the machine?"

"No," Mystery says. "Alas the machine's time has come and it has gone. We must move on to bigger and better things." Mystery holds his hand out and Tony places a file folder in it. "But first we must clean up after ourselves."

"We must?"

"Yes, Doctor, there are a number of loose ends with the machine and it falls to me to trim them." He hands the folder to Dr. Landsin who opens it to find a first-class plane ticket to the Bahamas.

"I don't understand," Dr. Landsin says.

"It's quite simple, Doctor," Mystery says. "You're holding a ticket for a plane which will later today, crash into the ocean." Dr. Landsin stares at the ticket as if it were a gun pointed at his face. "Clean up time begins with your death," Mystery says.

CHAPTER EIGHT

"Shelly," Spacer says, walking back into the house. "You here, babe?"

Spacer walks through the living room and into the kitchen where he last saw his wife. No Shelly, no ass-pillow. No surprise.

He hobbles back to the stairs and yells, "Honey? You up there?" No response.

He walks to the back of the house and steps through the screen door onto the deck overlooking the beach. The salt air brushes gently against him and he inhales deeply. This was what he was thinking about from the moment the bullet plunged itself into his bottom.

There's a single beach chair out on the sand with a single occupant. He leans against the railing and takes in the sight of his bikini clad wife, red hair brilliant in the morning sun, cascading over her shoulder to the swell of her right breast, only just held in check by the slight fabric of her favorite, white bikini top. The white of the suit almost perfectly matches the skin of his Irish lass and when she breathes in her breasts rise and fall almost with the rhythm of the tide.

He allows his eye to wander from her breast over her small torso, her belly button stretched into an oval the way she's reclined. He stares at her button for a long time, thinking about how he must trace his finger around it the first chance he gets.

"That was a long 'Mo' you took across the road," Shelly mutters without turning. Never spy on a spy.

"I met the neighbors," Spacer says.

"Yeah, I figured." Shelly absently flips the pages of the book in her hand and Spacer squints to make out the type.

"Really? Lady Chatterley's Lover?" he asks.

Shelly shrugs. "I figured it was time I found out what all of the fuss was about."

"What did you do with my pillow?" Spacer asks.

"Oh, you know that isn't how the game is played," Shelly says.

"Did you put it in the oven?" Spacer asks. Shelly says

nothing. "You did, didn't you? You know there may come a day when I use the oven, you really should stop hiding shit in there."

"I'll believe it when I taste it," Shelly says. "Strike that, I'll believe it when you taste it first."

Spacer hobbles inside long enough to pull his pillow out of the oven and then he makes his way back out to the beach. "Where are the chairs?" he asks.

Shelly points behind her to the railing where three more chairs are leaning, folded. Spacer lowers himself gently down the three steps to the beach and sets one up next to her.

"Mmm," he says, lowering himself into it, pillow first.

"You're getting old, moaning like that when you sit," Shelly says.

"I'm not getting old, I got shot."

"I've been shot, you don't hear me whining."

"You haven't been shot recently and, believe me, when you did, there was plenty of whining."

"Yeah yeah." Shelly lowers her book and considers him. "Still rocking the jammies, huh?"

"You know it." Spacer looks her over once more. "You know you can't be out here too long with your complexion."

"I'm wearing, like, SPF 3000. I'll be lucky if I even get a little color."

"You say that every time we come to the beach and every time I spend the entire first week slathering you with aloe."

"Yeah, like you aren't just waiting to get to do that again," Shelly says.

"I'll admit, it's not my least favorite thing." Spacer pulls off the T-shirt he slept in the night before and relaxes into his chair. "Speaking of ovens and not using them, I was thinking we could go out for seafood tonight."

"Seafood? At the beach? You rebel."

"So, you're in?"

"Why not," Shelly says, stifling a yawn. "What are the neighbors like?"

"They're nice people, Darren Whitman and family."

"And family?"

"Mm hmm, met the whole sampler."

"Really, you had to go with the Whitman's Sampler pun?"

"Darren thought it was hilarious."

"Yeah, not really selling him on me."

"All right, but they are nice. A little dull maybe, but very nice."

"Wait a minute," Shelly says, sitting up to get a better look at him. "It sounds like you are trying to sell me on him. What have you done?"

"Nothing?" Spacer says, perhaps a bit too defensively.

"Oh yes you have. When are we going over there for a nice home cooked meal?"

"I can honestly say I made no plans to have dinner at their place," Spacer says.

"Then you've made other plans. Spacer Alexander Sharpe, what have you signed me up for?"

"Please don't use the middle name, I do not want you and my mother to overlap in any way in the Venn diagram in my mind."

"I'll use it again if you don't tell me what we're doing with the neighbors and when."

"Okay, we're just going out on the town with them tomorrow night."

"With them, with the whole sampler?"

"See, it's hard not to pun."

"Spacer! Are we going out on a family fun night?"

"No, we're just going out with Darren and Si... and his wife."

"His wife who is named...?"

"Sissy."

"His wife is named Sissy? You want me to go, what, clubbing with Darren and Sissy Whitman?"

"Actually, that's exactly what I was hoping for," Spacer says. "Come on, please be cool about this, Darren had to bribe his wife quite handsomely to get her to go."

"Oh, so now I'm supposed to go out with someone who has to be paid to be seen with me?"

"No, it wasn't like that, it was..."

"Maybe you should go inside."

"But you'll think about it?"

"Spacer!"

"I'm going," Spacer says, pulling himself slowly out of the low chair and making his way back to the deck. He turns to plead his case a little more, but Shelly has returned her attention to Lady Chatterley and he decides it's better off leaving the two girls to themselves.

He makes his way slowly up the stairs and steps into the shower. He relaxes into the warmth cascading over his body, gasping a little as it runs over his wound but then adjusting to the sensation and finding a perverse sense of pleasure in the pain. He grits his teeth into it and smiles.

At last he cuts the water and steps out into the steam filled bathroom. He wipes the mirror until he can see himself, gauges the shagginess of his beard and decides to leave it as it is. Trimming is not a vacation activity.

He pulls on some shorts and stumbles to the bed which he eases himself down onto. He glances around for something to read, he'd brought Lady Chatterley for himself, and finds an old Reader's Digest in a basket by the bed. He flips it open to the Laughter is the Best Medicine section and is halfway through a joke he's already heard about a pig farmer when he drops off to sleep.

Spacer jolts awake and looks around the room. The shadows aren't long, it's early afternoon. Is Shelly still out on the beach? She'll be burned to a crisp.

He jumps to his feet and falls screaming back to the bed. "Oh yeah, the gun shot," he says.

He pulls himself slowly to his feet and grabs his cane from where he laid it against the dresser.

"Shelly!" he yells as he puts his foot on the first step.

"We're down here, dear?"

"Oh, thank God," Spacer mutters to himself. "Wait a minute, 'we're?' 'dear?' this cannot be good."

He shuffles down the stairs as quickly as he can without injuring himself further and when he gets to the bottom wheels around to the kitchen and stops dead in his tracks.

Sitting on the two bar stools in the kitchen, a pitcher of something most likely non-alcoholic on the counter between them, were his lovely wife still in her swimsuit with a sarong wrapped around her waist and Sissy Whitman in a sensible skirt and matching top.

"Ladies, hello," Spacer says.

"Oh my," Sissy says, turning and seeing Spacer standing in nothing but the shorts he fell asleep in.

"Spacer, honey, Sissy here came over with a whole pitcher of lemonade. Wasn't that nice?"

"I was… oh my," Sissy says.

"Sissy and I have been talking all about our plans for our big night out, tomorrow. We're both just so excited," Shelly says. She turns to Sissy and says, "Don't worry, dear, we'll both be wearing much more clothing tomorrow."

"You… you don't have to," Sissy says with a slight chuckle. "If I looked like you… either of you… well, I just might go around naked all of the time." She bursts into a loud giggle and her face glows crimson.

"Well, that is just so nice of you to say, Sissy,' Shelly says, reaching out and dabbing at a small pearl of saliva forming at the edge of Sissy's mouth.

"Oh, goodness, thank you," Sissy says, turning slightly away from Shelly.

A motorcycle approaches from down the street. Sissy jumps at the sound and whispers, "Oh no."

"What's wrong, Sissy?" Spacer asks.

"It's… it's nothing," Sissy says. She hops off of the stool and offers her hand to Shelly. "I hate to cut our little visit short but I'm going to have to dash now. Please, keep the pitcher and enjoy the lemonade, I'll come back for it tomorrow."

Shelly holds out her hand and Sissy gives it a quick, spastic shake before heading for the door. She nods at Spacer as she walks by and says, "You have a lovely home."

"Thanks, but it's not ours, we're just…" Spacer isn't able to finish the sentence because the door shuts behind the retreating Sissy.

"Darren!" Sissy can be heard yelling as she runs across the road. "Darren it's him again, it's Francis!"

Spacer arches an eyebrow at Shelly who shrugs and walks to the window. Spacer stumbles next to her and they watch as a kid, can't be more than eighteen, pulls onto the Whitman's yard on a motorcycle.

"What is that?" Spacer asks. "A Kawasaki with a Harley emblem glued onto it?"

"Suzuki, I think, but that's definitely a Harley emblem glued onto it. Kinda looks like it's been painted with house paint too," Shelly says.

The kid, wearing a denim jacket with leather trimmed sleeves, ripped jeans and a pair of pristine looking motorcycle boots climbs lazily off the bike and makes his way up the path toward the front porch.

"Where do you suppose he got the boots?" Spacer asks.

"You like the boots?"

"They're good boots."

Shelly pats him on the side of the face and says, "Well, maybe if you're good for the rest of the year Santa will bring you some."

"Ah, Santa never remembers the things I want all the way back in July."

The kid stops on the front porch and bellows, "Yo, Q, you ready?"

The door swings open and Darren stomps out.

"Ah boy, this can't be good," Spacer says.

"Mr. Sampler I presume," Shelly says.

"You and your bike need to get off of my property right now," Darren screams in his face.

"I should go give him a hand," Spacer says.

"We're keeping a low profile here, remember?"

"Look old man, this has nothing to do with you," the kid says.

"The hell it doesn't. That is my fifteen-year-old daughter in there and she is not going anywhere with you."

"The daughter's fifteen?" Shelly asks.

"Yup."

"Okay, I'm going to shoot the punk."

"What happened to a low profile?"

"I can do it. They'll have no idea where it came from. I'll use the silencer you got me for our anniversary."

"Daddy!" Quinn yells, running outside.

"Wait, that's her?"

"Yeah."

"I saw her sneak something into our mailbox earlier."

"Oh yeah, she said she'd get me a list of hot nightspots in the area."

"That was prearranged? I'm glad we had this chat, I had plans of maiming her in the near future."

Spacer shrugs, "At least one good thing's come of this."

Quinn tries to pull her father away from the kid. "He's not worth it, Q. Just come on," the kid instructs.

"She's not going anywhere with you," Darren says.

The kid shakes his head and turns halfway away as if pondering the facts in evidence. "Oh Darren, don't step in, this is the oldest trick in the book," Spacer says.

Darren takes a step toward the kid and the kid spins around, cracking his fist into Darren's jaw and dropping him to the porch.

"Okay, go beat his ass," Shelly says.

"Can't now, if I flatten him in front of Quinn right after he dropped her dad, Darren will never live that down."

"You're right," Shelly says, nodding in contemplation. "I'm getting my gun."

"Don't get your gun, I think there's another way we can help Darren out on this one."

"You're thinking of calling in Pete, aren't you?"

"He owes me one, several actually."

"You really want to blow a Pete favor on the Whitmans?"

"They're nice people, Sissy brought you lemonade."

"It's really good too," Shelly said. "I have to get her recipe… and then have her come over with the ingredients to use the recipe to make me more."

"Oh, look, here comes the cavalry," Spacer says.

An older man who apparently lives in the house next door

to the Whitmans runs into the yard, garden hose at the ready. "You get outta here you punk!" he yells.

"Seriously? Go back to your nursing home," the kid tells him.

"You asked for it," the older man says, depressing the release valve on the hose. Nothing happens. "Dag blame it, Henrietta, turn on the spigot," he yells back to his house.

"The what?" an elderly female voice yells back.

"The spicket, the spicket woman! Oh, never mind, I'll get it myself." The old man runs disappears around the side of his house.

"So close," Shelly says.

The kid saunters over to his bike and Quinn jumps on it behind him.

"Quinn, I forbid you from going with him," Darren yells from where he still sits on his stoop.

"Yeah, why don't you come over here and try to stop her, old man?" the kid says, revving the small motor of his disguised bike.

"What a guy, punches a middle-aged out of shape accountant and then threatens him," Shelly says.

"Don't act like you wouldn't have hopped right on that bike at her age."

"How can you say that?"

"I was there, remember?"

"Oh right, I keep forgetting we went to the same high school."

"Yeah, I wasn't a memorable part of your formidable years."

"I'm still plenty formidable, and you're a big part of my life now, don't you forget that," Shelly says, popping Spacer on the ass.

"Oh my God! Really?" Spacer says, grabbing his ass and collapsing against the wall.

"I'm sorry, I keep forgetting."

They watch the kid drop the bike into gear and pull away from the yard just as the old man runs back around the corner, spraying for all he's worth but just missing the departing kids.

Shelly and Spacer back away from the window before they can be seen by the Whitmans.

"Okay, so, revenge and then dinner, you think?" Shelly asks.

"That sounds good. Go on up and get ready, I'll make a couple of calls."

Shelly pecks him quickly on the lips before running up the stairs. Spacer plucks his phone off of the entry table and scrolls through his contacts to the Ps. He hits a number and waits for it to ring on the other end.

"What?" a voice says.

"Put Pete on."

"Who   the   hell   are   you?"
"Really?" Spacer asks.

"Hey, whoa!" he hears in the background and then the gravelly voice of Pete comes on the line. "Sorry about that, Spaceman. That's a… heh… that's a new guy."

"Yeah, keep him away from my phone," Spacer says, there is no humor in his voice, if Darren were to hear Spacer now he'd be putting extra locks on his door by nightfall.

"Will do, brother. What can I do for ya?"

"I'm in Bridges…"

"I'm sorry, man. What, you got dumped there? I can come pick you up. Is Shelly okay?"

"No, we're both here, we're here on purpose. It's a vacation."

"Really? If that floats your boat."

"So, listen, there's a dive just at the edge of town, it's where the townies go when they want to pretend they're dangerous."

"Yeah, I know where you mean."

"Meet me there with the boys in two hours. I've got a job for you."

CHAPTER NINE

"Ready babe?" Shelly asks, walking down the stairs.

"No, I've got to shower and…" Spacer says turning and seeing her for the first time. "What are you wearing?"

"My leathers," Shelly says. "I'll be riding with Pete."

"No, you won't."

"Um, we're doing a snatch and grab, I don't think it's a good idea to let Pete go unsupervised."

"Neither do I, but I'll be doing the supervising."

"Really? You'll be riding a bike with that extra hole in your ass?"

"I… well…"

"Didn't think about that, did ya?"

"Well, not as such, but…"

"And where were you planning on putting the cane, Grandpa?"

"I… would have figured something out," Spacer says.

"Uh huh. So, you'll take me into Havenboro so I can get the Ninja and then you can come back here and get all pretty for dinner." Shelly holds up her Glock 19 and slides a round into the chamber. "So, the only real question is, gun or no gun?"

"No gun, this kid is going to scare easy, trust me."

"Actually, I was thinking it would be good for keeping Pete in line."

"Oh, please, Pete's more afraid of you than the punk's going to be of him."

Shelly stares at the pistol for a moment and sighs, "Yeah, you're right. I just like it so much." She shrugs. "I'll put it away."

She runs up the stairs and into the bedroom.

"Why did you even bring your gun on vacation?" Spacer yells up the steps.

"Because we always wind up doing missions on vacation," Shelly says, walking back down the steps. "I brought yours too."

"You brought my gun?"

"Better to have it and not need it."

"I really don't think we do that many missions on our vacations."

"Trust me," Shelly says, throwing her leather jacket over her shoulder. "We do."

"Okay, but I promise, no missions on this vacation."

"What do you call this?"

"What, this little outing? This isn't a mission."

"I'm wearing my leathers and we're meeting up with Pete, this is a mission," Shelly says, walking through into the garage.

"Well if you count little things like this as missions of course we're going to be doing missions on our vacations," Spacer yells as he hobbles after her.

He catches up to her as she slides into the passenger seat of the Spyder.

"Is that the way it works?" she asks.

"I'm just saying, this is what we do, we can't just turn it off," Spacer says, crawling behind the wheel.

"Funny, I was under the impression that vacations were for turning off."

Spacer presses the button opening the garage door and backs down the driveway, drawing the eye of everyone on the street. "I told you we should have gone with something less flashy," he says. "We are attracting way too much attention."

"This place is supposed to be peopled by the uber-wealthy, we shouldn't be getting this much attention from the Spyder."

"It used to be the wealthy, now it's upper middle. We're in SUV country."

"The last time we were in a Land Rover we were being chased through the outback by Aboriginals. I'm not using one of those to go to the market for milk."

"It may surprise you to learn, but there is a middle ground between off road behemoth and asphalt peeling, sports coupe."

"If you think I'm getting a BMW to blend in with suburbanites you've clearly forgotten the lady you said, 'I do' to."

Spacer shrugs and turns onto the bridge leading toward Havenboro.

"I will admit, it's nice to be so close to all of our toys and accomplices if we do have to go on missions while vacationing," Shelly said.

"That's the spirit, but this isn't a mission."

"Mm hmm."

Shelly turns on the radio to an all eighties station and they let folks like Prince, the B52s and Duran Duran do the talking for them for the remainder of their drive to the warehouse.

Spacer pulls the car next to the warehouse and they step out in silence. Spacer unlocks the door and steps over to the bank of switches and flips on the florescent overhead lights, illuminating the spoils of a decade and a half of spy work; the armory in the back behind a locked cage, the array of listening devices hung on peg boards along the walls, the cabinets filled with bugs, cameras and disguises, and of course, the fleet of automobiles, bikes and a few light weight jets. The things they've seen and done over the course of their careers have left them both stripped of what faith they ever had in any sort of higher power but this, for them, is a place of reverence. This is their chapel and they maintain the decorum due it.

Shelly selects a helmet from the shelf, one with a full faceplate tinted so that no one can see her face behind it. Spacer steps up behind her.

"Quinn cannot know you're a part of this," he says.

"Yes, love, that's why I picked this helmet."

"It's not the helmet that concerns me; you have hair like no one else in the world."

Shelly spins and smiles at him. "Thanks, babe."

"I'm not complimenting you this time. How are you going to hide it?"

"I'll tuck it in the jacket and flip up the collar, she won't see a single lock." Shelly studies her husband's face, crinkled with concern. She reaches up and takes his chin in her hand. "Don't worry, Spacer, I've got this."

"It's not just the hair either, it's… all right, dammit, this is a mission and I'm not going to be there to back you up."

"This? This isn't a mission, it's an outing," she says, kissing him softly.

She steps back and flips her hair inside the jacket. "You just worry about getting us a good table. I'm not eating lobster next to the men's room."

She walks over to the Ninja and throws her long leg over it, settling onto the leather saddle. Spacer presses the button raising the garage bay door and walks next to her. She pulls the helmet on and raises the visor to look up at her husband.

"Really, Spacer, I've got this. It's a walk in the park."

"I can't help worrying."

"And that is why I love you," she says, popping him on the ass and making him wince. "Didn't forget that time," she says, winking at him before lowering her visor and cranking the machine to life. She revs the engine twice, lets out the clutch and peels out of the warehouse without looking back at Spacer. There comes a time when goodbyes must end.

Once on the open road headed back toward bridges her mind clears of distraction and she thinks only of the task at hand. She opens the throttle and kicks the bike into high gear.

Pete leans against the wall of the poser biker bar watching his men mill about growing more and more impatient. He could care less about his bored brethren, he's more worried about what it is he'll be doing. When Spacer needs a favor, it can mean anything from driving toys to a children's hospital to watching a captured head of some enemy state.

He looks up at the sound of a fast approaching bike and watches as a small framed rider peels into the lot, kicking gravel and slaloming around the haphazardly parked motorcycles without cutting the speed at all. The rider disappears around the side of the bar and he hears the squeal of the tire as the rider turns the bike 180 in what must be a tight doughnut before killing the engine.

"Fuck," he says.

"What's wrong, boss?" Rodrigo asks from his place against the wall next to him.

"It ain't him, it's her."

"Madre de Dios," Rodrigo mutters. "Are you sure?"

The small rider walks around the side of the bar, removing both her helmet and any doubt as to her identity. "I thought you said it would be him," Rodrigo says.

"That's what he told me."

"Well, lookey what we got here," one of his men says. It was Clint, the new guy.

She turns her head and glares at him. Pete grabs Rodrigo on the arm and shoves him toward Clint. "You shut that idiot up."

"What are you going to do, boss?"

"God help me, I'm going to go talk to her." He watches her disappear back around the corner of the bar and jogs to catch up with her. By the time he reaches her she's leaning against the brick wall tapping her helmet absently on her thigh. He swallows thinking about the time he saw her cave in a man's head with a helmet very much like that one.

"You have a new guy," she says, piercing him with her eyes.

"I… uh… yeah. I'm really sorry about that, Mrs. Sharpe, that won't happen again."

"Uh huh," she says. "What did Spacer tell you about this?"

"Well," Pete says, scratching at the back of his head and chuckling nervously, if she would just put down the damn helmet. "Not… not much actually, just told us to be here. We…" he chokes a little and takes a deep breath. "We thought we'd be meeting him actually."

"There was a change of plans," she says.

"Understood," Pete says. "You, uh, can I take your helmet for you?"

She smiles at him but her grey eyes don't waver. "Am I making you nervous, Peter?"

"Yes, Ma'am."

She nods. "What we're doing is a classic snatch and grab. There's a punk ass in there with a girl who shouldn't be. We're going to take her."

"Where are we taking her?"

"You don't need to know that. She rides with one of your guys and he follows me, just the one."

"She's not riding with you?"

"No, she rides with me and she's going to wind up feeling the girls," she says, grabbing her own chest. Pete swallows and hopes the full erection he's sporting isn't too obvious. Thank God he wore his chaps. "It's really important this girl thinks I'm just one of your boys."

"Okay, I'll take her," Pete says.

Shelly shakes her head. "Can't be you, I need you to stay and make sure your boys don't put the punk in the hospital."

"No?"

"No, Spacer and I are trying to have a vacation out here. We don't need the noise of a community wide outrage that would come of a motorcycle gang hospitalizing a townie."

"Okay, so just scrapes and bruises."

"Not even that if you can help it, I get the idea that this kid would go to the ER over a paper cut. The clothes are all secondhand, but the shoes are nice, I'm thinking he's a doctor's kid."

"Nice kicks, huh?"

"Yeah, matter of fact, see if you can find out what size they are. We may be taking the boots too."

"Got it," Pete says. "Scare the kid, take the girl, maybe the boots. How we doing this?"

"We'll surround the kid's bike, then you and a few of your guys go in, roust the punk and take the girl." She reaches out quickly and grabs Pete's vest pulling the big man down until his face is just an inch or so from her deadly eyes. "The girl does not ride with the new guy."

"No... no ma'am, I wouldn't do that. Rodrigo can take her."

She arches an eyebrow, considering. "He's the best choice?" she asks.

"If you can think of a better, you're welcome to him."

"No, no I guess he'll have to make do." She nods and lets go of Pete's vest. He straightens quickly and resists the urge to smooth it. "Go tell your men only what they need to know. I'll pull around in five and we'll do this thing."

Pete nods and backs slowly away from her. He's just about to turn and walk back to his boys when she yells after him,

"Peter."

"Yes?" he says, spinning quickly to face her.

"If he ends up in the hospital you will have me to deal with."

"Ye… yes ma'am," Pete says and runs back to his men to threaten them with their lives if anything happens to the punk or the girl.

"Okay," Pete says, staring each of his men in the eye. "You all know what you have to do. Do we need to go over it again?"

"We got it, boss. What the fuck, you think we're morons?" Clint says.

He should not have brought him along. Pete grabs him by the collar and pulls him close to his face. "You open your mouth one more time before we're back at the house and you're going to find out what the fuck."

Clint starts to say something but thinks better about it. The Ninja's motor cranks and soon she pulls around the side of the building, once again wearing the helmet and looking more like a small man than the rockin' piece of ass Pete would never have the balls to admit she was.

She pulls to a stop next to a piece of shit Suzuki with a Harley emblem glued onto it. Pete walks over to her.

"We ready to do this?" she asks.

"This is the bike?"

"This is it."

"I thought you said he came from money."

"I'm thinking he built it himself, probably followed some YouTube How To. It's a rebellion, I've seen a lot of pampered kids try it."

Pete considers the small machine.

"You… uh… you mind if I rip the emblem off in front of him?"

She looks up at him and raises the visor so he can once again see her slate eyes. "Peter, do the entire world a favor and rip the emblem off of this bike."

Pete smiles his first genuine smile since he got Spacer's call

66

and says, "Yes Ma'am."

Pete turns and walks toward the bar. Rodrigo and Clint fall in behind him as they planned. Clint probably isn't the best guy to bring in, but he'll be damned if he's going to leave the new guy outside with her.

He pushes the door open and lets the evening sunlight flood inside, trailing his long shadow. He takes a single step inside and feels every eye in the place turn to him. Just like he thought it would be, it is filled with kids in leather they probably bought on line drinking watered down beers they most likely charged to their daddies' cards. He sighs and walks inside, Rodrigo shutting the door hard behind them.

"Whose little Harley is that sitting outside?" he asks, his deep voice booming through the room, completely overtaking the sound of Born to be Wild blaring from the jukebox in the corner.

Everyone turns away in unison.

"I guess they didn't hear me over the music. Clint, do something about that," Pete says.

Clint picks up a bar stool, spilling its occupant onto the floor, walks over to the juke and slams it into the machine, killing the music.

"Hey," the bar tender yells but stops and backs away when Pete looks at him. That was the way people were supposed to behave around him.

"That's better," Pete says. "Now I was asking, who's little hog is that sitting outside."

"It's my boyfriends," a small but fierce voice says from the other end of the bar.

"Q, shut up!" a boy's voice yells.

Pete smiles and walks toward the sound. He sees the skinny kid, shitty clothes but Mrs. Sharpe was right about the boots. He's sitting next to a little whisper of a thing in a tank top who is staring directly at him. Something in the set of her gaze sends a quick shiver down his spine that he shakes off with a manly chuckle.

There's a kid sitting on the stool next to the punk. Pete unceremoniously plucks the kid from his perch and tosses him away. Pete slides onto the now empty stool and puts his meaty arm around the punk's shoulders. "So that's your ride, huh?"

"Um," the kid says, glancing up at him and then quickly away. "I… I guess."

"Francis, you don't have to take shit from this guy," the girl yells. "And get your hands off him."

She shoves Pete's arm but he doesn't move. Clint and Rodrigo crowd around the punk.

"I don't think I've ever seen a bike quite like that."

"It's… it's just a bike," the punk says.

"It's not just a bike," the girl yells. "Francis built it himself. Which is probably more than any of you dipshits have ever done."

"Built it yourself?" Pete asks, looking back at his boys and then to the kid. "Hey, that is pretty impressive. Why don't you come show us how you did that, Francis?" Pete leans in very close as he says the punks name.

"I… uh…"

"You don't have to go anywhere with these assholes!" the girl says.

"Come on, Francis, let's take a walk." Pete stands and drags the punk to his feet.

"Hey, quit it!" The girl yells. She turns to the rest of the patrons and says, "Hello, little help?" No one looks at her.

"Oh, don't worry about your boyfriend, girlie, you're coming too," Pete says. Clint moves in to grab her but Pete shoves him away. He picks the girl up by her waistband and drops her over Rodrigo's shoulder.

"What the fuck? Let go of me!" the girl screams, pounding on Rodrigo's back.

"Come on, Francis," Pete says, dragging the punk toward the door with his boys and the girl following closely behind.

Pete pushes through the door and blinks to readjust to the bright early evening. The punk stumbles under the weight of his grip but he doesn't lose his footing. Pete drags him to the small bike where Mrs. Sharpe and the rest of his crew wait for them in silence.

When they reach the bike, Pete lets go of the punk and says,

"So, you built this swee…" he stops for a moment, choking a little on the bile rising in his throat. He works it down and says, "this sweet ride all by yourself, huh?"

"Well… I had some help," the punk says.

"Why are you letting this jerk treat you like this, Francis?" the girl asks, scrambling her way off of Rodrigo's shoulder and over to the punk's side. "Tell him you built the bike and where he can shove his shit."

"Q, god dammit, will you shut up?" Francis says, slapping her across the face. "And it's Frank! How many times do I have to tell you?"

Pete jerks his head to Mrs. Sharpe who is slowly walking toward them. He jumps between the two kids, shoving Francis away from the girl. Mrs. Sharpe stops walking but stares at them.

"Why'd you go and do a thing like that, Francis?" Pete asks, reminding himself to breathe deeply.

"What the fuck, Frank?" the girl asks, tears forming in her eyes.

"How much did this set you back, Francis?" Pete asks, running his hand over the cracked plastic saddle.

"I don't… I don't know."

"You don't, huh?" Pete runs his hands up the engine. "I sure would like to have something like this myself." He snaps the Harley emblem off and holds it up to the punk. "Oopsie."

"You, um, you wanna buy it?" the punk asks.

"Buy it? Frank, you can't sell your bike, we're going to ride off on it and start our life together," the girl says.

"Well, jeepers Francis, I'd like to buy it but it's damaged," Pete says. He drops the emblem onto the asphalt and grinds it beneath the heel of his boot. "I just hate paying good money for damaged goods."

"But you…" the punk starts to say but shuts up and looks the other way.

"But I what, Francis? What do I?" Pete asks, leaning over the small man.

"I don't… I didn't…"

"I think what you probably meant to say was that I deserve

to just have it for free. Isn't that what you meant to say?" Pete asks.

"I... I..." now tears are beginning to form in the punk's eyes as well.

"Yeah, that's what I thought you meant," Pete says. "And I do appreciate the gesture, but I'm not sure I can ride it. You've probably noticed that I'm a pretty big guy. I may be too heavy. About how much do you weigh?"

"I don't know," the punk says, backing away.

"Yeah, I figured you'd say that. Boys, you wanna help him out?"

Two of the guys, Jerry and Nick, grab the punk, flipping him upside down and holding him by his legs. "Hey, come on, please?" the kid says, crying unashamedly now.

"Get a good feel, boys, I need an accurate weight," Pete says, walking behind the punk and glancing at the soles of his boots.

He walks slowly away from them to where Mrs. Sharpe stands. "Sorry about the slap, I didn't peg him for the type," he says.

She doesn't turn her head from the scene, but she says, "Yeah, all bets are off on the hospital now, fuck the community outrage."

"Really?"

"Try to keep him out of intensive care if you can."

"I'll do my best, ma'am," Pete says. "Oh, the boots, they're size eights."

"Eights? That figures. He can keep them."

"Actually, if you don't want them, I've got a kid I think they'll fit real nice."

Now she did turn to face him and said, "Pete, your kid is seven... and a girl."

Pete shrugs. "What can I say, she takes after her old man."

She turns her attention back to the dangling boy. "Well, you tell Caitlyn to wear them in good health. But it's time we got the girl on the road."

"Right, I'm on it."

Pete walks back to the punk and says, "So, boys, what's the

verdict?"

"He's pretty light, boss," Nick says.

"Yeah, I was afraid of that. Tell ya what, Francis. As much as I like your wheels, I think I like your girl a little better. Which one do you think I should take?"

"The girl!" the punk yells without pausing to think.

"Frank!" the girl screams.

Pete grins broadly. "You know, Francis, I can't tell you how happy you just made me."

He turns and nods to Rodrigo. Before Rodrigo moves Clint says, "I got her, boss!" clapping his meaty palms onto the girl and hoisting her over his shoulder.

"No!" Pete yells.

In a black flash Shelly leaps over the bike between them, slams her elbow into Clint's throat, spins and scoops the girl from his shoulder as he falls. She hands her off to Rodrigo and kicks the collapsing Clint in his face as he is crumpling to the ground scattering a half dozen of his teeth over the parking lot.

She walks silently back to her bike, sparing the quickest of glances toward Pete as she passes. She revs the Ninja again and pulls out of the lot, slowly until she is sure that Rodrigo is following her with the girl and then opening it up.

Pete sighs and runs a hand through his hair. He turns to Nick and says, "See if Clint is still alive."

Nick releases his hold on the punk and Jerry allows him to drop to the parking lot.

"He's alive, boss, but he ain't lookin' too good," Nick says.

"Yeah, well he's doing a lot better than most of the folk who piss off that lady."

Pete turns back to the punk who is pulling himself up off of the ground.

"O... okay," the punk says. "You got my girlfriend, now are you going to leave me alone?"

"Oh, we'll leave you alone, but before we do, there's one more thing we need to discuss. I told you how much I hate receiving damaged goods and you damaged that girl right in front of me. I'm afraid you're going to have to make that right with a few of your bones."

"What?"

Pete pulls a set of brass knuckles from his pocket and slides them onto his fingers. "Boys," he says, "step aside."

CHAPTER TEN

The man's hand is like a vice on Quinn's small stomach, holding her against him as they speed down the road. She couldn't pull away from him if she'd tried. She won't try anyway, they have to be doing eighty on the highway. The wind blowing in her face is so cold she doesn't know if she is crying.

Not that she doesn't have a good reason to cry, she is probably not going to survive whatever these people have planned for her. She doesn't want to think about what is going to happen. Frank's probably already dead. Fuck him though, the only thing that upsets her about that is that she won't get to kill him herself.

He'd just given her away to them like she was some thing he could replace whenever he wanted. He didn't even have to think about it, he chose his stupid, ugly motorcycle over her. He didn't even try to stand up to these bastards either. Sure, he could be a big man in front of her dad but...

Oh, her dad, her daddy, she'd been so terrible to him. She'd left him sitting there on the porch after that asshole, pussy, jerkoff had punched him over her. He'd tried to stop her from this, but she hadn't listened and now she's never going to have the chance to apologize. She'll never see him again, or her mom or little scout. She'll never see her room with her posters and her music. She'll never text Jamie or Sara or anyone ever again.

Wait a minute! She can text someone, she can call for help. Her phone is right here in her purse... where's her purse? What happened to her purse?

They swerve around some junk in the road and then man's hand slips just below her belt, but he quickly repositions it and glances at the small man riding just in front of them, probably hoping he hadn't seen it. That's the man who terrifies Quinn. She'd seen the way the others acted toward him, even the big guy at the bar who did all the talking was taking his orders from the little guy. The way he had beaten that man who'd grabbed her, he'd moved so quickly Quinn hadn't even known what was happening until it was all over. Whatever is going to happen to her, it will be on that man's orders.

The small man straightens on his cycle and twists his head around to look behind them. His hair pulls free from his jacket and it shines in the beam of their motorcycle's headlamp. It's the brightest red Quinn has ever seen, and it looks almost soft. All of the bikers have long hair, but theirs is greasy and stringy. This man's hair is cared for, lush and almost feminine. Could the small man actually be a woman?

He or she turns back around to face front and the hair disappears once more into the coat. He leans forward and speeds up even faster. The man driving Quinn matches his pace.

The small man turns off onto a road that Quinn knows very well, they're only two blocks from her house. Are they going to take her somewhere in her own neighborhood to kill her? The thought of being assaulted and killed on the same streets she'd ridden her bicycle on as a child hits her with a horrible irony and fresh tears spill from her eyes. No mistaking these for the irritation of cold wind.

The small man makes two more turns and the man driving her follows suit until they come to a stop in front of Quinn's own home.

"What's going on?" she asks as they pull alongside the small man.

"Don't say we never did you any favors, kid," the small man says, his voice a hoarse croak.

"You're... you're letting me go?" Neither man says anything. "How do you know where I live?"

The small man reaches into his jacket and pulls her clutch purse from inside it. She hadn't even felt him take it off of her, it must have been when he'd grabbed her from the other guy. He hands it and her drivers permit bearing her address back to her.

"But... why?"

"Just stay away from the assholes, okay?" the small man croaks without looking at her.

The porch light comes on and her daddy steps outside.

"What's going on out here, who are you people?"

"Daddy!" Quinn screams, unable to stop herself.

"Quinn? What are you doing with these men?"

"Oh daddy!" Quinn yells, running into his arms and embracing him.

The two bikers start their engines and pull away.

Shelly can't help but smile behind her visor as she drives slowly away from the scene. She'd like to have stayed longer and watch the whole homecoming, but questions would have been asked and she doesn't have answers for them.

Still, it's nice to have a definite win in her ledger.

CHAPTER ELEVEN

Rachel steps into the front hall of Mystery's expansive home. She stops short as one of the various black-suited thugs steps in front of her without noticing and hurries away to a back room. The energy in the house is higher than it had ever been during preproduction of one of their shows.

She's shoved from behind and turns to see the kid, Jason, stumbling past her, his face buried in the screen of his phone. She can't hear the video he's watching but it's something to do with motorcycles barreling dangerously down the highway. Rachel watches as his zombielike shuffle leads him closer and closer to the stairway. She secretly bets herself five dollars that he misses the step and face plants.

"Whoa there, Scooter!" the main thug, Tony, says as he steps out of Mystery's home office. He grabs the kid by the arm just before he has the chance to trip. "Can't have you falling and damaging that beautiful mind of yours."

"Huh?"

"Never mind."

"Where's the boss?" Jason asks. "I need to show him something."

"He told me to have you wait in his office. He had to bump the session a little later tonight. There's something he…" Tony's concentration falters as he looks over to see Rachel standing there. "Something he has to do," Tony says at last. Rachel doesn't know why, but the words send a chill to her very core.

"I think he'd really want to see this," Jason says, holding his phone out toward Tony.

"Huh?" Tony says, staring blankly at the kid for a half second before remembering where he was. "Oh, yeah, if you say so, you're pretty good with this stuff. But you're going to have to wait for a minute. He's going to seriously not want to be disturbed for the next little while. You get me?"

Jason nods. He's a smart kid, he won't press his luck. "Okay, can you let him know though?"

"Yeah," Tony says, ushering Jason toward the office door.

"Yeah, I'll let him know." He guides the kid inside the office and closes the door behind him. When he turns toward Rachel, he smiles beatifically toward her. The smile is as bad as the words.

"Hello, Tony," she says, keeping her voice even and cheerful.

"So good to see you," Tony says. "Did you just get in?"

"Yes, just now," Rachel says. "He called and asked me to bring by some of the receipts from the last show," she holds the brief case she's carrying up as exhibit A.

"Yeah, yeah he's expecting you," Tony says. "He's out back, I'll... um... walk you out."

"I know the way," Rachel says.

"Hmm? Oh, yeah. Yeah, I guess you do." Tony looks toward the back of the house and then back at Rachel. "I'll walk still with you. I've gotta, um, I've gotta deliver a message from the kid anyway."

"All right," Rachel says.

"So, um... after you," Tony says, gesturing meekly.

Rachel nods and steps in front of him, her breath catches as he falls in step behind her.

"Did, uh, did you have any trouble driving over?" Tony asks.

"No, I... it was fine."

"Well... that is good to hear."

Rachel stops and Tony very nearly collides into her. "You, you okay?"

"Look," she says, turning around and facing him. "I don't know who you are or what it is that you and Mystery are doing together, I don't, I don't want to know."

"Okay," Tony says.

"What I do know is that I have worked with him for a very long time and I think that the time we've spent together should warrant me a little more than..." Rachel stutters looking for the right word."

"You upset that he wants to see you out back?" Tony asks.

"Is he even out there?"

"Yeah. What? Yeah."

"Oh," Rachel says. She turns and starts to walk again.

"Wait," Tony says, putting a hand on her shoulder to stop her. His hand is heavy, but his touch is light. "What did you think was happening?"

"I… well," Rachel sighs, "I was pretty sure you were going to whack me."

"To   whack   you?"

"I don't know what the cool kids are calling it," Rachel says. "I was pretty sure that I was about to have a bullet in me. I'm not completely convinced I'm not."

"Yeah, that's what I was afraid you were thinking," Tony says. Is that a nervous tremble in his voice? "Without going too much into the details of my past, I have dealt roughly with people on a number of occasions, it doesn't really get to me."

Rachel takes a long breath. If he's trying to calm her it isn't working.

"Dealing with you, though, that's getting to me." Tony takes a long breath now and releases it slowly. "I may not have known him as long as you have but I've seen him with a lot of people. I've seen him with people he needed and people he didn't, people who were useful and hangers on he wanted to drop, but only one time have I seen him with a person he…"

"A person he what?" Rachel asks, her nerves were dissipating now but her curiosity was rising through the roof.

"Look," Tony shrugs, "I'm not here for counseling, not really one of my strengths. What I'm saying is that I need to take you out there and, when I do that, I need for you to be in a good place, emotionally speaking. If I take you out there like this, I'm going to have a meeting with him after you leave that I genuinely do not want to have." Yes, that is definitely a tremble in his voice. "So, what do I have to do to make you better before we go out there?"

"Actually, Tony, I think you just did."

"Seriously?" Rachel nods. "Thank God. Now come on, he expected us, like, five minutes ago."

Rachel walks out the back door with Tony following closely behind her. She takes the small footpath to the pool and stumbles to a stop when she sees Mystery lounging on a deck chair in a Megadeath T-shirt and flower print shorts. "What... happened to him?" she asks.

Tony sighs and shrugs.

"Mystery," Rachel says, stepping up to him.

"Rachel," he says, looking up from a book which she can now see is the latest John Grisham.

"How's the book?" she says.

"Hmm? Oh, it's all lawyers and south and stereotypes and if you'd made me read it for another minute you'd probably have found I'd drowned myself in the pool," he says, throwing the paperback into the pool instead. He takes a deep breath and says, "I'm sorry, I do not like these clothes."

Rachel nods at him and holds up the briefcase. "I brought the receipts."

"Yes, thank you," Mystery says. He looks at Tony, "Would you mind putting those in my office?"

"Sure thing." Tony takes the case and says, "Speaking of which, Scooter..." he bites his lip and says, "Jason is in there right now waiting to do the thing."

"Thank him for his patience."

"Will do. He also said that he found another thing about the other thing which you would probably be very interested in."

"I'm sure I will," Mystery says. "Now can we have a moment?"

"You got it," Tony says, vanishing into the house.

Mystery turns to Rachel and pats the lounge chair beside him. She sits but doesn't recline.

"What's going on, Mystery," she says.

"How do you mean?"

"How do I mean? You've shut down the show and you clearly have no intention of opening a new one any time soon. There are... I don't know... gangsters and one weird nerd crawling around your house. Tony who was always this dark figure you kept at arm's length is now attached to your hip. That is how I mean."

"Well, when you put it that way," Mystery says. He smiles a smile that would have been charming if the rough pony he'd pulled his hair into weren't pulling his features back like a bad face lift.

"What is up with your clothes?"

"These? Believe it or not, I thought they would put you at ease."

"Oh." Rachel says.

"Not one of my better ideas," Mystery says, mercifully pulling the band out of his hair and letting it fall to his shoulders.

"I don't know what's happening, Mystery. I… it scares me. I really thought that I was going to be killed tonight."

"What?" Mystery says. "Why? Did Tony say something?"

"No! Actually, he was really nice to me."

"Tony?"

"Yeah," Rachel says, finally allowing herself to relax a little. "I mean I'm pretty sure it's because he's afraid of you, but still."

"That is good to know."

"I… you don't… we," Rachel begins but she can't find the words to follow.

Mystery sits up and turns toward her. "You don't know how you fit in to the new operation, do you?"

"I don't."

"There's really not a delicate way of putting this but…"

"I don't," Rachel says. "I don't fit in to the new operation."

Mystery shakes his head.

"Well, I suppose that says it all," Rachel says. She sits up and looks around for her things before remembering that the only thing she had she gave to Tony. She takes a long breath, stands and says, "I guess I'll just show myself out."

"Rachel," Mystery says. "We've known each other too long for you to storm out of here like the heroine in a melodrama."

Rachel sighs. "You can fire a person or you can tell her how to leave your home. You cannot do both."

"I'm asking. Please, have a seat."

Rachel looks down at the man who'd hired her away from her life of waiting tables for shitty tips so many years ago. She never knew when he stopped being her boss and became her friend, bizarre friendship though it was. But he was her friend and, given the stuff going on in that house, she had a strong feeling that this might be the last time she ever saw him.

She sat.

"First of all, I want you to know that you won't be going back to waiting tables. I've provided for you."

"Mystery, I don't…"

"It's in your bank account and more will be coming regularly. Live on it, give it all to charity, do what you will with it but that's a thing which is happening."

Rachel nods. She's known him long enough to recognize a closed issue.

"Secondly," Mystery says, "I've had a lot of employees in my life, but I've never had a Rachel."

"That's not true," Rachel says with a grin, "you had that assistant, Rachel Mankowitz."

"No, she was terrible and not deserving of the name. I rechristened her. She is now Hildegard."

"Is she aware?"

"Doesn't matter." Mystery's smile softens. It isn't the charming, roguish leer he uses so often to get his way with everyone. It's one which Rachel is certain only a handful of people in this world have ever seen. "The point is that you are the only one I have ever met who I could…"

"Who you could what."

Mystery reaches under his lounge chair and produces a thick envelope. He holds it out to her. "The only one who I could trust with this."

"What is it?" Rachel asks. She stares at it, afraid to touch it.

"To be completely blunt, it is an immense responsibility," Mystery says. "One which you are in no way obligated to assume. Though, should you choose not to, I really can't imagine who would."

"Oh, for the love of God," Rachel says, snatching it out of his hand.

She starts to open it but Mystery stops her, "No, don't open it now. Wait for the opportune moment. At that point you can decide."

"How will I know the opportune moment?"

"You'll know," Mystery says.

"Okay," Rachel says.

Mystery takes her hand gently in his and envelopes it in his other. He looks into her eye and says, "I cannot express to you how much our time together has meant to me. It isn't something I say lightly. You are a truly special human being."

"You…" Rachel says with a small laugh. "You're not so bad yourself." She wipes at the tear as it streams over her cheek.

"Thank you," Mystery says and whatever reserve she has gives way and lets tears flowed freely.

"I… I really do need to leave now," Rachel says.

Mystery nods and relaxes once more into the lounge. There won't be any more words, why dull the impact of the perfect ones he's already said? Rachel stands and holds the envelop to her chest like a child's Teddy bear.

She walks out of the house and into the night.

CHAPTER TWELVE

Spacer shifts his hips, trying to find a comfortable spot. The pillow is not a very good fit with the wrought iron restaurant chairs. He crosses his legs and immediately thinks better of it.

A gasp rings out from a table next to him and Spacer watches as every head in the room turns toward the door. Smiling, he follows their gazes to see Shelly, still leather clad, walking into the room as if on a Parisian runway.

Spacer glances down at the white blazer he's wearing over the paisley button up and wonders if anyone is going to actually believe that she is there to meet him.

"I see you went with a Miami Vice motif," she says, striding up to his table and sitting across from him.

"Yeah, it's all I can do not to roll up the jacket sleeves,' Spacer says. "What kept you? I've been through, like, four baskets of these cheesy biscuits."

She relaxes back into her seat and takes a breath. She smiles at him and says, "So what inspired the outfit?"

Spacer shrugs. "I don't know, it seemed appropriate, what with us being at the beach and all."

"We're at the beach, we're not in Miami."

"Close enough."

"We're, like, a thousand miles from Miami."

"We're not a thousand miles, there is no way that Miami is a thousand miles from the North Carolina coast."

"If it's not, it's close."

"It's like three thousand from coast to coast. You really think we are one third of the country away from Miami?"

"I really do."

"That's it, I'm Google Mapping this," Spacer says, digging in his pocket.

"Oh no you aren't."

"Ah, not so sure any more."

"No, I'm plenty sure, but I am not having my date playing on his cell phone when he's out to dinner with me. It's a thing for me, a thing called courtesy."

Spacer takes his hand out of his pocket without his phone.

"Fine, but I'm looking it up when we get back to the house."

"You're really that desperate to be wrong?"

"I really am," Spacer says with a smile. "How did it go?"

"And, are you two ready or will you be needing another moment?" the perky waitress asks. Spacer jumps. Every waitress he's ever had has been better at sneaking up on him than every single assassin who'd ever tried it. Not that he's complaining, but if they only knew the windfall they are missing   out   on.

"Steak, bleeding," Shelly says.

"Okay, and what would you like on the side?"

"I don't care," she says.

"All righty then," the waitress says, giggling nervously. "And for you, sir?"

"I'll do the lobster with the mixed green salad," Spacer says.

"Very good, I'll put those right in"

"Where were we?" Spacer asks.

"You wanted to know how it went."

"That sounds like me," Spacer says with a nod. "So… how did it go?"

"Well, for starters Pete has a new idiot."

"Yea, I talked to him on the phone, he brought that guy along?"

"Yupper, at one point he got a little handsey with the girl, I stepped in."

"Does Pete still have a new idiot?"

"If you're asking me if the idiot is still living, I think so, but he'll be on a liquid diet for the next little while. If you're asking if Pete's kicked him out of the group, the answer is if he ever wants to work with me again he has."

"Either way, that's on Pete. He should know better than to bring along unproven guys on anything we do," Spacer says.

"You'd think."

"What else happened?"

"The girl got slapped."

"Oh," Spacer says, taking a deep breath. "The new guy?"

Shelly shakes her head. "The punk. I didn't know it was

going to happen until it was over."

Spacer takes a long drink of his water and asks, "He in the hospital?"

Shelly nods. "I told Pete to keep him out of ICU." She turns her head and looks at the floor, "If possible."

"There'll be some noise about that; you know that kid's been coddled."

Shelly nods her head slowly. "I won't apologize."

"I don't think you should, it was your call and you made it. I'm just saying, there's going to be noise." Spacer clears his throat and fingers the empty bread basket.

"Did you really eat four baskets worth of biscuits while you were waiting for me?" Shelly asks.

"No, I ate, like, two biscuits, I went through four baskets."

"What did you do with the rest of them?"

Spacer reaches below the table and pulls out a large GAP shopping bag. He holds it in front of her and shakes it so that she can hear the bread rustle inside.

"Why do you have a huge GAP bag?"

"For swiping cheesy biscuits. I would have thought that was apparent."

"You brought a bag just so you could steal bread?"

"Bitch, I bought a sweater which I will never wear just so I could have a bag to steal bread with," Spacer said with a smile.

Shelly laughed in spite of herself and covered her mouth self-consciously. "What did you do with the sweater? Spacer shrugs and peers inside the bag. "It's in there somewhere."

"You are certifiable," Shelly says.

"I won't apologize," Spacer says.

Shelly kicks him playfully in the shins. She takes a drink of her water. "She may have seen the hair."

"Huh?"

"The girl, Quinn, she may have seen my hair. I'm not sure, it was dark, but it definitely pulled out a little when I turned to check on her."

"Not much we can do if she did."

"Yeah, still I hate to be the weak link. I probably shouldn't be here dressed like this but I got the feeling the Whitmans were all tucked in for the evening and that it would be safer to stow the bike and come kill some time here before heading back."

"Where's the bike?"

"A safe place."

"Which would be…?"

"Safe."

"Really? That's all I'm getting, safe?"

"That's all you're getting."

"I guess I'll have to live with that. How'd you get here?"

"Took a cab."

"From   the   safe   place?"
"From A safe place."

"I love you when you're cryptic."

"You love me when I'm anything," Shelly says, smiling at him.

"That I do."

"All righty, here we go," the waitress says, approaching them with a tray. She sets a plate in front of each of them and asks if there is anything else she can get for them.

"No thanks," Spacer says as Shelly picks up the serrated steak knife from her plate and, with the quick flick of her wrist, conceals it in a pocket sewn into the lining of her sleeve for just such a purpose.

"Really?" Spacer asks.

Shelly shrugs. "I like to be armed and you talked me out of bringing my gun."

Spacer nods to the steaming meat on her plate. "You could have stolen it after you finished your steak."

"Then it would have steak yuck all over it. I'm not having that in my jacket and having every dog in the neighborhood follow me around."

"Okay, but how are you going to eat your dinner?"

Shelly picks the steak up with both hands and tears into it, her white teeth sinking slowly into the flesh, a primal, almost feral glint in her eye, blood running down her chin and onto the plate. Spacer stares silently, the lobster claw he'd been working with the nutcracker entirely forgotten.

"Oh god," he says.

Shelly drops the meat onto her plate and dabs daintily at her chin with her napkin. "You like?"

"I like very much," Spacer says.

"If you give me the keys, I'll do it again."

"How about if I just promise to let you drive but don't give you the keys? It... um... it may not be good for me to be playing around in my pockets just now."

Shelly skids onto the road to their rental house and then peels into their driveway, not slowing until slamming the Spyder to a stop inches from the back of the garage. She runs a hand through her hair, straightening the few out of place strands and smiles at Spacer as she presses the button to lower the automatic garage door.

"We talked about this and you promised to only use evasive maneuvers when we're actually being followed," Spacer says.

"I didn't trust that kid."

"The one on the Huffy?"

"That was a Schwinn and you know it." Shelly smiles at him. "Babe, I can't tell you how much I needed that."

Spacer looks in the area behind the seats. "Well, I hope it was worth it, we lost the majority of my biscuits."

Shelly grabs the lapels of Spacer's sport coat and pulls him close to her, "Surely there must be some way I can make it up to you," she says.

Spacer smiles and says, "Perhaps there is one thing you can do." He grabs her jacket and pulls her into him, kissing her.

Shelly pulls back. "Uh uh, no, no I'm sorry."

"What's wrong?"

"No, I want you, I want you now, but I really want you to be gentle tonight."

Spacer stares at her, his jaw a little slack. "Gentle? That would be a twist."

Shelly smiles at him and shrugs. "It's what I want right now."

Spacer traces her jaw with his finger, stopping under her chin. He guides her toward him this time and softly presses his lips against hers. "Then it is what you shall have," he says, running his hand down her back.

"Are you sure you're up to this?"

"When have I ever failed to rise to the occasion?"

"I'm not talking about that, it's your ass I'm worried about."

"You let me worry about my ass."

"I always worry about your ass."

Spacer undoes his seatbelt and leans toward Shelly, she lays back, pulling him into her arms. His elbow brushes against the horn and it belts out a sharp blast causing them both to jump.

"We should do this inside," Spacer says.

"No," Shelly says, "we must do this on the beach." Without another word she steps out of the car and through the back door.

"The beach it is," Spacer says to himself, popping open his own door and forcing himself to walk, rather than hobble, outside after his wife.

CHAPTER THIRTEEN

Mystery takes a moment to center himself before stepping back into the cacophony of the house. "Boss!" says one of the guys, Mystery can't place the name. "So I had a few ideas about the…"

Tony claps a hand on the guys back silencing him. "The kid's waiting in your office, boss."

Mystery nods and walks toward the office door. He glances furtively at the stairs leading to his bedroom and, within that, his closet. He would love nothing more than to get out of these clothes but he'd kept Jason waiting far longer than he should have already. Most likely Jason neither cared nor noticed, he had his phone to entertain him, but Mystery will not become the sort of person who left people waiting.

He hates those people, the messy people. He hates how close he's become to being one of those people. He hadn't foreseen the spies interrupting the construction of the machine and he is paying for his lapse. It is a mistake he does not intend to repeat.

He opens the door to his office to find Jason with his nose buried in his tiny screen. "I apologize for my tardiness," he says.

"Huh?" Jason says, looking up. "Oh, that's cool."

"No, it is not, but I appreciate your saying so."

"No biggie."

Mystery steps inside and closes the door behind him. He considers the boy who has already returned his attention to the device. Jason is unlike anyone he's before encountered. He's brilliant in a way that Mystery must admit he himself is quite stupid. But Mystery has known brilliant men before and he's been able to find their weaknesses each and every time. Jason though, his weaknesses aren't so obvious. He has no desire for power, he hates most people far too much to want fame or recognition. Even money isn't much of a motivator for him. He cashes the meager checks Mystery cuts for him each week but if he spends any of it at all, it never shows in his outward appearance.

He is here because Mystery has access to cool toys with which he is given free reign. The thing about boys and their toys though, there is always a cooler one just around the corner.

Mystery walks around the desk and sits in his chair. "Where did we leave off last time?"

"We'd just made it through your mid-thirties," Jason says.

"Yes," Mystery says, rubbing his temples. "All right, my thirty-seventh birthday was…" He stops when he realized that Jason is not opening his tablet and settling in like usual. "Is there a problem?"

"No, I mean, there's this thing…"

Mystery stares at him for moment before remembering. "Oh! Yes, Tony said that you had something interesting to show me."

"Yeah," Jason says. "I mean, maybe." He taps his phone a few times and then holds it out to Mystery.

Mystery takes it and looks at the screen. There's a parking lot filled with cheap motorcycles and one impressive Ninja. "What am I looking at?"

"It's a biker bar in Bridges, NC. That gang is about to hassle some kid whose Dad is making an impassioned plea that the gang be brought to justice."

"Why are we watching it?"

"The dad is some rich guy, made his money when he invented the winky emoji with its tongue sticking out."

"He   invented   emojis?"
"Not all of them, just the one."

"Really? There's that much money in a single emoji?"

"Yeah," Jason says.

"Why am I watching this?"

"Oh, well I'm not sure but I think that might be one of your spies," he says, pointing at a small figure in the crowd.

"Him?"

Jason stares at Mystery arching his eyebrow. "I'm pretty sure that's a 'her' dude."

"What makes you say that?"

"Well, I guess it's not so obvious while she's just standing there but once you see her move and you check out her ass, I… well, I've already jerked off to it twice."

It isn't often that Mystery is taken entirely by surprise but that did it. "Is… is that a figure of speech?" he askes hopefully.

"Huh? Oh, no, I rubbed a couple out to her."

"Where?"

"Here."

"Here? In my office?"

"Nah, I went into the bathroom," Jason says, pointing to a door in the far wall. "I mean, I cleaned up after."

Mystery looks down at the father pleading from the small screen in his hand. "Well, that's a relief," he says, placing the phone on the desk and moving his hands as far from it as he can without drawing attention to it. He glances at a desk drawer which he knows contains hand sanitizer but decides against it. It would be rude. Not quite as rude as pleasuring one's self in another man's personal bathroom, but rude none the less.

"Oh, this is the good part," Jason says, pointing at the phone.

Mystery glances down to see the woman, a blur in the poor resolution of the security camera, leap over the bikes and drop a man more than twice her size. Without thinking he scoops the phone up from the desk and bends over it, watching as the woman straddles the Ninja and peels out onto the road.

He looks up at Jason. "How do I rewind that?'

Jason holds his hand out for the phone and Mystery remembers what this particular phone has just been used for. He tosses it quickly to the boy.

Jason taps and slides his finger over the screen and tries to hand it back to Mystery. Instead of accepting it, Mystery stands and watches the phone as Jason holds it out. When it's over he sits once again and says, "I think you have something here. I'm going to check this out in person tomorrow."

"It's on the other side of the country," Jason says.

"That it is." Mystery presses a button and when he speaks his voice is amplified through speakers placed strategically around the house, "Rachel, can you…" He releases the button remembering a moment too late that Rachel was no longer a member of his staff.

"I guess I'll have to make my own plane reservations now," he says to Jason. He turns to his computer, opens a browser and stares at it. "I'm actually not sure how to do that."

"You want me to?" Jason asks.

"Is that… something you can do?"

"Yeah, I'm not an idiot." Jason pokes at his phone for a moment before realizing what he'd just said. "Oh, um… I didn't…" he stammers.

"Get the earliest you can, I need to be back in time for tomorrow's session."

"You? I mean, we could probably skip a day."

"No, time is something we are running quite short on. If anything, we need to double our efforts."

The door opens and one of the guys sticks his head inside. "Hey, boss, that lady, Rachel, isn't here any…"

He stops as Tony walks by and grabs the back of his neck, pulling him out of the office without breaking stride.

"There's a four AM flight if you want one that early," Jason says.

"Perfect, put me on and afternoon flight back. Do you need my card?"

"Nah, I've…" Jason looks sheepishly at him. "I mean yeah."

Mystery sighs. "Would it even do me any good to cancel that one and get a new number?"

Jason shrugs, "It might make you feel better." He puts down his phone and takes out the tablet. "You're set. You ready?"

"Yes," Mystery says. "My thirty-seventh birthday."

Two hours later Mystery steps out of the office and signals Tony over. "I'm going to be away for the majority of the day tomorrow. Just keep everyone on task for me and, um, do you have the number for Harriet?"

"Harriet the cleaning lady? I think I can dig it up. You want me to have her in with all of the guys here?"

"Yeah, don't let her see too much but have her do a general tidying. You know, kitchen, bathrooms, maybe extra attention on the bathroom in my office."

"Extra   attention?"

"If she scrubs away the tile that's something I'm willing to live with."

"Do I want to know?"

"You do not."

"I'll take your word for it," Tony says, pulling out a pen and small note pad and scribbling a note. "Anything else I can do?"

"No," Mystery says, turning toward the stairs. He stops and turns back, "Actually, you can." He pulls the T-shirt over his head and tosses it to Tony. He yanks off the shorts and hands those over as well. "You burn those," he tells him, standing naked in the middle of the busy room. "Burn them and gather the ashes and, if you can figure out how, burn those as well."

"Burn ashes," Tony says, still scribbling. "Got it."

"I'm going to bed," Mystery says, climbing the stairs. "Wake me if you need me but try very hard not to need me. I have an extremely early flight tomorrow."

CHAPTER FOURTEEN

Spacer stirs and a smile spreads over his face when he realizes Shelly is still curled in his arms. It's a rare thing for her to snuggle against him all through the night and it's a treat for him regardless of the complete numbness in his right arm.

He stretches luxuriously and pulls one leg out from under the beach towel they'd used as a blanket the night before. "Man," he says aloud to himself. "I've got sand in my… everywhere."

He nudges Shelly and she mutters something without waking.

"Babe, I've got to get up, I need to check on the Whitmans."

Shelly raises her head and stares at him with the one eye she bothered to open. "That is not the way a girl likes to start her day after the night we had," she tells him.

"I know, luv, but we've gotten them tied up in our shit and I need to know what's happened with them."

Shelly sighs and pulls herself off of the beach chair, taking the towel with her and leaving Spacer entirely to the elements. She looks down at him. "Well, what are you waiting on, go see the Whitmans."

"Maybe I'll shower and put on pants first, what do you think?"

"I think it'll break Sissy's heart, but if it'll make you comfortable, go for it."

"I'll just have to come up with some way of making it up to her," Spacer says, pulling himself gently to his feet.

"Just make sure it's not the same way I made up for biscuit ruining."

"That reminds me, I really should get those out of the car."

He takes a few halting steps until he reaches the banister leading up to the porch. "I didn't hurt you, did I?" Shelly asks.

"Oh no, babe, it was all good," Spacer says, forcing himself to hop up the two steps and turn with a bow.

"Hmm, maybe I should go into physical therapy," Shelly says with a wink.

"That would be a happy trauma ward," Spacer says, walking inside.

Cleaned and clothed in Khakis and a white cotton button-up, Spacer makes his way slowly down the stairs, not bothering with the cane until he steps off of the last step. He walks into the kitchen where Shelly sits, still wrapped in the beach towel, sipping coffee.

"I see the cane is back," she says.

"Well, don't want to show off, people will be asking about my miracle cure and I've decided I don't want to share." Spacer pours a cup for himself and leans against the counter.

"I'd cut you in on whatever I made," Shelly says, sliding a folded newspaper across the counter to him.

"I really do feel much better, surprisingly better, actually," Spacer says, picking it up and flipping it open.

"That's not for reading."

"Come again?"

"It's not ours, it's the Whitmans'."

"Why did you steal the neighbors' paper, you know we get one of our own."

"I figured you would need an excuse for going over there again. You can take it back to them and blame the paper boy."

"Ah, that's pretty clever."

"I'm a clever girl."

Spacer grabs the paper but stops when the picture on the front page catches his eye. "Did you see this?" he asks Shelly.

She nods.

He lowers himself into a chair and stares at the face of the man he'd very recently dangled with off of the end of a crane under the heading "Renowned Physicist Dies in Plane Crash." He looks at Shelly and says, "That can't be a coincidence."

Shelly takes a deep breath and shrugs. "Seems unlikely."

"Mr. E?"

"Unless he's angered another mysterious master villain."

Spacer peruses the article, he rubs at the throb developing in his temple.

"If they need us they'll call," Shelly says.

Spacer nods and folds the paper. He grabs his mug and it's almost to his lips when he stops and says, "Wait a minute, you went across the road wearing a towel?"

"Yeah." Spacer arches an eyebrow at her. "What? It's seven thirty on a Saturday morning, who do you think saw me?"

Spacer walks to the window and pulls open the curtains, outside are a dozen boys on bikes, the tallest with a news bag strapped over his shoulder, the smallest on a Li'l Tykes tricycle. They sit motionless, staring mutely at the house, the only movement is the gentle waving of their hair in the breeze.

"Dear God," Shelly says, joining him at the window. "It's like a scene out of Hitchcock."

"Mm hmm," Spacer says. "I think the folks on our side of the road are going to have a long wait for their paper today."

Shelly shrugs, "I'll go get rid of them."

"No, I think you and your towel have done enough. I'll shoo them off on my way over."

"Whatever you think is best, Darling," Shelly says, pecking Spacer on the cheek and then walking to the stairs. "Just remember, while you're over chatting with Darren, I'll be upstairs cleaning off all of this sand, including what's in the hard to reach places."

"That wasn't nice," Spacer says.

"I never claimed to be…" Shelly says, dropping the towel and walking slowly up the stairs, "…nice."

Spacer watches her until she is out of sight and then lets a small groan seep out from deep inside "Yeah, we've got to take care of this Mr. E stuff so I can plan on not leaving this house for the rest of the month," he tells the smug looking cartoon cat on his coffee mug.

The cat does not respond.

Spacer steps outside with the paper under his arm, he still uses the cane but he's able to put far less of his weight on it, the workout from the night before seems to have done wonders for his wounded muscle.

He approaches the boys who do not move or even look at him. "All right, fellas, show's over, you can all go home now," he tells them.

At last the paper boy looks up at him and says, "Mister, is the lady going to come back outside?"

"Not for a while, she's in there taking a shower," Spacer says and instantly regrets it.

"Wow," the boys all say in unison.

"Can we go in and watch?" another kid asks.

"No, you can't go watch," Spacer says. "Why would you want to watch? Don't you kids have the internet?"

"There's nothing like her on the internet," another boy says. "Believe me, I've looked."

"Well, you're not going to see any more today, sorry guys. Go on home."

"I'll give you a dollar," yet another boy says.

"Really? That's your opening bid?" Spacer asks.

"How much then?" the kid asks.

"That was a joke. Seriously, it's time to disperse."

"Mister, can I marry her?" the kid on the trike asks.

"Sorry, pal, you're too late, I already married her."

"Oh," the kid says, looking down at his sneakers. He looks back up, a hopeful gleam in his eye, and says, "Are you going to stay married to her?"

"That's the plan."

The kid's smile turns to a grimace and he peddles quickly, slamming his trike into Spacer's shin. He rolls backward, looking up at Spacer, daring him with his eyes to do something about it.

Spacer laughs and says, "Actually, I kind of understand that."

The kid peddles at Spacer again, but Spacer catches the handle bars and stops him. "I understand it, I'm not going to let you keep doing it though." He turns to the rest of the boys, "Seriously, go home now, you may all want to talk to your parents, you probably have some questions for them."

"I don't have any questions," says the boy with the internet. "Except, how can I get one of those?"

Spacer shrugs. "I chalk it up to dumb luck and living a virtuous life."

"Lame," the paper boy says, climbing at last onto his bike and peddling off down the street. The other boys, reluctantly and with many glances back at the house, follow suit.

Spacer walks across the road and steps quickly up onto the Whitmans' porch without thinking about it. "Wow," he says, looking back down the whole two steps, "That was easy. I have got to have much more sex with my wife."

He steps over to the door and looks from the paper in this hand to the door knocker. He raises his fist to knock but thinks better of it. He looks around himself, shrugs, and leans against the doorbell for half a minute.

"What in the world?" he hears Darren yell from inside.

He unfolds the paper and scatters them about the porch, bending over to pick them up just as Darren, house coat hanging from his shoulders, pulls open the door. "Do you have any idea what time it…" Darren bellows. "Spacer?"

"Hey there, neighbor," Spacer says, grinning sheepishly up at him.

"What are you doing?"

Spacer shrugs and holds up the scattered pages he'd managed to retrieve. "Sorry about that. The paper boy must have given us yours by mistake."

"So, you threw it all over my porch and rang my buzzer for half an hour?"

Spacer chuckles guiltily. "I am so sorry, I was bringing it over here, I was just going to pop it in front of the door and head on back but, well, I got a little tripped up coming up the steps and I, gosh, I feel like such a moron, I must have fallen into your doorbell.

Darren raises an eyebrow at him. "I know, what did you ever do to deserve a clumsy neighbor like me, huh?" Spacer says with a shrug.

"No," Darren says, bending over to help him pick up the pages. "No, I'm sorry I was short, it was really neighborly of you to bring it back over. Why, do you know some of our neighbors across the way actually come over and steal it from us?"

"No?" Spacer says, gasping.

"I'm afraid they do," Darren says with a solemn nod. "Sometimes I wonder just what kind of world I'm leaving to my children."

Spacer hands Darren the last of the crumpled pages and Darren says, "I'm just sorry you had a little spill, are you okay?"

"Oh, I'm fine, just not used to the hardware still, I suppose," Spacer says, holding up his cane.

"Well, why don't you bring yourself and your hardware inside and I'll get you a cup of Joe. You do drink coffee, don't you?"

"Oh, I absolutely drink coffee, but I don't want to impose."

"Nonsense, I should be up now anyway, I just... well, we had something of an adventure last night," Darren says, stepping aside from the door and gesturing for Spacer to walk on in.

"Adventure?" Spacer says, stepping by him with a nod. "That sounds exciting."

Darren chuckles sardonically as he follows Spacer inside and closes the door behind them. He walks into the kitchen and Spacer follows. "Clearly you haven't had many adventures."

Darren picks up the coffee maker and turns it around in his hands. "You... um... you know how to operate one of these contraptions?"

"Hmm?" Spacer says. "Which contraption?"

"This thing," Darren says, holding it out to him. "To tell you the truth, I'm only pretty sure it's the machine that does the coffee. It is, isn't it?"

"You've never used your coffee maker?"

"Oh good, it is the coffee machine." Darren sighs and shrugs. "Sissy takes care of the kitchen things."

"What about before you were married?"

"Well, I was engaged to Sissy when I left home and joined up, after the army it was only a few months and, hell, I was lucky I even had a sink in the place I was renting, I wouldn't have dreamed of making coffee in my home. I made do with the stuff from the diner."

Spacer chuckles, not at him, really, just at the weird innocence of him. "Yeah, I've brewed a pot or two in my day," he says. He walks over and takes the coffee maker from Darren. "Any idea where Sissy keeps the grounds and the filters?"

"Oh yeah, I guess you would need those," Darren scratches his head and looks around, bewildered. "Nope, it's no good, I'm just going to wake her up."

"Hang on," Spacer says. "Most people keep them pretty close to the coffee maker." He opens the cabinet directly above the spot where the coffee machine sat on the counter to reveal a can of Folgers and a pack of coffee filters. "Violà," Spacer says.

"Say, that's pretty impressive," Darren says. "I guess you younger fellas all have some experience in the kitchen, you probably watch a lot of that food tv, yeah?"

"I do like my contessas barefoot," Spacer says.

"Huh?"

Spacer chuckles again as he fits a filter into the machine and begins scooping in grounds. "Never mind."

"Well, I just hate that you're my guest and I've got you doing all of the work. Is there anything I can do?"

Spacer hands him the coffee pot. "You can fill this with water if you like."

"Water? Yes, that I know where to find." Darren takes the pot and walks over to the oven. "Oops, no water there," he says, raising his voice and octave and bobbing his head.

"Good one," Spacer says.

Darren fills the pot from the sink and hands it back to Spacer who pours it into the reservoir and turns on the machine. "It'll take a couple of minutes, then we can go on a hunt for mugs," Spacer says, leaning against the counter. "So, tell me about this adventure."

Darren sighs and turns away, when he speaks he doesn't look at Spacer. "Well, I'm sure that you saw the... ugliness on my front lawn yesterday."

"I'm not sure what you're talking about," Spacer says.

Darren shakes his head. "It's kind of you to say, but you'd

have to have been deaf and blind to miss it."

Spacer shrugs, "Didn't see it."

"Okay, if you insist," Darren says. "Quinn has been... seeing a boy named Francis, he's nineteen and he rides a motorcycle."

"Every father's dream for their fifteen-year-old," Spacer says and is surprised when Darren genuinely laughs.

"You sound like you have one."

"Nah, but it doesn't take a genius."

"Well, he certainly isn't my choice for my little girl. He rode by yesterday afternoon to pick her up even though I'd strictly forbidden her to see him."

"Uh huh."

"He and I got into it a little, there was quite a ruckus, even Martin from next door came over with his hose the poor old fool."

"The hose didn't scare him off? Wow, the kid is tough," Spacer says, forcing a smile.

"Yeah, can you believe it?" Darren sighs and looks sheepishly at Spacer. "Anyway, I... I let the punk get the better of me during our fight and he punched me in the face." A strong blush blooms on Darren's face and he rubs a hand over the dark bruise on his cheek that Spacer had been intentionally not noticing. "That's where I got this," he says.

"It was a cheap shot," Spacer says, then remembers he wasn't supposed to have seen anything. "Probably."

Darren raises an eyebrow at him but says nothing.

"Well, that sounds like quite an adventure," Spacer says, hoping to restart the conversation.

"Oh, that wasn't the adventure, that was just... well, it was what it was. Quinn rode away with him and, apparently, they ended up at the Vroom Shack. Do you know the place?"

"Hmm? Is that the place right on the edge of town?"

"Yeah, it's... well, it's not doing the town's reputation any favors. Anyway, they were at this bar... I can't believe my own little girl was at a bar..."

"I imagine you bent your elbow a few years before the law said you could, I know I did."

"Yeah, but neither of us were ever fifteen-year-old girls. I know that isn't PC to say but there's a huge difference between a seventeen-year-old boy sneaking into a dive and a fifteen-year-old girl doing it. At least in my mind there is."

Spacer shrugged, wishing he could fast forward the social commentary.

"Anyway, they were at this place and some bikers, real bikers I mean, from out of town, dangerous folks. You know the type?"

"I'm aware that some folks exist," Spacer says. The coffee finishes and Spacer opens a cabinet door in search of a mug. "Anyway, what about them? The bikers?"

"Well, they came in and, according to Quinn, for no good reason, start hassling him... Francis... the punk."

"Oh no."

"Yeah, well, that's what Quinn says, I don't know, Francis is the sort of guy who just knows how to stir up a hornets' nest. Although, I don't actually have any trouble believing that they just didn't like his face."

"Probably not too hard for you to imagine," Spacer says, nodding.

"So, these guys, they wind up taking Francis and Quinn outside to look at his bike. Francis, of course, is a sniveling prick about it."

"Of course."

"So, they start roughing him up a bit and when Quinn steps in to defend him he..." Darren's face grows dark. Once again, he isn't looking at Spacer but this time it's not because he's ashamed. He's gone someplace in his mind, likely the parking lot of the Vroom Shack, creating the scene from his daughter's words and replaying it in his mind. When he speaks his voice sends shivers down the spine of a man who once spent three days tied to a chair in North Korea being "interrogated."

"The jackass slapped her in the face," Darren says.

Spacer stares at the man who is not looking at him, the tension in the air threatens to become alive if he doesn't do something quickly. "How do you take it?" he asks.

"I don't know, how would any man take a thing like that?"

Darren says.

"No, I mean your coffee, how do you take it?" Spacer asks, holding up the mugs and the now full coffee pot.

"Oh! Oh, yes, I'm sorry, black is fine," Darren says.

Spacer fills the two mugs and takes a careful step across to the counter. "Here ya go," he says.

"Thank you," Darren says, taking the mug. "I'm sorry, you've been on your bad leg all morning, let's have a seat at the table."

"You don't have to ask me twice," Spacer says, walking around the counter and joining Darren at the table. He drops into the hard kitchen chair and gasps, realizing he forgot his pillow. He takes a deep breath and relaxes into the pain.

"Are you okay?"

"No, I'm fine, I actually am okay," Spacer says, realizing that he's telling the truth.

Darren nods and drums his fingers on the table, apparently debating whether or not to continue. At last he sighs and says, "So the guys, the bikers, they rough Francis up a little, break that ridiculous Harley thing he glued onto that monstrosity and then they ask him if they should take the bike or... the bike or my daughter and the no-good, ass... ass..."

"Ass-wipe?" Spacer suggests.

"Yes, that will do nicely. The no-good ass-wipe, without a single thought, tells them to take my daughter instead of his precious piece of shit."

"Oh my God, is Quinn..." Spacer starts and then pauses for dramatic effect.

"No! No, she's fine, she's upstairs now. I'll get to that in a moment."

"Thank God."

"Believe me, I have been, all night," Darren says.

"So, they didn't take her?"

"They did, that's one of the more puzzling things about it. When that... well, you know, when he told them to take her they didn't waste a minute grabbing her up, though apparently there was some tussle over which of them exactly would get to take her, apparently one of the bikers was quite badly injured which didn't make Quinn feel any too safe."

"I imagine not," Spacer says, wondering now if maybe he should have pumped Shelly for a little more info regarding her "stepping in" with the new guy. "How did she get away from them?"

"She didn't."

"But… didn't you say…"

"Yes, she's snoozing away in her bedroom as we speak, believe me, I've been up all night checking on her."

"So, what happened with the bikers?"

"They brought her home."

Spacer forces a chuckle as if he can't believe his ears. "I'm sorry?"

"I'm not, I've never been more happy to have motorcycles pull up to my house," Darren says, his smile beaming.

"That's amazing."

"I know, I can't figure why they'd do it."

Spacer leans back in his seat trying as hard as he can to look as if he's contemplating the possibilities. "Well, now that I think about it, there is a certain logic to it."

"There is?"

"Spacer nods. "I don't know if you know or not, but we have a lot of book readings and signings and that sort of thing at the store…"

"I didn't."

"Okay, well, now you do. Anyway, we try to get colorful people to come in and once we had a guy who used to ride with a motorcycle gang and he'd written a memoir about them, though he never mentions them by name, part of the code."

"Uh huh."

"I say the code because that was what he kept referring back to in his book, that and the 'life.' Those were two big points." Darren nods but says nothing. "So, he goes on about the life and how there are those in it and those out of it and, as part of the code, they tried not to involve those who weren't in the life in any way. Does that make sense?"

"No," Darren says, shaking his head.

Spacer chuckles. "Okay, say there's a gang leader and he

has a girlfriend or a… I hate to use the word in your lovely kitchen here."

"No, please, go ahead."

"Well," Spacer says, leaning over and whispering, "bitch."

"Ah," Darren says, nodding knowingly. "That is what they call their women."

"Indeed. At any rate, the bitch, of course, is part of the life and if a rival gang were to kidnap her to send a message to the gang leader, well, as someone who was part of the life, all bets would be off. However, if some regular guy, say, me for example, were to somehow cross a gang leader, of course they'd want to make an example of me, it's a point of pride…" Spacer stopped and covered his mouth forcing a cough to cover the laugh he couldn't suppress.

"Yes, I can see that,' Darren said, urging him with his eyes to go on.

"So, anyway, they'd probably rough me up some, but they'd leave Shelly out of it because she isn't a part of the life, you see?"

"Yes, but why would they take Quinn in the first place?"

"That was probably more to scare… what was the ass-wipe's name again?"

"Ass-wipe is good."

"Okay then, it was probably more to scare ass-wipe than anything."

"Well, it scared Quinn something awful too."

"I'm sure. I'm sorry it had to happen."

"To tell you the truth, I'm not," Darren says. He leans back in his chair and takes a sip of coffee, allowing that to seep in. Spacer looks at him, trying to slack his jaw enough to connote the appropriate amount of surprise.

"Huh?" he says.

"Well, of course, no one wants their little girl to be scared, but it showed her the true nature of Ass-wipe before she got in too deep and, really, there was no harm done to her. As a matter of fact, if I knew who was responsible for last night, why, they'd be welcome at this very table right now."

"That's fortunate," Spacer says.

"How's that?"

"That you can see the silver lining in such a thing."

"Oh, yes, I suppose that it is."

"I'm almost afraid to ask but, did anything else happen last night?" Spacer asks, leaning in and studying the man closely. This is the part of the story he doesn't already know.

Darren shrugs. "Well, of course we filed a police report, we really couldn't see any way around it. It turns out that, after they took Quinn away, the bikers did quite a number on asswipe. He's in the hospital now with a broken leg, two broken arms and his jaw is wired shut." Darren grins unashamedly. "Couldn't happen to a nicer guy," he says, once more rubbing his cheek.

"So the cops were here for a while?"

"Oh, it seemed like they would never leave. They kept asking Quinn to describe the men but all she would give them was that they were big and rode motorcycles, I don't think that narrowed it down much for them." Darren leans toward Spacer confidentially, "She's usually brilliant with detail, to tell you the truth, I think that she feels the same way I do about them."

Spacer nods. "Could be."

Darren yawns. "Excuse me. It's been a long night, but I don't really feel it. I hope I don't crash in the middle of our night out tonight."

"Oh," Spacer says. "In all the excitement, I'd entirely forgotten. Listen, we can do that anytime, why don't you spend tonight with your family?" He doesn't say, "and give me time to figure out what the death of a scientist I once saved means for me."

"I suggested that, but Quinn would not hear of it. She said that she wouldn't allow her own foolish decisions to wreck the first night out that Sissy and I have had in... well, I don't even want to admit how long it's been." Darren thinks for a moment and says, "She's feeling very guilty about the scene on the front yard yesterday, she thinks she has something to make up to me for. I'm just so grateful that she's..." Darren's voice cracks and he goes silent.

Spacer nods.

"Anyway, she said she'd never forgive herself if we didn't keep our little date with the two of you. So, I promised her that we would," Darren says. "You... you're still willing to go, aren't you?"

"Of course," Spacer says because he can't think of anything else to say. "You just try and stop us."

CHAPTER FIFTEEN

"Anything else, Hon?" Sarah asks, topping off the coffee in Gerry's mug.

Gerry sighs as he looks at his bran muffin sitting all alone on his plate. "No thanks," he says.

"All righty," she tips Jim a wink and walks away to her other customers.

"You saw that, right?" Jim says. "I think I could hit that."

"You can't," Gerry says, not taking his eyes off of the dry, stale thing he was calling his breakfast. He picks at the wrapper hoping that it won't come off for some reason, giving him an excuse for tossing it in the trash. The wrapper doesn't want to have anything more to do with the thing than Gerry does and falls immediately to the table.

"Why not?" Jim says.

"Huh?" Gerry asks.

"Why couldn't I hit that?"

Gerry looks back at Sarah bending at her small waist to fill another patron's cup, her breasts all but spilling out of the pink, tight fitting blouse of her uniform. He turns back to Jim, whose gut actually spills out from the bottom of his sweat stain t-shirt and well over the waistband of his grease stained blue jeans.

"You know what, I was wrong. Go hit that," Gerry says.

"Well, not right now."

"Yeah," Gerry says. He sniffs at his muffin and looks longingly at the picture of the breakfast sampler on the menu stacked against the wall at the edge of their booth. He tells people that he's been eating the muffins on his doctor's orders, but the truth is that since the film industry left and he isn't able to find any other driving jobs, even a ten-dollar breakfast is a luxury he can no longer enjoy. Washing dishes just doesn't pay the same amount as transporting Hollywood highbrows. Julie hasn't had a paying photography gig in weeks and Jenni is going to need braces. Knowing that still doesn't make dry bran taste like bacon, sausage, eggs and hash browns all smothered in some kind of yellow goo everyone agrees to pretend is cheese.

"All I'm saying…" Jim says. He trails off into silence.

Gerry looks up and sees him staring blankly out the window. He follows Jim's gaze and sees a man in skin tight black pants and a pink blouse with a ruffle down the front stepping out of a rented Miata.

"What do you make of that?" Jim says.

Gerry shrugs.

"Seriously, what would make a…one of them, even want to come to a place like this?" Jim asks. "I mean, they have to know they're not… welcome."

Gerry rolls his eyes.

"What? You're okay with that… lifestyle? You spent too much time with those Hollywood weirdoes."

"All I want to do is eat my shitty muffin in peace," Gerry says.

The man walks into the dinner and passes Gerry's booth. Gerry can't help but notice all of the rings he's wearing. There weren't that many rings in the cabinet when he'd bought Julie's engagement ring.

"Did ya check out all da blang blang?" Jim asks, affecting some sort of dialect though, hard pressed, Gerry couldn't have even guessed which one.

"I saw it," Gerry says.

Jim cranes his head to look at the stranger and, against his better judgement, Gerry looks as well. Sarah approaches him and the man smiles at her. She leans over to speak.

"I hope she don't get too close," Jim says. "God knows what diseases that guy is walking around with."

"You're a classy guy, Jim," Gerry says.

"Seriously, what could they possibly have to say to each other?"

"Well, just off hand, I'd guess he's telling her the food he'd like to eat and pay for," Gerry says.

"Nah, there's nothing on the menu that takes that long to order."

Gerry sighs and turns his attention back to the muffin. He takes a big bite and instantly regrets it. It's like every drop of spit he once had saw the muffin coming and ran. The taste, such as it is, is neither terrible nor great, it just is, but the experience of chewing is akin to walking miles over a desert on his tongue. He takes a sip of coffee which somehow disappears somewhere between his lips and throat.

Sarah steps up to his table and slides a plate full of all of the best grease traps the diner calls breakfast smothered in the yellow goop. Gerry looks up at her, tries to speak around the muffin, gives up and shrugs at her.

"From the fella in the booth over there," she says, nodding toward the stranger.

"There something you haven't told me about, Ger?" Jim asks.

Gerry glares at him. He tries to swallow but the muffin catches in his throat. He coughs and shoots the wad of dry muffin into his napkin. "I don't want this," he says to Sarah, pointing at the plate of cheese-ish stuff.

Sarah shrugs. "Don't tell me, tell your boyfriend."

"Gerry?" Jim says.

"Shut up, both of you," Gerry says. He slides out of the booth, grabs the plate and walks over to the stranger. "Do we know each other?" he asks.

The stranger looks up at him and smiles. Gerry is certain they've never met but, staring at him up close, he actually does look somewhat familiar. Amateur musician maybe, low rent reality star, something along those lines.

"I haven't had the pleasure," the man says, extending one of his ringed hands. Gerry has never seen fingers as long as those.

Gerry slides the plate onto the table and says, "Do you mind explaining this?"

The man glances at the breakfast sampler. "Given a thousand years I could not conceive of an explanation for that, but I'm given to understand that it's quite popular with the locals."

Gerry sighs. He hates talking to people who think they're clever. They're so busy proving their cleverness they never come to a point. "Why did you send this over to me?"

"I thought you might enjoy it," he says. "I've never seen a man battle a pastry like you were with that muffin."

"So, what, you just drive around righting breakfasts which once went wrong?" Gerry says.

The man smiles, "Would that I had the time and resources to do just that," he says with a chuckle. "What a life that would be."

"Look, just tell me, what do you want with me?"

The man nods and gestures to the bench on the other side of the booth.

"Don't do it, Ger," Jim says.

Gerry jumps and turns to find him standing not even an inch away. "What the hell, Jim?"

"I thought you could use some backup."

Gerry looks down at the man twirling the salt shaker absently between two fingers. "I think I can handle myself," he says.

"Sorry, hon," Sarah says, walking up to the booth. "Cook says kale will never darken the doorstep of his kitchen."

The stranger smiles at her. "Well, we both knew it was a long shot."

"Is there anything I can get you?"

"You know what, I've changed my mind. I will have that cup of coffee."

"Coming right up."

Sarah walks off to fetch the coffee and the stranger again gestures to the bench. "I have a business proposition for you," he says to Gerry.

"He's propositioning you, Ger," Jim says.

"Yeah, I heard," Gerry says.

"People who have real job offers don't use the word proposition," Jim says.

"It doesn't matter whether or not it's real because I..." Gerry stops himself when he realizes that he's speaking to Jim instead of the person he should be speaking to. "I'm sorry, I'll have to pass. I already have a job."

"I hoped you did," the man says. "As a matter of fact, holding a position which would place you prominently in public is a prerequisite to my job offer. You have such a job?"

Gerry shrugged. "I wash dishes at a place down town. The place is public but I'm pretty much tucked away in the back."

"That couldn't be more suited to my needs."

"He wants you to suit his needs, Ger!" Jim says.

"Hear me out," the man says to Gerry. "The worst-case scenario is that you have the breakfast you want while listening to an offer you turn down."

"Here you go, hon," Sarah says, placing a mug in front of the stranger. She sets a container of cream next to the mug and points out the sugar packets on the far side of the table.

"Thank you," he says.

"Anything else?"

"No, I'm fine."

"Actually," Gerry says. "Could you do something about..." he gestures toward Jim leaning in over his shoulder.

"Sure thing, sweetie," she says, walking past Gerry and hooking a finger in Jim's collar pulling him with her as she departs.

"Hey," Jim mutters. "I've gotta..."

Sarah deposits him back into his booth and glares at him when he tries to climb back out. "You stay," she says.

"Look, I..." Jim says.

"No, you stay and be a good boy." She winks at him and says, "If you're good, you just may get a treat."

"But you don't..." Jim starts then says, "Wait, what?!?"

She smiles and walks back to Gerry. "That should keep him put."

"You don't have to... treat him, just so I can have a conversation," Gerry says.

Sarah shrugs. "He's been giving me puppy dog eyes for a month. He's a nice enough guy, I figured I'd give him a shot eventually. This way kills two birds."

Gerry looks back at his friend, staring at them from his place on the bench, not daring to move an inch. "Thanks, Sarah."

He slides into the booth and pulls the breakfast sampler toward him. "All right," he says, plunging a fork into the center mass and spearing whatever it was lying below, "let's hear this offer I'm going to turn down."

The man plucks the creamer up from the table and pours a healthy portion into his coffee. He stirs, the cream forming into concentric circles traveling around his mug. Gerry watches the circles spinning slowly, almost lazily.

"I'm looking for two people," the man says, "a man and a woman. Have you seen them?"

"Not that I know of," Gerry says. How do those circles stay so uniform? Shouldn't there be some variation?

"Oh, you would know," the man says. "They tend to stand out." The spoon continues its trip around the cup, the circles flowing in step. Shouldn't the cream be mixing into the coffee? "You might say they ain't from these parts."

"Oh, we have a vibrant tourist industry," Gerry tells him sleepily. "Actually, since our wise leaders ran the movie companies away, it's just about our only industry." Gerry can feel his temper rising as he remembers his old life that was ripped from him.

"Be that as it may," the man says, his voice gentle and calming yet undeniable. "These two would stand out. If they are here, I want to know. I will pay you handsomely for any information you can provide. If you tell me where they are, you'll never have to worry about money again."

Gerry moans and furrows his brow. He doesn't like what he is hearing but he wants to hear more. "Why do you want to find them?" he asks.

"That is not your concern. Your concern is caring for your family. How many do you have at home?"

Gerry doesn't want this man and his circular cream to know anything about his family. He's let him in too much as it is. "One, a little girl," he says.

"I'll bet she's a handful. Have you hit the braces stage yet?"

"She's getting them next week."

"One phone call, and you can stop worrying about that," the man says. There's something in Gerry's hand, he looks at it and sees a card with a telephone number on it. In his other hand is a fork with something on the end dripping yellow onto the table. He drops the fork in disgust.

"Well, there's my offer," the man says, picking up his mug and taking a sip. "Think it over and, should the opportunity arise, give me a ring."

The man stands, walks to Sarah and hands her two bills. "Breakfast is on me all around, you keep whatever is left over from that."

"Wow," Sarah says. "Thanks."

Gerry looks down at the breakfast sampler, the cheese-like stuff already congealing on the meat and biscuits. He wishes he had a bran muffin.

Mystery steps outside the diner and pauses before getting into his car. His stomach rumbles and he takes a long breath, remembering the two dozen coffees he's had, one for each diner he recruited an agent in. There has to be a less ulcer inducing way of doing this. He forces a burp and gets into his car. Just five more and he'll be happy.

CHAPTER SIXTEEN

"More coffee?" Darren asks.

"No, I should be getting back," Spacer says.

"No!" Quinn blurts, bursting into the kitchen and typing furiously on her phone. "No!" she says as she types, pausing long enough to open the fridge, take out a can of Starbucks iced coffee and head back toward the living room. "OMG, no!" she says as the door between the rooms swings closed behind her.

Spacer raises an eyebrow at Darren who jumps up from the table and follows her through to the living room. Spacer follows, catching the door behind Darren and leaning against the doorframe.

"Is that Francis?" Darren asks.

"Huh?" Quinn says. "As if that would happen ever. The jackass traded me for his shitty bike!"

Spacer smiles as Darren fights his natural impulse to correct his daughter's profanity.

Darren takes a deep breath and says, "Then who is it?"

"Um, it's my business is who it is," Quinn says.

"Quinn, please," Darren says.

Quinn looks at her father for a moment, sighs and says, "Fine, it's Stephany, Jenny, Hillary, Tim, Brooke and Jessifer."

"Jessifer?" Spacer asks.

"Spacer?" Quinn says.

"Touché," Spacer says with a nod.

"What are Stephany, Jen..." Darren begins but stops himself with a sigh. "What are they saying that's upsetting you?"

"They're just being idiots. Some guy is going all around town offering to pay people for information on two strangers who he just says, 'You'll know when you see them.' They want me to drive all over town with them and watch him. As if."

"Why do they..." Darren begins but Spacer interrupts him.

"What two people?" Spacer says.

"Weird people, who knows," Quinn says. "If it were me I'd be like, 'Give me half now cause I'm looking at one of them."

Darren chuckles. He turns to Spacer and says, "Kids right?" He pats Spacer on the shoulder, "You sure I can't talk you into one more cup of the coffee you made?"

"Huh?' Spacer says. "Oh, no, I really need to get back to Shelly."

"Got you on a tight leash, eh?"

Spacer just smiles.

Spacer walks inside their rental and notices the hallway door leading to the garage standing open. He peers inside, the ninja is resting on its kickstand right beside the Spyder. "That's odd," he says closing the door.

The smell of bacon reaches him from the kitchen wiping all thought of the motorcycle from his mind. He walks back through to see Shelly sitting at the table with a huge spread of pancakes, bacon, sausage and eggs laid out in front of her. "You cooked?" he says.

She laughs a sharp, sarcastic laugh and wipes her face with her napkin. "I picked up."

"You picked up an entire breakfast?"

"You'd rather I picked up a partial breakfast?"

Spacer shakes his head and takes a seat across from her, helping himself to a piece of toast on which he spreads a jam which is dark red, almost purple. "My God, this jam is delicious."

"That it is."

"What is it?"

"Jam."

"Seriously, what kind of jam is it?"

"The delicious kind."

"And where did you find an entire breakfast to go?"

"A place?"

"Same place you left the bike?"

"Could be," Shelly says.

"I'm not going to find out about this place, am I?"

"You know too much already," Shelly says, sipping from

her mug. "A girl has to have some mystery about her."

"Yeah, because if there's one thing you lack, it's mystery."

"How are the Whitmans?"

"They filed a police report, we should tell Pete to stay away from Bridges for a while."

"That'll break his heart," Shelly says with an eye roll.

"We're also still on for tonight," Spacer says, hiding as much as he can behind the toast.

"Really? Quinn didn't want mommy and daddy to stay in tonight and hold her hand?"

"Nope, they offered, apparently she insisted they go out as planned."

"Hmm," Shelly says, considering. "That'll make looking into the Mr. E stuff a little harder."

"About that," Spacer says.

"Yeah?"

"I think I'll call in Bruce."

"Ugh," Shelly says. "In that case, I am definitely getting away for the evening."

Spacer smiles at her.

"I seriously don't like that guy," Shelly says. "Him and his nicknames."

"Ah, the nicknames aren't that bad."

"Yours isn't. You get to be Spy Guy. I'm stuck with Hot Ass."

Spacer shrugs, "He calls em as he sees em."

"Sometimes the indirect approach is best," Shelly says. "Is he available?"

"I don't know, hope so," Spacer says. "I think someone is asking around about us."

"Who?"

"Don't know. Someone strange enough to attract the attention of disaffected teenagers."

Shelly nods, "That takes some doing."

"I'm guessing he wants us to know he's looking for us. I'd to have some backup."

"Give Bruce a call."

"Actually, I think I'll drive into Havenboro and see him in

person. He'll want a down payment."

"You think he'll have to get physical?"

Spacer shrugs. "I have no idea. But I'd like to have eyes on our place and the Whitmans' as well."

"Take cash," Shelly says.

"I know the drill. You don't care to stay around and keep tabs on things while I'm gone, do you?"

"Well, I was planning on cracking that Christopher Moore novel but, hey, vacation surveillance can be fun too."

"I thought you were doing Lady Chatterley."

"Please, that was yesterday."

"Ah yeah, I forgot."

"You run along and have fun with your friend; I'll be here if anything goes down."

Spacer crams a last piece of bacon in his mouth and stands. He turns to walk toward the garage, but Shelly stops him. "Oh, sweetie," she says in her sweetest, 1950's homemaker's voice.

"Yes, muffin?" Spacer answers in kind.

"I've cleaned and pressed your Colt, it's on the table by the door."

Spacer glances at the large pistol waiting for him in a shoulder holster lying on the table. He smiles at her and says, "I really don't deserve you."

"You can say that again."

Spacer pulls to a stop outside a three story walkup and climbs out of the car. He looks up at the second level where the PI's office is located. Nondescript is what the guy is going for and he achieves it. There is no signage, no flashing neon eye in the window, the whole thing looks residential, which is appropriate seeing as, as best as Spacer can tell, the guy lives in his office.

Spacer steps inside the building and is instantly assaulted by the smell of cabbage and fish. The Chinese place next door must vent directly into the building. He walks up the steps, noticing morebounce in his step than he has had in days. He's hardly relying on the cane at all. He comes to the door of the PI's office. Again, there is no sign, you have to know where to find the guy.

He pounds on the door and a voice from inside says, "It's open."

Spacer turns the handle and steps inside to see an empty office.

"Spy guy?" someone says from behind him. He turns to see Bruce, "The Havenboro PI" Perry standing there holding large piece of wood over his head.

"PI?"

"How's it going?"

Spacer shrugs, "Not bad, you?"

"I've been worse."

Spacer nods. "Okay, I'm just going to say it, how come you're hiding behind the door holding a heavy, blunt object over your head?"

"Usually when folk pound on my door the way you did, it means they're coming in to kill me. If you'd been one of those folks, I'd have brained you with it by now."

"The people who want to kill you knock first?"

"You'd be surprised how often they do."

"No one who tries to kill me ever knocks. We live in very different worlds, you and I."

"And yet, our paths cross an awful lot," the PI says. He lowers the wood, "I think I'm going to just put this down now."

"I'd appreciate that," Spacer says. "What is that anyway, a piano leg?"

"Yeah, it's left over from a case I worked. Probably best that you not ask."

"I wasn't going to."

The PI nods at the cane and says," How's the lumber working for you?"

Spacer picks it up and considers it. "Not bad, thanks for the loan. I've been meaning to ask, why the duck head?"

"Because when I bought it, it had a duck's head on it."

"Makes sense," Spacer says. "I probably won't be needing it much longer though."

"Yeah, you found yourself a quick cure for being shot in the ass?"

"You could say that."

"Hot Ass?"

Spacer smiles, "She has something to do with it."

The PI drops the piano leg in the corner and walks around his desk. "A woman like that, she'll make you forget your troubles." He points to the chair across the desk and Spacer takes a seat. "Of course, she'll bring you twice as much as you had before you started forgetting."

"I can't argue with that, but she makes it worth the pain."

The PI shrugs. "So, I'm guessing you didn't come over to talk about your ass."

"Got a job for you."

"I'm listening."

"You free tonight?"

"Depends on the job, and the price."

"I need a sitter."

The PI smiles but only because it seems the thing to do. "I don't do diapers."

"Actually, I need you to set up on a house. I'll pay time and a half your hourly rate."

"Anything specific I'll be watching out for?"

"Yeah, some guy's been asking around about folks who might be us. Ordinarily I wouldn't think much about it, but we sort of stuck our necks out for the neighbors last night and may have wound up shining a spotlight on them."

"And you want me to…?"

Spacer shrugs. "If they set up surveillance or something, let em. I don't want to tip our hand. Thing is, there's kids in the neighbor's house and things could turn sideways in a situation like that."

"So, any static between the creeps and the kids and I step in."

"First you call me. You know which number."

"I do."

"Then you step in and stay in until I get there." Spacer clears his throat and says, "Is there any chance I can get you to go armed with more than a piano leg?"

"I don't do guns, I tell you that every time."

"And I think it's stupid every time. This time kids could get hurt."

"It seems to me that, if keeping kids safe is your goal, you'd want to reduce the number of guns present, not increase it."

"Fine," Spacer says.

"You know my policy about getting physical."

"I do," Spacer says, reaching into his pocket and producing fifty $100 bills wrapped in a rubber band. He drops them on the desk between them.

The PI slides the money into his desk drawer and locks it dropping the key into his pocket. "That's nonrefundable, even if I don't have to get my hands dirty."

"You're not going to count it?"

"You've worked with me enough not to screw me over. You know you're going to need me again someday."

Spacer nods. "So, I want you hidden but I want to see you. I'll be leaving the house at eight o'clock."

"You'll get a signal," the PI says. "So where is this place?"

"The address is on a slip of paper under the rubber band."

"What rubber band?" The PI says, then looks at his desk. "The one on the money?"

Spacer shrugs, "I was sure you would count it."

The PI sighs and digs in his pocket for the key. "You couldn't have stopped me before I locked it?"

"No, by that point it was just funny."

"You're a real bastard sometimes, Spy Guy."

Spacer walks into the rental and says, "Bruce is lined up and you..." looks at Shelly curled up on the recliner with a paperback. "You are reading Lamb with a glass of Chardonnay."

"Mm hmm, it turns out that accommodations can be made when doing recon in one's own front room."

"Looks comfy." He glances out the bay window at the house across the street. "Has there been any movement?"

"Sissy and the girl went out about an hour ago, no sign of Darren or Carlos."

"Carlos?"

"You never told me the boy's name, so I have named him Carlos."

"It's Scott, don't call him Scout."

"Seriously, are you writing a biography on these people?"

"People talk, I listen, what can I say?" He turns back to look at Shelly. "Any movement that isn't family related?"

"Nothing outside of the mailman, which reminds me," Shelly scoops a piece of paper off of the table beside her. "I grabbed the girls list of suggestions out of the mailbox, most of it is utter shit but there are a few places that I've actually been meaning to try. I got us reservations for Les Bon Cher."

"The place the French ambassador recommended?"

"The very one."

"How did you even get reservations? It's booked for months."

"I know the French Ambassador, do I really have to say more?"

"I thought we were laying low, here. You're dropping Henre's name?"

"Where would you have us go, Aw Shucks, night club by night/oyster shack by day?"

"Possibly... is that really a thing?"

"It's really a thing."

"Well, okay, not there, but there has to be some middle ground."

"I don't do middle ground."

"I don't know, Shelly. I mean, he hasn't said so, but I get the impression that Darren is going to try to pick up the tab. He's pretty proud and there is no way he could swing Les Bon Cher for himself, let alone four people."

Shelly drops the book on the table and stares at him. "Look, we may be in the middle of a stupid mission that neither of us wanted, but this is still my vacation and I am not going to limit myself to the salary of a CPA. You boys can tussle over the check when it comes." She readjusts herself and picks the book back up, "I laid out your Armani."

"Really, you want me to go Armani?"

"I'll be wearing Vera Wang."

"Which Vera Wang?"

"The red one, with the open back."

"The one you wore for the Russian Prime Minister?"

"Yes, but I don't think there's much danger in our running into him tonight."

"You really know how to fly under the radar." Shelly smiles and returns her attention to her book. Spacer walks into the kitchen. "Is there any of that jam left?"

"There is not."

CHAPTER SEVENTEEN

Spacer steps through the door and leans his cane against the wall to straighten his jacket. He glances across the road in time to see a flash of light twinkle in the tree line behind the Whitmans house. The PI is in place.

He runs a hand over his suit coat, wishing for the comfort of the bulge his Colt would bring. There is no way he can wear it without calling attention to it. He has the derringer in his ankle holster, but that does not bring with it the same feeling of relief.

"I'm going to hop on over there," he yells back into the house.

"Go ahead, I'll be out in a sec," Shelly yells back.

Spacer steps down onto the walkway, cane first. He's needing the support less and less to the point that the cane is almost more accessory than aide. It's the first time he's really dressed up since his shooting and there's a dapper quality to the entire look that he cannot deny.

He stops when he reaches the end of the walkway and waits for a few cars to pass by. There's been very little activity on this road since they got here but apparently Saturday is when people on this street come to life.

When it's clear, he crosses and makes his way quickly up to the Whitman's porch. He rings the bell and in a moment the door is answered by Darren in an off-the-rack suit from Men's Warehouse from the look of it. Spacer instantly regrets his own tailored designer label.

"Well," Darren says, "you clean up right nice."

"Back 'atcha, big guy," Spacer says.

Darren laughs deeply and pops him on the arm, "Look out ladies, there are two Tomcats on the prowl tonight, eh?"

"Now, now, let's not get ahead of ourselves," Sissy says. "You Tomcats will be escorting two ladies." She appears at the door in a flowing, silver dress which has probably been in storage for a while given the tightness around certain less flattering areas. Her hair is pinned up and the grey has been professionally removed. The effort she's put in is obvious and

Spacer smiles his warmest smile at her.

"Sissy, you are breath taking."

"Oh," Sissy says, a blush forming on her cheeks as she turns away from him.

"Yep, I'm afraid I'm going to have to watch all the other fellas out tonight. I'm going to have the prettiest girl in the place on my arm."

"I think you're right," Spacer says.

"Don't you be getting any ideas," Darren says, chuckling. "Say, where is your lovely wife, I still have not met her or even seen her up close."

"She's just getting ready, she'll be…" Spacer stops as he realizes the scene that is just about to play out behind him. Darren and Sissy gasp.

Spacer turns to see Shelly stepping out of the house, bare right leg, from the slit that runs to her thigh, first. As if she has command of nature itself, a breeze blows just as she steps outside, playing with her hair, tousling it and causing her to smile in that way she, somehow, does not realize is impossible to look away from.

She steps down onto the walkway, one long leg before the other, her stride is confident, determined, her dress, accentuating all of her best features, flows around her.

Boys who had not been anywhere in sight, pull their bikes and scooters to a halt on the sidewalk and stare shamelessly at her as she advances. A VW Beetle comes to a stop in the middle of the road as does a small Ford Ranger. The cars behind them start to blare their horns but soon stop when she comes into view.

"She stopped traffic," Sissy says, the shock plain in her voice. "Cars literally just stopped because she stepped out of her house."

Shelly, for her part, pretends to notice none of this. She continues in her stride, until she has crossed the road and is standing on the Whitman's porch. She runs her arm around Spacer's and the tableau behind them slowly comes once more to life.

Spacer smiles sheepishly at the Whitmans, he staring slack

jawed at this Venus come to life on his front porch, she trying very hard to hide her true thoughts. "Sissy," Spacer says, "you've already met my lovely wife, Darren, I'd like to introduce to you Mrs. Shelly Sharpe."

Darren says nothing; he merely continues staring at her as if he's lost all motor function. Sissy jams an elbow into his ribs. "Hmm!" he says with a start. He blinks twice and offers his hand, "Uh, yes, Darren Whitman, it is a true pleasure, Miss…. Ma'am!"

"Darren," Sissy says.

"Oh, yes, and this is my wife, Sissy."

"She already knows that, we met yesterday."

"Ah, yes, someone should have mentioned," Darren says.

"Spacer did, just this very minute," Sissy says.

"Ah, yes, of course he did," Darren says. "Say, I could use a drink, anyone else care for a drink? Let's have a drink." Darren walks quickly, if a tad awkwardly, inside the house. When he thinks no one is looking, he jerks on his pants, readjusting himself. Everyone is looking.

Spacer shrugs and follows Darren through to the kitchen. Shelly glances at Sissy who stares back at her. "Shall we?" Shelly says.

"Yes… please… let's let my husband see more of you," Sissy says, walking inside. Shelly remains on the porch for another moment debating and then follows her.

"So, what'll you have?" Darren asks.

"Scotch would be great," Spacer says, "although anything in the whiskey family will do."

"Oh," Darren says. "We… um, we don't really keep a lot of liquor in the house, what with the kids, I was thinking soda or maybe some of Sissy's lemonade."

"Oh, yeah, that'll be… of course," Spacer says.

"No, no I think," Darren says, turning to Sissy. "Didn't you get a bottle of something for those whiskey brownies you made for that bachelorette party you went to?"

"Seriously, whiskey brownies?" Spacer asks. "That sounds like the best thing ever."

"Oh, they were all right. You see, you simmer the whiskey

and then melt the chocolate chips in it," Sissy says.

"Oh, Sissy, how I regret that you were already taken by the time I met you," Spacer says.

"Yes," Sissy says, glancing at Shelly. "I'm sure you've somehow managed to accept your situation."

Shelly looks from Sissy to Spacer and then Darren, "So you say there IS whiskey in this house?" she asks him.

"Where is that, Sissy?"

"Oh, I think I crammed it way back in the cupboard," Sissy says, rooting around in their pantry. She pulls out a barely used fifth of Old Crow whiskey. "Honestly, I'm surprised I didn't toss this out."

Darren takes it from her. "I have to admit, I'm not very up on my whiskeys, is this a good one?"

"It'll do in a pinch," Shelly says. She takes the bottle from him and swigs directly from it. "Oh... my goodness, that is... that is something."

Sissy hands Spacer two glasses and he takes the bottle from Shelly, pouring three fingers of the stuff into both and handing the second to his wife. "Will you guys be joining us?"

"I think we'll start out with the lemonade," Darren says, pouring a glass for himself and Sissy. He holds his out and says, "To a great evening with new friends."

"Salud," Shelly says, tinking her glass with his, Spacer and Sissy join in the toast and they and Darren sip while Shelly throws hers back swallowing it in a single gulp. She closes her eyes tightly and slams her fist on the counter, "Damn, that is... something."

"Yeah," Spacer says, grimacing. "Something all right." He forces the rest of his drink down as well.

"So, we've been discussing places we could take you to," Darren says. "And I think we have a few pretty good suggestions."

"Oh, about that, it turns out that there is one place we've been meaning to go to right here on the island, Les Bon Cher," Spacer says.

Darren and Sissy look at each other and share a chuckle. Darren turns back to Spacer and says, "We don't mean to laugh at you, it's just that that place has a waiting list a mile long. If we'd made reservations four months ago we'd only have a chance at getting in."

"We hate to disappoint you, but that simply isn't going to happen," Sissy says.

"We have reservations at 9:00," Shelly says, refilling her glass. Spacer arches and eyebrow at her. She shrugs, "It's kind of growing on me," she says, taking a long swig.

"How in the world did you manage that?" Darren asks.

"I know someone," Shelly says.

"Who?"

"One of her cousins… her distant cousin, is a busboy there," Spacer says quickly. "He was able to get us in."

"I had no idea that the busboys had so much pull there," Sissy says.

"Well, he's very good at his job," Spacer says.

There are footsteps on the stairs and Quinn yells, "Mom, Dad, are you guys still here?"

"We were just about to take off," Darren yells back. "Come on in and meet Mrs. Sharpe."

Quinn walks into the kitchen and gasps when Shelly turns and smiles at her. "Hi, Quinn, I'm very glad to meet you," Shelly says.

"Your hair…" Quinn says.

"Yes, it is pretty amazing, her hair," Sissy says, flatly. She pours some of the Old Crow into her now empty lemonade glass and takes a sip. "Oh God! No!" she says, holding the glass away from her as if it were an animal which might bite at any moment.

"Let me help you out with that," Shelly says, plucking the glass from her and throwing back the whiskey.

"I'm seriously becoming concerned about you," Spacer says. Shelly shrugs.

"Quinn, hon, is everything all right?" Darren asks.

"Huh? Oh, yeah, Dad, everything's great." Quinn backs slowly out of the kitchen, never taking her eyes from Shelly. "You guys have fun tonight, me and Scout will be just fine."

"I thought we weren't supposed to call him Scout," Shelly

says.

"He'd prefer we didn't, they can get away with it, they're family," Spacer says.

Quinn turns and runs back up the stairs without another word.

"You'll have to forgive her," Darren says. "I suppose Spacer has already told you about her harrowing night."

"Oh yes, it was as if I'd been there," Shelly says, Spacer glares at her.

Darren glances at his watch. "Well, I suppose if we have to make 9:00 reservations we'd best be moving along." He looks up and says, "Whose car are we taking?"

"Ours," Shelly says, quickly.

"Ours only has two seats," Spacer tells her.

"And, you have both been drinking," Sissy says.

"What, this? You call this drinking?" Shelly asks. "I once drank Vladimir Putin under the table and then drove a team of..."

"Vladimir Putin was the nickname of my college roommate," Spacer says. "The kid could drink." He turns to Shelly and lowers his voice, "But that was back when we were less responsible adults."

Shelly rolls her eyes at him. "If you're willing, we'd be happy to take your car," she tells Darren.

"Excellent, the Whit-mobile it is," Darren says, leading them through the living room and into the garage where they find a Dodge Caravan.

"A minivan," Shelly says. "Wonderful."

"It may not be as sporty as that thing you drive, but it certainly serves our purposes," Sissy says, climbing into the back seat.

Spacer pulls Shelly aside and whispers, "What are you doing? Why are you being such a pill?"

"I'm sorry, luv. I can literally feel the mediocrity crawling all over me. It makes me a little bitchy."

"Could you maybe not make them suffer for not being a super hero like you?"

"I'll be nice." Spacer squints at her. "I will, now let's go."

Shelly walks to the van and Spacer opens the passenger door and allows her to climb in.

"What a gentleman," Sissy says, looking pointedly at her husband.

Spacer shuts the door and crawls in next to Sissy. Darren cranks the car and opens the garage door with the remote clipped to the sun-visor above his seat. "Now, am I mistaken or is there dancing at Les Bon Cher?"

"You are not mistaken," Shelly says.

Darren turns to look at Spacer. "Are you going to be able to handle that? It's not going to aggravate your canyon injury, is it?"

"Canyon injury?" Shelly asks.

"Oh yes, what did you say when he told you he'd fallen into a canyon?" Sissy asks her.

"Oh... I'd say I was pretty speechless," Shelly says. "In fact, it still surprises me. Hearing you all talk about it, it's like hearing it again for the first time."

"It's a unique situation, indeed," Spacer says. He turns to Darren, "I may be sitting out most of the dances tonight, but we'll still have fun."

"You got that right, my friend," Darren says, pulling out of the garage.

Darren pulls the van up to the valet station outside Les Bon Cher and the valet walks quickly to his lowered window. "You folks need directions to someplace?" the valet asks.

"No, we have reservations here," Darren says with a chuckle.

The valet raises his eyebrows. "Um, are you... sure?"

"Yes," Shelly says, looking around Darren. "We're certain."

"Oh... oh, I see, now," the valet says, running around to the passenger side and opening the door for her. Spacer pulls open the sliding back door, steps out and offers Sissy his hand.

"Why, thank you," she says, stepping out."

They join Darren on the other side of the car as he hands a dollar bill to the valet, "Thank you, my good man," he says, laughing.

The valet looks at the bill and says, "Um, sir…"

Spacer catches his eye and shakes his head at him. Shelly leads the group to the door followed by Darren and Sissy, arm in arm, and lastly by Spacer who stayed behind to slip the valet a twenty unnoticed.

The maître' de looks up as they approach and smiles. "Reservation for Sharpe," she says.

"Of course," he says, looking past her at Darren and Sissy. "I have you here for a party of four?" he says.

"That's right."

"And this would be your party?" he asks.

"It would."

"Very good," he says, his smile faltering just a little. "Please, follow me."

As he leads them into the dining room Darren falls back to speak with Spacer. "I just want to say up front that tonight is on me."

"Oh, no, I can't ask you to do that," Spacer says.

"No, I won't hear another word on the subject. We are supposed to be showing you a good time, we can hardly expect you to pay."

Spacer starts to say something else when he hears the maître d' say, "I trust this is to your liking."

"It's fine," Shelly says, as the man pulls out a chair for the ladies.

"Oh, we've got to get over there, now," Spacer says.

"Why, what's wrong?" Darren asks.

"Your waiter will be by shortly, but can I start you off with a drink?" the maître d' says.

"Seriously, we have to…" Spacer starts but Shelly stops him when she says, "Yes, a bottle of Dom Perignon for the table."

"Before that happens," Spacer said.

"Very good," the maître d' says.

"What just happened?"

"Shelly just ordered champagne for the table," Spacer says.

"Oh, it's a celebration, we should have a little bubbly," Darren says, slapping him on the back. "Don't worry so much." Darren chuckles but it seems forced. He clearly doesn't know exactly how much a bottle of Dom costs, but he's heard it can be quite a bit.

They join the ladies at the table and Spacer leans into Shelly and whispers, "Dom? Really?"

"I told you, I am not limiting myself."

"This restaurant is so snazzy, I have to admit, I feel a little out of place," Sissy says.

"Nonsense," Spacer says. Shelly cuts him a look which he ignores. "There's no place which can't be improved by your presence."

"Well, that's kind of you to say," Sissy says. She looks at Darren, "Why can't you say things like that."

"Hmm?" Darren says, visibly distracted.

"Hi, I'm Jonathan, I'll be your waiter this evening," a young man in a perfectly pressed white shirt says as he approaches with four menus.

"Hi, Jonathan, I'm Darren and I'll be your customer," Darren says, chortling. Shelly looks again at Spacer and again he ignores it.

Jonathan hands Spacer a menu and holds one out for Darren. Spacer shoves his into Shelly's hands and snatches the one offered to Darren. "Thank you, Jonathan," he says.

"Sir, those are for…"

"I know what they are for, Jonathan," Spacer says, leveling a dead stare at the boy that could rival Shelly's. "They are for ordering food."

Jonathan swallows and nods at him, handing the remaining menus to the Whitmans. Darren raises an eyebrow at Spacer but says nothing.

"Your champagne will be right out. Can I get you anything else while you wait?"

"I could really use a Glenlivet," Spacer says.

"Of course, anyone else?"

"You don't have any Old Crow do you?" Shelly asks.

"Um, no ma'am, I'm afraid we don't."

"Fine then, I'll have what he's having."

"Very good," Jonathan says. He looks at the Whitmans.

"Nothing for us just now," Darren says.

"I'll have those out in a jiff," Jonathan says before walking away.

Shelly opens her menu and peruses the options, each with a considerable price next to it. She shakes her head and whispers, "What good do you think giving them the menus without the prices is going to do?"

"I'm not sure, but I need a little time to figure this out without the accountant doing the math," Spacer says.

"Ooh, I'm going to have the forty-dollar salmon," Shelly whispers.

"You don't even really like salmon."

"Somehow, knowing it's worth forty dollars makes me like it so much more," Shelly says. "I should make you give me the men's menu with the pricing every time we go to one of these places."

"Honey, I don't see prices," Sissy says.

"Oh," Darren chuckles. "A place like this doesn't put something as common as prices on their menus. If you can't afford whatever, you shouldn't be in here."

"I don't know."

"Just, don't you fret, order whatever you feel like."

"Hmm, the salmon looks good, I'll bet that isn't too pricey."

"Don't you go ordering what you think is cheapest, Sissy. You'll make us look ridiculous. Get the shrimp, you like shrimp."

"I'm allergic to shrimp."

"Well, eat around it."

"Eat what around it?"

"You know, the other stuff."

Jonathan returns with the two Scotches and the bottle of champagne. He places the drinks in front of the Sharpes and picks up the bottle. "Shall I pop the cork?" he says.

"Absolutely," Shelly says.

Jonathan wraps a towel around the cork and pulls, making a loud "POP" which causes Sissy to jump.

"Oh my, I wasn't expecting that."

Jonathan smiles at her as he fills four champagne flutes.

"Have you had time to decide?" he asks when he is done.

"Yes," Darren says, "I will have the sirloin, well done, and my wife would like the shrimp."

"Yes, I would like the shrimp," Sissy says.

"Very good," Jonathan says, and turns to Shelly. "For you?"

"Let's start with the oyster tray…" Shelly says.

"Really?" Spacer asks.

"Mm hmm, I'm thinking an aphrodisiac might be just the thing this evening. Maybe we'll even get you out on the dance floor," Shelly says with a wink. "And for my main course I will have the salmon."

Sissy glares at Darren.

"And for the gentleman?"

"What the hell, I'll do the sirloin as well, but make mine rare," Spacer says.

"Of course." Jonathan jots their orders on his pad and walks back into the kitchen.

Spacer raises his champagne and says, "What should we drink to now?"

"I say we drink again to a great evening," Darren says, raising his own.

"I say we drink to our health and we make our own great evening," Shelly says.

"Oh, I like that," Darren says and the four of them clink their glasses.

The music that has been playing in the background kicks up in tempo as they each drink and Shelly looks around. "That's a tango," she says. She spins on Spacer and says, "Think you're up to it or is the canyon wound still bothering you?"

"I'll sit this one out," Spacer says.

"Then it just became your lucky day," Shelly says to Darren, grabbing his hand and pulling him out of his seat despite his protests.

"This is… this is very kind of you, but I really wasn't talking about a tango when I said I wanted to dance. I… I'm not sure I'll be able to keep up," he whispers into Shelly's ear as she drags him behind her.

She spins on him and stares at her, flames behind those grey eyes. "Can you catch?" she asks.

"What? I mean… yes, I suppose I can."

"Then catch this." She throws her leg up until she is doing a vertical scissor split. Instinctively Darren grabs her ankle and she leans into him. "Now walk backwards," she says. He does as he is told, dragging Shelly's remaining foot behind them and clearing the area around the center of the dance floor. "Now duck," she says, kicking off of him and spinning her leg around, her stiletto heel slicing the air where Darren's head had been half a moment ago.

Darren cowers on the ground as Shelly twirls around him, he closes his eyes and tries not to do anything disastrous. Strong hands pull him from where he stoops and spin him until he is once more face to face with Shelly. "Retreat," she tells him.

He backs away from her and she advances, twisting and twirling, her arms and legs a blur to him. She grabs him by the collar and he stops. She melts into him, sliding down the length of his body.

"Well, they certainly seem to be having fun," Sissy says. Jonathan delivers the tray of oysters and she grabs one and slides it down her throat.

Spacer looks at his cane, runs a hand over his sore thigh and says, "Fuck it." He grabs Sissy by the hand, pulling her from her chair and twirls with her onto the dance floor.

Shelly is in the middle of a Mexican hat dance, using the once more cowering Darren for the hat, when she sees that she has some competition. Spacer stops his twirl in the dead center of the floor and pulls Sissy close to him. He leads them into a tango, marching to the rhythm all around the dance floor, stopping long enough to spin Sissy before locking, once more, into synchronized step.

Shelly pulls her partner from the floor and, grabbing his hand, spins before him, a dervish possessed by a demon.

Spacer stops his tango, slides Sissy through his legs and tosses her into the air and over his head, turning just in time to catch her, spin her again and lock back into their tango.

"I am very much regretting having eaten that oyster at this

moment," Sissy says to him.

"Do you want to stop?"

"Not if I'd eaten a thousand oysters."

Spacer smiles at her, "That's my girl."

Shelly takes two steps back from Darren and runs two fingers over her eyes while shaking her hips. Spacer tangos over to her and says, "The Batoosi? Really?"

"You have to admit, I make even this look good," she says.

"Dammit, she's right," Sissy says, immediately covering her mouth as if she could force the words to go back in. Spacer throws his head back and laughs.

He straightens and dips Sissy, swaying to the left. Shelly leans over her and says to Spacer, "Big finish is coming up, are you ready?"

"I'm more ready than you are," he says.

"Hope that canyon injury doesn't act up on you."

"Hope your partner's a good catch."

"Um, Spacer, a lot of blood seems to be flowing to my head just now," Sissy says, her face almost purple from prolonged dip.

"Oh my God, I'm so sorry," Spacer says, pulling her to her feet. "I'm going to spin you to the other side of the dance floor. On my signal, run at me and jump, I'll do the rest."

Shelly gestures for Darren to back up as she and Spacer do the same until both couples are on either end of the floor.

"It's very nice of you to bring Sissy out here," Shelly says. "But you aren't over doing it, are you?"

"No, I really am feeling much better after last night."

"Maybe tonight we can administer another treatment."

"Really, the mood you've been in I figured I didn't have a chance in hell."

"Well, I will be eating oysters, very soon."

Spacer nods at Sissy and Shelly breaks into a run at the same time. Shelly, the faster of the two, passes Sissy when she is only a quarter of the way across the room. She jumps and Darren holds up two trembling hands to catch her. Sissy stops in her advance and turns to watch with everyone else. Shelly ignores Darren's hands but springs off of his shoulders in a handspring. Darren panics and bolts for the safety of the crowd. Spacer breaks into a run as Shelly summersaults in midair, sliding the last few feet on his knees so that he can catch her as she lands in a perfect split.

"My hero," she whispers in his ear.

"Couldn't let you have all of the glory," Spacer says. She kisses him hard on the mouth and the crowd erupts into applause. Still kissing, Spacer stands with Shelly in his arms and the applause grows even louder. At last she breaks from him and whispers, "Not until later, lover," and he lowers her to the floor.

The kitchen staff break into applause. It isn't often that something would pull the entire staff away from their duties, but no one was willing to miss that. Now they are slowly drifting back to their assigned stations, all save for one dish washer.

Gerry reaches into his pocket and pulls out his phone and a pack of cigarettes. He steps outside, lights a cigarette and removes the business card he'd slipped into the pack just after breakfast. He lights the cigarette, takes a long drag and lets the smoke out slowly.

"Where the fuck is Gerry?" he hears his manager yell from inside.

The phone buzzes and he looks at the text coming in. Don't Worry About My B-Day his wife says. We Need Milk More.

Gerry feels his face go red. Fuck 'em, what does he owe those assholes. He types the number on the card and listens as it rings twice on the other end. "Yes?" a voice says.

"I… um, I was given this number in case I saw something strange."

"You calling from Bridges?"

"Yes!"

"What did you see."

"I… well, it was dancing."

"Go on."

"I mean, it was really good dancing. Like… um, there were gymnastics involved."

"Hang on."

The voice disappears for a moment and Gerry takes another drag off of his cigarette. Soon the familiar, melodic voice of the stranger he'd met this morning comes on the line. "Gerald," it says.

"Yeah… wait, how did you know?"

"That's not something you need to concentrate on. These athletic dancers, tell me about them."

"Hmm?" Gerry says, coughing and dropping the cigarette.

"Tell me about them, did anything stand out apart from the dancing?"

"Uh, yeah, I mean, I don't know if they're movie stars, but it wouldn't surprise me. You know, they've got that look. And I know movie stars, I used to drive them."

"I understand. Tell me more about the look."

"Well, he's… I mean, don't take this wrong, but he's a good-looking guy. And she… holy God, I wouldn't kick her out of bed for eating crackers, you know. And the hair…"

"What about the hair?"

"I don't think I've ever really seen hair like it. Red doesn't even describe it it's…"

"Thank you, you've been most helpful," the voice says. "You'll find I am very appreciative when you check your bank balance tomorrow."

Gerry takes a deep breath and lets it out in ragged chuckles. "I'll appreciate your appreciation."

"Just one more thing and you can walk away from those dishes of yours and never again worry about a bill. Tell me how I can find them."

"Hmm?" Gerry says, "Well, I mean…"

"Is there a problem?"

"Look, they're here with a local fella and, he's an all right guy. Used to use him for my taxes. I don't want to, you know, jam him up in this."

"Well, if that's your decision, I can certainly respect it," the voice says. Gerry hears liquid sloshing as if coffee is being stirred. Suddenly that confounding circle fills his vision and he needs to know why that damned cream just won't mix. He hears himself from far away giving the man Darren Whitman's address.

"Thank you, Gerald," the voice says before breaking the connection.

"God dammit, where the fuck is Gerry?" Gerry's manager bellows. Gerry shakes a new cigarette from the pack, lights it, and decides it is time to shop for his wife's birthday.

Shelly and Spacer make their way through the throngs of onlookers shaking their hands and patting them on the back until they reach their table where the Whitmans are already sitting. "That was some display," Darren says.

"We couldn't have done it without the two of you," Shelly tells them.

"Still, something tells me that this is not the first time the two of you have cut a rug together."

"Maybe not the very first," Spacer says.

"Well, it was certainly a first for Sissy and me," Darren says, picking up an oyster and examining it. "Say, has this been cooked?"

"It's a raw oyster platter," Shelly says.

"Raw?" Darren puts the half shell back on the platter. "That's a first experience I don't think Sissy or I want to have."

"Not a first for me," Sissy says, throwing back another oyster.

"I... Sissy?" Darren says.

"They do take some getting used to," Spacer says, picking up an oyster and dousing it with hot sauce.

"Does the hot sauce help?" Darren asks.

"Well, if you like them, it's a good compliment, if you're trying to hide the oyster entirely, that would take a lot of sauce." Spacer throws back his own oyster and says, "Probably more than would be healthy."

"Or you could just go au natural," Shelly says, tipping one to her lips and allowing it to slide gracefully down her throat. Both men stare at her shamelessly, even Sissy has a hard time looking away.

At last, Sissy clears her throat and says, "I'm going to check in with the kids." She stands and excuses herself to the alcove next to the bathrooms.

Spacer whispers to Shelly, "I'm going to check with the sitter."

"I'll keep daddy company," Shelly whispers back. He excuses himself from the table and walks toward the kitchen so that Sissy won't overhear his call.

He keys in the number and, after one ring, the PI says, "Nothing yet, Spy Guy... oh, hang on."

"What's up?"

"Well, could be nothing, but it ain't nothing."

"Tell me."

"A van just did a drive by. They were definitely casing the place."

"Still there?"

"Nah, wait, yeah. One guy is sneaking back through the yard."

"Can you take him out?"

"I could, but you may not want me to. It looks like he may be planting some bugs. If I move, whoever he's working for is going to know you're on to him."

Spacer sighs. "Okay, we'll go with that. If it takes a turn you know what to do."

"Yeah, I've got the piano leg"

"How are you not dead yet?"

"I'm good at what I do."

Spacer disconnects and is about to return to his table when he hears raised voices inside the kitchen. He peeks inside to see a man in a grey, pinstripe suit addressing two men in solid black ones. "You cannot do this to me," he says.

"Face it, Pierre, it's happening. We'll be back in a week, either every guy here without proper paperwork is gone or we're shutting you down."

They turn and walked toward the door, shoving past Spacer. "Out of the way, twinkly toes," they tell him.

Spacer smiles at them and steps aside, mentally cataloguing

all of the ways he could kill them without breaking a sweat. He turns and walks into the kitchen.

"I'm sorry, but you can't be back here," the pinstriped suited man says.

"I couldn't help but overhear. I'm guessing a lot of the kitchen staff are undocumented," Spacer says.

The man laughs a shrill laugh, "The only one I had that wasn't just took off on me."

"Actually, I may be in a position to help you, the name is Spacer... Spacer Sharpe."

The man looks at him without recognition.

"My wife is Shelly Sharpe."

The man gasps. "Shelly Sharpe, the friend of the ambassador? She is your wife?"
"Yes, she is my wife."

"Do you think you could speak to her about speaking with the ambassador and arranging visas for my staff?"
"Well, I could do that, or I could just speak to the ambassador himself."

"Probably better it comes from a friend of his, don't you think?"

"I'm a friend of his, I introduced him to Shelly!"

"You did?"

"Yes, I'm just not as quick to brag about it."

The man grabs Spacer's hand and shakes it vigorously. "Oh sir, if you could do this you would never pay a single tab in my restaurant, ever, starting tonight."

"I was so hoping you would say that. You get me a list, I'll get on the phone." Spacer steps through the door to the kitchen when something hits him. He turns back. "Actually, what if you just charged us... oh, let's say a hundred bucks for this evening?"

"What? Why would you want to pay for something I'm giving you for free?"

Spacer shrugs. "It's sort of involved. Do you think you could do that? Just make up a bill for a hundred bucks... well, not a hundred even, that would look suspicious, like, a hundred and two and change maybe."

"I… this is a very unusual request."

"It's a kind of unusual situation."

"I don't know, comping is a thing that all restaurants do. But, if there is a piece of paper out there with my name on it and everything you have had tonight coming to a mere one hundred dollars, I could not show my face if that were to get out."

"Oh, don't worry, the receipt won't leave this building, I promise you that."

One half hour long call later, Spacer returns to the table to find everyone almost finished with their meals. "Hey, chief, we were starting to get worried."

"Yeah, I wound up getting involved in a work call, I'm so sorry."

"Is everything okay with the shipment?" Shelly asks.

Spacer shrugs, "A little issue with the van, but nothing inside was harmed."

"Well, that's good."

"I'm afraid your steak must be stone cold," Sissy says.

"That's alright, I can eat meat pretty much any way I get it," Spacer says.

"A man after my own heart," Darren says, daintily removing any piece of gristle from the last bite of his steak.

"Will there be anything else?" Jonathan asks.

"Just the bill, please," Darren says.

"Ah yes," Jonathan says, taking a leather folder from his apron, opening it and staring at it quizzically. Not for the first time from the look of it.

"Thank you," Darren says, reaching an unsteady hand out to take it. He takes a deep breath and opens it slowly. "Oh," he says quickly. "Well that's not too bad at all." He pulls a card from his wallet and places it in the folder which he hands back to Jonathan.

Shelly raises her eyebrows at Spacer who looks only at his cold steak as he cuts into it.

"I have to admit, I thought for a bit that a place like this would take quite a dent out of the old checking account."

"Many people think that," Shelly says.

Jonathan returns with the receipt which Darren signs and hands back to him. He picks up his copy of the receipt but Spacer snatches it out of his hand and holds it over the candle. It bursts into flame in a way that makes him wonder if they used extra flammable paper for it.

"What was that about?" Darren asks.

"Never save a receipt after a night like tonight," Spacer says. "You should walk away with memories only."

"That's beautiful," Sissy says.

Spacer smiles at her and looks back at his steak.

CHAPTER EIGHTEEN

Darren pulls into his garage and kills the engine, still chuckling. "I just… I just haven't had so much fun in such a long time, I hate for it to end."

"How about we come in for one last drink?" Spacer says.

"You know what, that sounds like a fine idea," Sissy says.

Spacer crawls out of the van and helps Sissy out. He open's Shelly's door and leans in to kiss her on the cheek. "We need to do a search, if there are any listening devices I want to know about it. Can you do the upstairs?"

"Why can't you?"

"I may have over done it on the dance floor after all."

"I told you." She steps out and they follow the Whitmans into the house.

"You know, I just remembered a recipe for a toddy my mother used to make that I'll bet will make that whiskey we have tolerable," Sissy says, walking into the kitchen.

"I think I'm going to need to make a rest stop Spacer says. He points down a hall running next to the stairs. "It's this way I'm guessing."

"Just like your place," Darren says. He turns to Shelly and says, "I hope you don't mind my abandoning you for a moment." He points to his shoes and says, "These clod hoppers are killing me, I'm going to slip into something a little more comfortable." He laughs and says, "Oh, listen to me, I sound like a starlets from the fifties."

"You go on ahead," Shelly says. "I do just fine on my own."

She waits for him to walk up the stairs and into his bedroom and then she runs upstairs, taking them three at a time without making a sound. Darren turned left at the landing and so she hangs a right. The far most room on the upstairs in their place is a guest room, she assumes the same is true for this one. She opens the door and Quinn gasps.

Oh yeah, they have kids.

"I am so sorry, I was just giving myself a tour, I didn't realize this was your room," she tells the girl.

"It's… it's okay," Quinn says, her voice shaking. "Um, can

144

I ask you a question, Mrs. Sh…"

"Quinn, honey, this room is amazing!" Shelly says quickly before Quinn can say her name for any potentially listening ears.

"Oh, um, thanks, but… okay, this may seem really weird but… are you in a motorcycle gang?" Shelly forces herself to laugh as if that was the craziest thing she'd ever heard. She grabs a Hello Kitty themed pad and pen from Quinn's dresser and scribbles on it as she says, "That is just the silliest thing I've ever heard. Did your Uncle Felix tell you that? You know he is always making things up just to cause trouble." She hands the pad to Quinn who reads it: JUST GO ALONG WITH THIS, I'LL EXPLAIN IN A MINUTE.

Quinn raises an eyebrow but forces her own laugh and says, "Yeah, I guess I should have realized it would be Uncle Felix telling another one of his dumb jokes."

Shelly smiles at her.

"But you were serious when you said you'd give me a hundred dollars… for books, right Aunt Nicolette?"

Shelly's smile grows even broader. "Absolutely, I never joke about money." She walks around the room, looking for small holes which may have been drilled from the outside. "So, tell me about school."

"Oh, it sucks."

Shelly lets go with a genuine laugh and says, "Trust me dear, it gets so much better." She opens the window saying, "Can you believe what a wonderful night this is?"

"It's pretty nice, I guess."

Shelly runs her hand along the edge of the window and says, "You know, your Uncle Felix and I shared our first kiss on a night very much like tonight." She squints at a particularly odd and dangerous looking insect crouched on the wall next to the window, the sort of bug that people would avoid at all cost and leave to its own devices so long as it did not come inside.

"You did?" Quinn asks.

"Mm hmm, I still remember it, it was a magical evening," Shelly leans toward the insect, it doesn't move. What's more, it seems to be humming. "You know what," she says, leaning back into the house. "I'd love to show him the way the moon looks from this very spot, would you mind?"

"Um… I guess not."

Shelly walks quickly out of Quinn's room, stopping just long enough to admire the trophy sitting on a shelf above her bed. She runs down the stairs where she finds Spacer standing with Darren discussing… discussing the wallpaper?

"We were thinking teal for the hall, but in my heart, I knew that it was more of a beige," Darren says.

"You made the right call," Spacer says, without a hint of irony. How does he do it?

"Babe," Shelly says, "Quinn was just telling me all about the speech contest she won and I thought you really needed to hear it." Spacer nods and holds up a finger. "Seriously, we need you there, now."

"Hey," Spacer says, smiling at her, "I never pass up a speech story."

"She never talks about that," Darren says, "let's all go."

"Actually,' Shelly says, "she said she doesn't like to tell it in front of you, it feels like bragging."

"Really?" Darren asks. "Well, I don't want her to feel bad. Sissy and I will be in the kitchen when you're done."

Shelly walks back up the stairs, slowing her pace to accommodate Spacer, and then leads him to Quinn's room which she walks into once more without knocking. She spins to Spacer and says, "Here it is, Felix dear, the moon I was telling you about."

"Wha… Oh!" Spacer says, "yes, the moon, glad you brought me up here. That's not the sort of thing you can see from just anywhere."

"Oh, come to the window, see how much it looks just like the moon we shared our first kiss under."

"You know what, I'm willing to bet that IS the same moon we shared our first kiss under," Spacer says, joining Shelly at the window.

"Oh, you big goof," Shelly says. She points to the bug which still hasn't moved and is still humming slightly. Spacer rolls his eyes and laughs silently.

"You're right," he says, reaching into his interior jacket pocket and pulling out a set of tweezers and an eyeglass repair kit. "It is just like our first kiss. Thank you for showing me this." He kisses Shelly quickly on the mouth, hoping the smooching sound is realistic enough for those prying ears. "What was the song that was playing on the radio that night? Something Latin, wasn't it?"

"You know, I think that it was," Shelly says.

Spacer hooks his foot under Quinn's bed as an anchor and leans out the window. "I'd really like to hear that song again, see if you can find it on the radio, hon."

Quinn looks up and points to the radio, Shelly shakes her head at her. "I'm on it, dear," Shelly says.

Spacer prods the insect with the tweezers, it still doesn't move. He pulls a jeweler's glass affixed to eyeglass frames from his pocket and sets them on his face. Peering through the small magnifier, he works the tweezers along the back of the insect until he finds a small hatch which he opens to reveal circuitry. He puckers his lips in a silent whistle, admiring the tech inside.

"Oh Darling?" he says. "How is the music coming?"

Shelly shrugs, "Coming right up."

He smiles at her and works a tiny dial inside the insect with the eyeglass screwdriver. After a quarter turn he closes the hatch on the insect and pulls himself back in the window. "Okay, we can speak freely," he says. "I tuned the bug to the Latin radio station. They may question our choice of music for a while, but I don't think they'll realize what's happened until it's too late to do anything about it tonight."

"What about tomorrow?" Quinn asks.

"Tomorrow all of this will be over," Shelly says. "Felix and I will see to that."

"Okay, what is the deal with this Felix stuff?" Spacer says. "That's the best fake name you could come up with?"

"I like it," Shelly says.

"So, how do you know you set it to the Latin station if you can't here it?"

"It's not my first time," Spacer says with a wink.

Spacer nods to Quinn, "How much does she know."

"Not as much as she is about to," Shelly says.

"Are you sure that's a good idea?"

"I think she deserves it." Quinn surprises herself by smiling broadly at the compliment.

"All right, I'll leave you to it," Spacer says. He turns to Quinn, "I don't want to tell you to lie to your parents but…"

"Lie about this to Mom and Dad, got it," Quinn says.

"Told you," Shelly says.

"All right then." Spacer walks to the door but Shelly stops him.

"How much cash do you have on you?" "Couple of hundred, why?"

"Because one of those hundred belongs to Quinn."

Spacer shrugs, "I'm just going to trust you on that." He pulls a hundred dollar bill out of his wallet.

"She's a kid, babe, small bills," Shelly says.

"Fine," he replaces the hundred and digs out five twenties. He shows them to Shelly who nods. He holds them out to Quinn.

"Really?" she says.

"I told you, I don't kid about money," Shelly says.

"Wow, thanks Mrs. Sharpe," Quinn says, grabbing her purse and stuffing the bills inside.

"You earned it."

"So, I think I know where the other bug is," Spacer says. He nods toward the window. "That one is really powerful, if they put the other one anywhere near it they would interfere with each other. It's got to be spliced into the phone cord in the attic. I'll probably just have to kill the phones for this evening." He turns to Quinn. Do you guys use your land line a lot?"

"Our internet comes in on it, we have DSL."

"Really? Still?"

Quinn shrugs, "Dad can't see any reason to change."

"Well, now we have one," Spacer says. "I'm afraid you're going to have to miss out on Twitter tonight." Spacer walks out of the room.

Shelly closes the door behind him and turns to Quinn. "All right, what DO you know?"

Quinn shakes her head and says, "I don't know what I know. I thought you were the leader of a motorcycle gang but now you and Mr. Sharpe are in my room and you're doing things with... is there a bug outside my room? Like a real spy bug?"

"There is," Shelly says. "And I know that can be really upsetting, but trust me, Spacer and I are going to take care of the men who put that there."

"What is happening? Why did you beat up Francis and why do people want to put a bug outside my window?"

"Okay," Shelly says, sitting next to Quinn on the bed. "The people who put the bug outside your window are looking for Spacer and me, you guys have just been drug into something you never should have been and I'm sorry. I can't really tell you much more than that."

"So, you and Mr. Sharpe, you're like... secret agents or something?"

"Something like that."

"I knew you guys wouldn't own a lame-oid bookstore like the Black Box Book Shop."

"No, that part was true, we really do own and operate the book shop."

"Oh," Quinn says, shrinking away from her. "It's very nice... I'm sorry... please don't kill me."

Shelly smiles at her. "I'll let you off... this time." Shelly glares at her a little as she says it and Quinn scoots away from her. "Sorry, that was supposed to be funny. Humor is more Spacer's thing, I tend to stick to razor wit."

Quinn nods but doesn't move closer. "But... but you are part of that biker gang too, right? You're like their leader?"

Shelly sighs. "No, I'm not part of them, but that was me you saw yesterday. Just out of curiosity, what gave me away?"

"Your... your hair pulled out of your jacket. I've never seen hair like that. It's really beautiful."

"Thanks," Shelly says, not really listening. She replays the

149

events of the prior night in her mind. The kid is observant. "Man, I was really off my game yesterday."

"Did..." Quinn starts but hesitates. "Why'd you do it?" "Look back? Just wanted to make sure the good hands you were in stayed good."

"No, I mean, why did you and those bikers come into the bar and hassle us? Why did you pick on Francis? Why did you put   him   in   the   hospital?" "Those are two different questions, actually," Shelly says, leaning against the wall. She takes a deep breath and lets it out slowly. "When Spacer met your dad he... he kind of took a shine to him. He does that, he adopts people."

"So when Francis punched him, you decided to beat him up?"

"Not exactly. We saw what went down between Francis and your dad and Spacer, being who he is, decided we should step in."

"But couldn't he have just come over and punched Francis? I mean, I'm guessing if you're both agents or whatever you know more about fighting than Francis does."

"Oh, honey, we could have sent him home in tiny pieces right then."

"So why didn't you?"

Shelly arches an eyebrow at her. "You're a bright kid, work it out."

Quinn relaxes a little as she thinks about the ins and outs of the previous afternoon. "If Spacer... Mr. Sharpe..."

"It's okay, call him Spacer."

"Well, if he'd come over, hobbling on his cane from the canyon accident," when she says, "canyon accident" she holds her fingers up in air quotes.

"Yeah, that was really lame, I've got to work with him on his phony excuses."

"What really happened? Was he shot?"

"As a matter of fact, he was."

"Oh my God."

"Price of doing business. Now, go on, you were saying..."

"Well, if he'd come over and beaten up my boyfriend... ex-boyfriend, after Dad had been punched out, that would make Dad look even worse."

"Bingo."

"But you beat him up anyway."

"That wasn't part of the original plan. We just wanted to show you what he was really all about. Things changed."

"It was when he slapped me, wasn't it? That was when things changed." Shelly nods, slowly. "But it wasn't that hard a slap," Quinn says, rubbing her cheek which was a light purple beneath the concealer she was wearing.

"I don't care if it was a gentle breeze, I don't let that shit slide," Shelly says, her voice a low rumble.

Quinn takes a deep breath but doesn't break eye contact.

Shelly puts her hand gently on Quinn's knee and Quinn forces herself not to jerk away. "Quinn, what you just said about it not being a very hard slap, that is exactly why I told those men to do what they did to him. He's a bully, he picks on the weak and then exploits their feelings so they will defend them afterword." She removes her hand. "I'm not saying that what I did was right or wrong, you'll find that, very often, those two ideas do not come into play out there in the world. There is only what you do and what you don't do. It was my call and I made it."

"But, when I went to see him today..."

"You went to see him?" Shelly asks so quickly, her gaze so narrow, that Quinn presses herself back against the headboard.

"Yes, I'm sorry."

Shelly sighs and forces herself to look away. "Don't apologize. It was your call and you made it, it's just not something I would ever do."

"Yeah   but   you're..."
"I'm what?"

"You're awesome," Quinn blurts. "You're gorgeous and you're brave and you can do all kinds of stuff. If Spacer ever hit you I'm sure you..."

"I would put him right beside Francis... actually, he would probably be downstairs."

"Downstairs?"

"I'm assuming the morgue is downstairs, it generally is."

"Would you really? You guys are so in love."

"We are, and one of the reasons I do love him is that he would never do that to me." Shelly smiles gently at her. "There are all kinds of men in the world, I sort of won the jackpot with mine, but if I was ever proven to be wrong, if he ever lifted a hand to me to do anything other than stroke my hair from my face, I would put him in the ground. He would get worse than anyone for making me believe in him."

"But I'm not you, I can't be like that."

"You are a lot like me, Spacer has been saying it since he met you and the way you stood up to Pete yesterday…"

"The big guy who was hassling us?"

"Yeah, that's Pete, he's an ass-wipe but I've got him on a very short chain and he's useful at times."

"If he ever tried to hit you?"

Shelly barks a short, harsh laugh. "I'm sorry, but the idea of Pete growing the set that would require is just too ridiculous." Quinn surprises herself by actually giggling at this.

"Still," she says. "And I'm really not trying to defend him, but I got a slap that I walked away from, Francis has two broken legs, a broken arm, his ribs are crushed… did you have to have them do all of that?"

Shelly runs her hand absently through her hair. "I didn't have to, I chose to. If things had worked out like they were supposed to and Spacer had been there, Francis probably wouldn't be in the place he is right now. But Spacer, as good a guy as he is, has never been a woman. He's never walked into a shopping mall and had to hope that the guy leering from the corner of the food court will be satisfied with just the eyeful and not try to grab a handful."

"I hate that," Quinn says softly.

"I know. He doesn't realize how, every time a woman steps out of her house, she is constantly on guard against an unwanted advance, how so many men see us as conquest that they have every right to conquer and have no fear about doing it. If Spacer had seen you get slapped he would have hated Francis too, but he would have tempered his hatred and kept

Pete and his boys in check. That would have been his call and it wouldn't have been right or wrong either. But my call was to take out one of the bastards who feel they have the right to lay hands on a woman."

Quinn nods. "Do you think it will teach him a lesson? Being beaten up like that?"

Shelly shakes her head quickly. "Those guys don't learn lessons, not that easily anyway. I think it was just a bit of justice is all."

"And the man who grabbed me, the one you... well, you know."

"Him? He was an idiot who couldn't follow orders. I just needed to shut him down before he could take us somewhere I didn't want us going." She winks at Quinn. "It's doing that sort of thing that keeps guys like Pete in line."

"I wish I could do that sort of stuff," Quinn says.

"That can be learned. What can't be taught is having the guts to do it and, sister, you've got those coming out your ears."

Quinn smiles broadly at her. "I spit on him," she says quickly.

"Huh?"

"Francis, I spit on him. When I got to the hospital I could see him through a window, lying on his bed, casts over, like, his whole body, and I asked my Mom to let me go in alone. When I went in he looked up at me, he couldn't really move, you know, traction, but he shifted his eyes up at me and said, 'Q,' that's all he said but I kept hearing him tell those guys, Pete I guess, to take me instead of his stupid ugly bike and I spit on him, right in his face."

Shelly smiles at her. "I know it doesn't feel like it, but that was the kindest thing he ever did, saying that. It showed you who he really was."

Tears begin to fall unnoticed from Quinn's eyes. "The whole time I was riding with that other man, I was so scared. I was sure you were going to rape me and kill me and all I could think about was how this was what Francis wanted. So I spit on him."

"Do you think that was wrong?" Shelly asks.

Quinn shrugs, "It was the call I made."

Shelly nods and pats her on the leg.

"So, do you think, in a way, when Spacer saw my Dad get punched, he was kind of feeling like you felt when I got slapped?"

"I hadn't really thought about it but, yeah, in his own way it probably was. I think one of Spacer's greatest fears is being like your Dad." Shelly stops and replays her words in her head. "I'm sorry, that was really insulting. Your father is a good guy, he…"

Now Quinn leans over and pats Shelly's leg. "It's okay, I think I know what you mean. But, yeah, my Dad really is a good guy. If he had been there, Pete would have to have ripped off both of his arms before he'd have let them take me."

"I believe you're right about that," Shelly says. "I guess I should head back down to the party." She stands and stretches and heads toward the door. She turns back and says, "Look, I know you promised Spacer you wouldn't tell your parents about this but, if it comes down to it, it'll be your call to make. Don't let uninformed promises keep you from making it."

Quinn nods and Shelly walks to the door. "Mrs. Sharpe," she yells after her. Shelly turns and looks at her.

"Yeah?"

"Just… nothing."

"Okay," Shelly says, stepping out of the room and shutting the door behind her.

She walks down the stairs to find Darren fiddling with the receiver on the phone and Sissy in the living room dancing a Samba by herself while holding a steaming mug. Spacer stands next to Darren, observing.

"Shelly?" Sissy says when she sees her. "You have got to try my toddy."

"Okay," Shelly says, sending Sissy dancing unsteadily into the kitchen.

"I just don't understand what's happened to the phones," Darren says. "There haven't been any storms that could knock them out."

"It's a mystery," Spacer agrees.

Sissy returns with a second mug which she hands to Shelly. Shelly takes a sip and coughs, it's like drinking melted butter.

"It takes some getting used to," Sissy admits. "But when you do get used to it, whoa mama!"

Shelly tries to speak but her vocal chords seem to slip in the butter. She swallows hard and says, "I may have to take your word for that."

"Your loss," Sissy says, taking Shelly's mug and sipping from each alternately.

Spacer looks at her and says, "They're having trouble with the phones."

"I hate to ask, but would you mind running to your place and seeing if you have a dial tone."

"Phones aren't turned on over there," Spacer says. "I don't know when they were last, but we just use the cells."

"Well, crackers. I hate to have to wait around for a phone guy tomorrow, it's Sissy's and my anniversary..."

"Well, congratulations," Spacer says.

"Yes, well, thank you. We were going to take the whole family out on a fun day but now I don't know. On a Sunday too, I'll probably have to wait all day for them to show."

"Let us do it," Spacer says.

"What?"

"Shelly and I can come over, house sit and wait for the guy, it's the least we can do after the evening you two gave us."

"Well... no, I couldn't ask you to do that on your vacation."

"We were just going to lay around the house tomorrow anyway, we'll just lay around yours instead. I even know a guy I can call, he won't cost you an arm and a leg."

"Shouldn't we just call the phone company?"

'Nah, they'll find a way to spike your bill. Trust me, this guy is a genius with this stuff. You've gotta let us do this for you."

"Well, what do you think, Sissy?"

"Ducks quack most often when Spain is playing soccer, I find," Sissy says, staggering a little and leaning against the wall.

"I think that means yes," Darren says, chuckling. "I'll get you a spare key, just come on over whenever you can, and thank you."

"It'll be our pleasure," Spacer says.

Shelly pats him on the back. "I hate to call it a night, but I think it's time I got this one to bed," she says.

Darren glances at his watch. "Goodness, two in the morning? I guess it's time we all went to bed." He looks at Sissy and then at the stairs. "If I can get her up those things, that is."

"Best of luck with that," Shelly says, leading Spacer to the door. "We'll chat tomorrow." She walks him outside to the porch, turns him and kisses him hard on the mouth.

"That was nice," he says.

"Mm hmm," Shelly says.

"Is there a particular reason for that?"

"I was upstairs talking to the kid and she helped me realize what a really good guy you are."

"Huh, you should speak with her more often."

"Well, I could go back up there for a chat, but I was thinking of just taking you across the road for another," she pats him gently on the ass, "treatment."

"Oh yeah, let's do that instead."

CHAPTER NINETEEN

Mystery flips the top card on the deck and smiles at the three of clubs. "Just the bastard I was hoping to see," he mutters. He sighs. It's a little depressing to think how long he'd worked on perfecting this shuffle and now he'll never get to use it.

There's a knock on the door and he says, "Come in."

"You wanted me, boss?" Tony says stepping inside.

"Did I ever tell you about the first trick I mastered?"

"Um…" Tony says, shutting the door behind him. "I don't think so."

"It's called bank heist," Mystery says, smiling at the memory. "It's a simple palm but it's pretty impressive to adults when a six-year-old does it for them. I lost count of how many of their dinner parties I performed at." He fixes his stare at Tony, "Do you think I'll know that? After I mean."

Tony shrugged. "Does Scooter know it?"

"I've told Jason but telling isn't living. Is it?"

"I guess we'll find out." Tony says. Mystery shuffles the cards absently and Tony turns his eyes away from them just to be safe. He clears his throat and says, "Did… you need me for anything, Boss?"

"Oh," Mystery says, bringing himself back to the present. "They found the bugs,"

"That was fast," Tony says. "We sure?"

"Either they have. or we are dealing with the only teenage girl in the world with a Santana fetish." Mystery presses a button on a laptop sitting by his elbow and the sound of Black Magic Woman fills the office.

"Good song," Tony says.

"It loses something the fifteenth time you hear it."

"What about the other one?"

"It went dark around the same time this one landed south of the boarder."

Tony nods. "I'd say you're right. Want me to activate the twister?"

"Already done, but I do want you on the ground out there."

"Yeah?"

"The guys I've got out there right now I trust just far enough to set the bugs. For the next phase, I need you there to make sure things don't go off the rails."

"We ready for the next phase? You and Scooter all finished up?"

"I'm finished. Scoot... Jason has work to do, polishing, but I can't be of service to him any longer."

"You sure you can trust him to finish on his own?"

"I am," Mystery says. "There's a financial incentive for him built in but I don't think he cares about that. I've spent a lot of time with him and I'm pretty sure he'd do it for a year supply of frozen burritos and only want those so that he didn't have to leave the project for food. Oh..." Mystery snaps his fingers. It's an unconscious habit Mystery has when remembering something he'd forgotten but Tony jumps and discretely checks his watch to make sure he hasn't lost any time. "That reminds me, before you go can you get a big box of frozen burritos from Costco?"

"Sure thing."

CHAPTER TWENTY

Spacer stretches and rolls his head on the pillow to watch Shelly sleeping next to him. The beach had been fun, but it is definitely a nice change to wake up with her in their bed. He looks at the clock, 8:00 AM, if they are going to figure out what Mr. E is up to, they probably better get started. He thinks about waking Shelly but decides he can let her sleep, at least for as long as it takes him to hop in the shower.

He pulls himself up from the bed, amazed at how smoothly his muscles move together. He still feels a little sore, and the dancing certainly didn't do him any favors, but last night's workout has done its magic and he thinks he won't need the cane at all today.

The warm water rushes over him, easing what soreness he was feeling, and he reviews the plans for the day. Drop by the warehouse, get guns - many guns - then make a call to a known associate, Pete since they're probably monitoring that line given the recent notoriety and their proclivity for planting listening devices, and drop a hint as to his whereabouts. Then they just have to wait for him to show up and they can finally put this thing to bed. There is no reason for Mr. E to be chasing them at all, but maniacs do stupid things. Sometimes you just have to out-maniac the maniac.

He hasn't discussed this with Shelly, but he knows she's thinking it too. He wouldn't be shocked to find out she'd come up with exactly the same details.

He turns off the water and steps out of the shower. The room is filled with steam and he writes, "Love ya, Babe," on the fogged mirror with his finger. She'll probably say it's ridiculous, but she'll love him for doing it.

He walks back into the bedroom and glances out the window, the Whitman's minivan is pulling out of the driveway. They really are getting an early start to their day of fun.

Spacer slides onto the bed and rubs Shelly's back. "Come on, Shelly, we've got idiots to kill."

She grumbles at him, "You're wet."

"I didn't complain about you last night," he says with a smirk. She rolls over and punches him in the chest. He grimaces and rubs the spot where she'd nailed him. "Come on, we've got a big day ahead."

"I swear, this is the last vacation we go on," she says, sitting up and trying to focus on him.

"Go on, I saved you some hot water."

"Yeah, we'll see how much," she says, standing up and striding across the room to the bathroom. Watching her walk, completely unmindful of her nakedness, Spacer whistles at her. She flips him off and shuts the door behind herself and he waits, counting the moments until she glances at the mirror. "That's ridiculous," she yells through the closed door.

He smiles to himself. "She loves me," he says to the empty room as he pulls on a pair of jeans.

Spacer, the colt snug in the shoulder holster under his blazer, leans against the car waiting for Shelly. When she steps into the garage, she is once more clad in her leathers. "You wanna take the bike?" he says. "We need to get quite a bit of stuff, I think this is more of a car trip."

"Yeah, I'm going to follow you," she says.

"Okay,   mind   if   I   ask   why?"
"I don't know, really," she says. "I just think we'll be better off if we both have a vehicle."

Spacer shrugs. "Okay," he says. He watches her climb onto the bike and place the helmet on her head. "You following me?"

"Yeah," she says.

He climbs into the car and pulls out of the driveway, followed closely behind by Shelly on the Ninja.

He pulls onto the road, his mind already thinking about the incredible vacation he's going to make sure they have after this silliness is done. He passes a fun park with mini-golf, batting cages and go carts and makes a mental note to bring Shelly back here. She pretends that she doesn't like this sort of thing but loves to show off her insane skills by running frat guys off the track every chance she gets. He notices the

Whitman's minivan in the parking lot and squints to see if he can pick them out inside.

Then he sees him. Working his way from person to person, showing each of them a piece of paper, is Dr. Landsin. "What the hell?" Spacer yells.

He cuts the wheel hard, pulling the sports car into a tight U-turn in the middle of the road, almost running a VW Beetle off the road, and peels back toward the entrance of the fun park. As he passes Shelly she holds a hand out, asking what he's doing. He cuts into the entrance and pulls to a stop as she turns the bike and follows him into the parking lot.

"So, no time for me to sleep, but we've got plenty of time for a round of putt-putt?" Shelly asks, ripping her helmet off her head.

"Follow me," Spacer says, walking to the entrance. He takes a fifty out of his wallet and, without pausing, hands it to the kid at the ticket booth. "That's for me and her and let as many people in out of what's left as you can," he tells him.

He pushes through the crowd milling about the entrance and looks around.

"When do I get to find out what we're doing here?" Shelly asks, catching up.

Spacer spots the man as he approaches the Whitman's, just teeing up on the first hole. He points him out to Shelly. "That son of a bitch!" she says. "Wait, are those the Whitmans? Why is he talking to them?"

"Because life actually is a Dickens novel." Spacer walks toward the Whitmans, Shelly steps back into the shadow of the entrance alcove.

Dr. Landsin pulls out the piece of paper he's been showing everyone. "Well, yes," he hears Darren say. "We have seen them, but what business is it of yours?"

"It isn't his business," Spacer says, stepping up to the men and ripping the paper from Dr. Landsin's hand. He glances at it, it's the photo of them they have on file with the agency. He must have swiped it when they weren't looking. He turns to show it to Shelly and notices at last that she hasn't followed. "Wait, where did she go?"

"Oh, is your lovely wife here?" Darren asks.

"Aren't you supposed to be waiting for the internet guy?' Sissy asks.

"Thank goodness you're here," Dr. Landsin says.

"You might want to hold off on your thanks," Spacer says. "What are you doing here?"

"Seriously, did the internet guy already come?" Sissy asks.

"No... I fixed it for you," Spacer says.

"I'm looking for you," Dr. Landsin says.

"Why are you looking for us?" Spacer says. "More importantly, how are you alive?"

"He's not supposed to be alive?" Darren asks.

"You can fix internets?" Sissy asks.

"I am alive, through no help of your precious agency," Dr. Landsin says. "They gave me absolutely no protection and allowed that mad man to find and try to kill me!"

"According to the paper he did," Spacer says.

"I'm sorry, what agency is this?" Darren asks. "Is this a book selling thing?"

"If you can fix internets, why didn't you just do that yesterday?" Sissy asks.

"I'd been drinking," Spacer says. "You don't fix internets after drinking. Everyone knows that."

"He tried to kill me," Dr. Landsin says. "He actually thought that he could hypnotize someone as intelligent as I and that I would just walk onto a plane which I knew would crash into the sea."

"Oh, my word, are you LAPPING right now? Is that what this is?" Darren asks.

"What?" Spacer says.

"Jeez, Dad, it's called LARPing," Scott says.

"Yes!" Spacer says. "That is the thing we are doing." He smiles and says, "Could you excuse us for just a moment? We need to LARP in private for just a minute." He grabs Dr. Landsin by the elbow and pulls him away from the Whitmans to where Shelly is standing in the shadow of the entrance.

"I wondered where you got to," Spacer tells her.

"Darren saw me drop off his kid in my leathers,
162

remember?"

"Oh, shit, I totally forgot about that."

Shelly nods at Dr. Landsin. "What's this about? It's traditional to wait three days before rising from the dead."

"Apparently Mr. E fancies himself a hypnotist and tried to make the good doctor get on a plane which he knew was going to crash into the sea and he was clever enough to not get on the plane or even warn any of the other 150 souls who went down with it." Spacer turns to Dr. Landsin, "Is that about right?"

"Yes, I suppose that's the size of it. Except that it's Mystery."

"What?" Shelly asks.

"The man who tried to kill me, his name is Mystery."

"That's what I said," Spacer says.

"Yes, but, is it?"

"Yes, I said Mr. E."

"See, you did it again. You're putting the emphasis on the E, like you're saying Mr. E."

"I am saying Mr. E."

"Then you're saying it wrong. It's Mystery."

"I've got to tell you, I'm not hearing the difference."

"Really? You can't tell the difference between Mr. E and Mystery?"

"No, I hear absolutely no dif... wait, are you saying Mystery?"

"Yes."

"Like Scooby Doo's van, Mystery Machine, Mystery?"

"That's correct."

"Like that Vegas magician Mystery?"

"Exactly like him."

"You mean it is him?"

Dr. Landsin looks at Shelly, "Is he always this quick on the uptake?"

"Leave him alone, homophones are tricky," Shelly says.

"He sent us letters taunting us and he signed them Mr. E," Spacer says.

"It's possible that he employed a pseudonym."

"He changed Mystery to Mr. E? What kind of an idiot would fall for that?" Spacer says. He looks from Dr. Landsin to Shelly and clears his throat. "Okay, I guess it was kind of effective."

"Most of his plans are," Dr. Landsin says. "He is a brilliant and brutal man and I am terrified by the idea of what he might do to me once he learns of my betrayal. I've sought the both of you out to ask for your protection."

"Oh, good God," Spacer says.

"Why did they report you died?" Shelly asks.

"What?"

"The paper reported that you were among the casualties of the crash. They wouldn't have done that if you hadn't gotten on the plane."

"Oh, well... I, well, couldn't just NOT get on the plane. If I'd done that he would have known before I could find you."

"You convinced someone to take your seat," Shelly says.

"You'd be surprised how easy it is to give away a ticket to Hawaii," Dr. Landsin says with a chuckle.

"So not only did you not lift a finger to save 150 people, you added one to the mix who shouldn't have been there," Spacer says.

"You're on your own," Shelly says.

Dr. Landsin frowns at them. "You know I can help you with Mystery, I clearly have more intel, like his name."

"Finding things out is sort of what we do," Shelly says.

"Do you think you can find them out before the thing happens?"

"What thing?" Spacer asks.

Dr. Landsin cocks an eye at him, "I'll tell you at the safe house you put me in."

Spacer cuts his eyes to Shelly who stares blankly at him. "He's got a point," he says.

"We don't need him," she says.

"We might... wait a minute," he holds the picture up to Dr. Landsin. "How many people have you shown this to?"

"What is that?" Shelly asks.

"A file photo of us he swiped from the agency."

"Good God, those people are in charge of national secrets!" Shelly says.

"How many?"

"I don't know, 6 or 7 businesses."

"You asked the owners of six or seven businesses?"

"Owners, customers, street people hanging about outside; you are two very difficult people to find."

"We're supposed to be!" Spacer yells, causing Dr. Landsin to flinch from him.

"He's been flashing our picture all around town, somebody is bound to have seen us out with the Whitmans," Spacer says to Shelly.

"Couple that with the weird guy whose description remarkably matches that of a Vegas magician…"

"Yeah, we've really been off our game," Spacer says.

"And something tells me that Whitmans shouldn't return to their house until this is over," Shelly said.

"Agreed," Spacer says. He turs and walks back to the three Whitmans, "Look guys, I…" Three Whitmans? "Hey, where's Quinn?"

"She met a little friend of hers," Darren says. "They said they wanted to get some Star-Deer…"

"He means Starbucks. He thinks that joke is hilarious," Sissy says.

"Oh, it is, you agree don't you, Spacer?"

"Mm-hmm," Spacer says through clenched teeth. "But hey, what's the rest of the Quinn story?"

Darren shrugs, "She said she really needed some girl time, but secretly I think she's planning a surprise for Sissy and me." Darren looks at Sissy and takes her hand. "The poor thing feels really guilty about the other night."

"So, this would be a surprise that would happen at your house?" Spacer says.

"Yes, I'm surprised you didn't see her when you were over there fixing our internet."

"Yeah, what kind of game are you playing?" Sissy asks.

"Don't mind her, think she's still a little…" he glances at Scott, "happy to see you."

"Excuse me for a moment," Spacer says. He runs back to the alcove, but Shelly isn't there. Her bike is missing from the place she left it too. The only trace of her is the sound of a motor cycle engine in the distance trailing away.

Dr. Landsin clears his throat, Spacer glares at him for a moment before saying, "When this is over, you and I are having a discussion about the people you let die." He turns and walks quickly back to the remaining Whitmans.

"Darren, today is going to be a big one for surprises I think," Spacer says. "I seriously don't have time to explain, please trust me when I say that I need for you and your family to hop into your van and follow me."

"Look, Spacer, you're starting to trouble me a bit."

"I'm sorry, I hope I'll be able to make you understand soon, but for now, just trust me."

"I don't know…"

"Like we trusted you with our internet?" Sissy says, the sound of her own voice apparently driving spikes into her head.

"Darren," Spacer says. He levels a stare at the man which has caused warlords to second guess themselves.

"Oh! Very well then," Darren says. "I… guess we'll return our clubs and…"

Spacer takes the clubs and tosses them to the side of the putting green. "They're returned. We should go now."

Spacer walks ahead of them but Dr. Landsin soon catches up to him. "What about me?"

"Oh, you are definitely staying where I can keep an eye on you," Spacer says. He digs into his pocket and pulls out a cell phone. He dials a number quickly and his call is answered on the second ring. "PI, Spy Guy," he says quickly as he climbs into his car. "Listen, drop whatever plans you have for today, I'm opening a tab.

CHAPTER TWENTY-ONE

Shelly pulls up to the Whitmans's house, jumps off the bike and runs up to the porch. "Quinn," she yells, pounding on the door. "Quinn, I need you to come with me right now."

Quinn opens the door in a flour stained apron with a bowl in her hand and gasps.

"Shit," Shelly says, ripping her helmet off of her head. "I'm sorry, it's me, it's Shelly."

"No, I... knew it, it was just kind of a shock seeing you like... you know, like that."

"I know, I should have thought about that. I really am sorry, but right now I just need you to come with me."

"Oh no you don't, you hoodlum!"

Shelly turns at the sound and is instantly doused with cold water, the old man from next door.

"Mr. Carlson!" Quinn yells.

"I won't let him take you away again," the old man says.

Shelly walks up to the old man, the spray never moving from her face until she grabs the hose from his hand.

"So, you like it up close and personal, do ya?" the old man says raising his fists. Shelly glares at him. "Wait a minute," the old man squints at her. "You... you ain't the hoodlum... are you his mom?"

"His mom?" Shelly asks. "The hose I could forgive but I'm about to take you up on the fist fight now, old man."

"Mr. Carlson, this is Shelly Sharpe, she's renting the house across the road. She's friends with Mom and Dad," Quinn says, running up.

"Oh, I'm sorry, you see, we've had a bit of a problem with folks on those type machines and I..."

"Yeah, don't worry about it," Shelly says. She turns to Quinn and says, "You need to come with me right now, I'm taking you to your parents."

"Is everything okay? Have they been..."

"They're fine, Spacer is with them, but something has happened with the men I told you about yesterday and we need to get all of you to a safe place for at least a day or two."

"But… but I can't leave, I'm in the middle of baking. The oven is on and everything."

"It's okay, as soon as you guys are safe, Spacer and I will be coming back. We'll take care of everything."

"That doesn't sound very fire conscious to me," a voice says, walking up the driveway.

They turn to see a large man in an expensive suit. He is flanked by a quartet of armed men almost as large as he.

"Mystery?" Shelly says.

"No, but… wait, how did you know about…" he tilts his head to the left for a moment. "Landsin, I knew there was something off about that autopsy!"

"What's this all about?" Mr. Carlson yells, trying to retrieve his hose from Shelly. She bats his hand away.

"What do you say we discuss what this is all about inside like civilized people?"

"Fine," Shelly says. "Let the girl and the old man go and we can have tea and crumpets."

"Hmm," the man says, turning to the others. "What do you think? Should I release the two vulnerable hostages and trust the lethal assassin who has already killed so very, very many people?"

"Well, when you put it that way, boss, I really think…" one of the men starts to say.

"That was rhetorical," the man says with a sigh." He gestures toward the house. "Shall we?"

"We don't have to, do we?" Quinn asks.

"I think we should," Shelly says.

"Oh dear," Mr. Carlson says.

Shelly steps toward the house but stops beside the man. "This doesn't end well for you," she says, loudly enough that only he can hear.

"That's not the first time I've been told that."

"May well be the last." Shelly continues into the house followed by Quinn and Mr. Carlson.

Spacer pulls into the lot outside the warehouse and turns to Dr. Landsin. "You stay right here."

"Where are you going?"

Spacer ignores him and steps out of the car as Darren pulls the minivan beside him. He motions for Darren to join him as he pops the trunk and pulls out a large gym bag.

"Where are we? What is this place, Spacer?" Darren asks.

"Okay, I know I lost my cool a little at the mini-golf course. I think I may have freaked all of you out just a little bit and I'm afraid that what you are about to see isn't going to help that. I debated maybe having you just wait in the car while I ran in there, but I think this might be the only way for you to know just how serious a situation you are in."

"Spacer, I don't mind telling you, you're beginning to frighten me."

"Yup," Spacer says, "that's only going to get worse."

Spacer walks to the passenger side of the Spyder as Sissy and Scott climb out of the van. He taps Dr. Landsin on the arm through the open window.

"Ouch," Dr. Landsin says. "That spot has been tender since you rescued me. I think I may have been grazed by a bullet."

"Yeah, that happened and you just didn't notice," Spacer says.

"Really?"

"No," Spacer says, rolling his eyes. "Out of the car."

"So now I CAN get out."

Spacer walks away without a word. He slides his key into the door and says, "Okay Whitmans what you are about to see will likely shake your trust in me, but I'm really going to need you to stick with me for the next little bit. Afterward, you can never talk to me again if you want."

"After what?" Darren asks.

"You'll be finding out, all too soon."

Spacer opens the door and cuts on the lights.

"Whoa, this is so cool!" Scott yells, stepping inside and seeing all of the cars, gadgets and guns.

"Oh my God!" Darren says.

Scott tries to run into the warehouse, but Sissy stops him.

"Spacer, what on Earth is happening?" she asks, stone sober now.

Spacer turns. "I'm a spy. That's my real job and these are the tools of the trade."

Darren steps in front of his family and backs them through the doorway. "And why have you brought us here? We couldn't have known too much, we didn't know anything until you just told us."

"You don't understand."

"You're damned right we don't!"

"Daddy!" Scott says, Sissy hushes him.

"I'm not holding you hostage," Spacer says, holding his hands out to his side. His jacket opens and they see the gun in his shoulder holster.

"Please," Darren says, "if you need a hostage, take me, let Sissy take the boy and drive away."

"No, I said I'm not..." Spacer starts before realizing his hardware is showing. "Oh, that."

"Can they please go, sir?" Darren asks.

"Yes," Spacer says. "As a matter of fact, you can all go. Just don't go to your house."

"Why, what are you doing to our house?"

"I'm not... God, we don't have time for this." Spacer jerks the colt from its holster and the Whitmans scream. "No, no screaming," Spacer says, laying the gun down on a nearby table. "Just removing the distraction."

Spacer pulls out a folding chair and sits. "I told you it was going to be scary, but I'm still the same guy I was yesterday."

"What do you want from us?" Sissy asks.

"I want to keep you safe. You have to believe me."

Darren and Sissy look at each other. Suddenly Sissy gasps and says, "Quinn! Quinn is at home right now."

"Shelly's on that," Spacer says.

"Shelly is a spy too?" Sissy asks. After a moment's thought she adds, "Actually, that's the first thing about all of this that makes absolute sense."

"I just... How can we trust someone who was hiding... all of this?" Darren asks.

"I don't know. Maybe we shouldn't," Sissy says. "But, if he wanted to hurt us, he's had ample opportunity. How many times has he been alone in the house with us? I mean, even with his canyon fall wound he could probably... oh."

"That wasn't from falling into a canyon, was it?" Darren asks.

"Gunshot wound," Spacer says.

"Dear God," Darren says.

"Even though he was still hurting, he took me on the dance floor because I was feeling bad watching you and Shelly," Sissy says. "That's not something someone who's trying to trick us would do, it's something a good person does." Sissy walks into the warehouse and takes a seat on another chair. "Now, tell me what you are protecting our family from."

"Sissy," Darren says.

"Sit down and let him tell us what is going on," Sissy commands. Darren sits.

"Can I go look around?" Scott asks.

Sissy looks at Spacer who shrugs. "The dangerous stuff is all locked away."

"All right, dear, but don't break anything. I get the feeling a paper clip in this place is worth your father's annual salary."

"Awesome," Scott yells, running into the warehouse.

"Okay," Spacer says as Darren takes a seat. Dr. Landsin skulks by the door. "I have to make this story short so I can load up on arsenal and we can meet Shelly and Quinn."

"What happens after we do that?" Darren asks.

"You guys, as a family, go someplace safe. Do you have any family close by?"

"The only relatives we really speak with are Sissy's parents and they're in Miami, that's a thousand miles from here."

"Actually it's 778 miles, I Googled it," Spacer says.

"Why did you Google the distance to my parent's house?" Sissy asks. "Are they a part of this?"

"Not to your parent's house specifically, just to Miami."

"Why did you Google the distance to Miami, is it a part of this?' Darren asks.

"No, it was a bet with Shelly, not everything I do is a part of this."

"Oh," they both say at once.

"I know it sounds extreme but going that far out of town wouldn't be a bad idea," Spacer says.

"All right, we'll go," Sissy says.

"Sissy! We can't just…"

"Look around you, Darren. There are swords and guns and God knows what else in here. I do not want to be a part of this. I want to get my daughter and get a thousand miles away from this." Spacer opens his mouth to say something and Sissy cuts him off. "Sorry, 778 miles away from it."

"Fine, we'll drop in unexpectedly on your parents," Darren says, crossing his arms over is chest. "Happy anniversary to me."

"But you will tell us why first," Sissy says.

"That's fair," Spacer says. "The last job we did was to rescue that man from a terrorist organization."

Sissy gasps at the word terrorist and turns to look at Dr. Landsin. "And why was he holding you prisoner."

"I happen to be the leading robotics mind in the world. Data point!" Dr. Landsin says.

"I see."

"There's a machine that this man needed the doctor to help him build," Spacer says.

"What sort of machine?" Darren asks.

"Don't worry over the details, just know that it would help him take over the world. When Shelly and I rescued the doctor, construction on his machine stopped. This is a man who, apparently, does not do well with disappointment. He's already attempted to kill the doctor and he'd like to kill Shelly and myself as well."

"And how did we fit into all of this?"

"You are his link to Shelly and me," Spacer tells her. "I'm sorry we've put you in the middle of all of this. If we'd known he'd hold a personal grudge we'd have stayed miles away from anyone." Spacer looks the two of them in the eye and says, "What we need to do now, is get you and your family out of the equation. Shelly and I can take it from there."

"But, if he's the sort of beast you say he is, how will the two of you stand a chance against him?" Darren asks.

"Oh, we have our ways of dealing with people like him," Spacer says, looking around the large warehouse. "Which reminds me, I've got some packing to do."

CHAPTER TWENTY-TWO

"Where you want them, Tony?" one of the goons asks the large man.

Tony sighs. "As close to earshot as they can be when you're saying my name."

"You… you think that's a good idea?"

Tony nods to another one and says, "Take the old guy into the kitchen and check him for weapons."

"Yeah," the guy says, "he may be packin' a squirt gun."

"Hilarious," Tony says.

"O—okay," the guy who'd made the corny joke says, pulling Mr. Carlson by the arm into the kitchen. Tony turns to Shelly and gestures to the first guy who'd spoken. "Pat her down, I'm certain she's armed."

He steps toward Shelly who opens her jacket to reveal the Glock in her holster. "There's that and a dagger in my boot," she says.

The man pulls the gun from the holster and pries the dagger from her boot, both of which he hands to Tony.

"We appreciate the assist, Mrs. Sharpe," Tony says, admiring Shelly's gun. "But I think we'll check for ourselves just to be sure." He nods at the goon, "Larry."

The man steps back up to Shelly who leans in to him and says, "Pat me down if you must, but I'm remembering every place you touch and for each place, I will break one of your bones." He tries to laugh at her, but it comes out forced and shaky. He looks back at Tony whose pale blue eyes glare into him. He turns back to Shelly and finds even less comfort in her slate grey eyes.

"Get on with it!" Tony says.

Shocked, Larry grabs Shelly's sides with both hands. "That's two," she whispers.

He runs his hands quickly over her torso and down both legs, taking great care not to linger on any of the parts which might get his bones extra broken. Shelly can think of at least a dozen places she could easily have hidden a blade or, in some cases, small pistol that he entirely over looks. She should use that line more often.

He backs away from her and Shelly catches his eye with hers. "It's twice as bad for anything you do to the girl."

He looks at Quinn, shaking a little and cowering away from him. "They're both clean," he says to Tony.

Tony rolls his eyes. "No wonder people kill you all so easily, you are worthless. Will you at least tie her up?"

Quinn leans against Shelly, shaking. Shelly takes off her jacket and puts it over the girl's shoulders. "We're going to be fine," she whispers.

Larry steps up quickly and grabs Shelly by the arms. She turns her head and whispers, "That's an even thirty." He tightens his grip silently, but Shelly can't miss the fact that his palms are sweating, quite a lot actually.

Quinn screams as another guy grabs her by her arms. "Where do you want the girl?" he asks.

"Take her upstairs," Tony says, and the guy drags Quinn, kicking and jerking to the stairs.

She twists enough to sink her teeth into two of the guys fingers. He screams, jerks his hand out of her mouth and slaps her across the face.

"You don't want to do that again," Shelly tells him.

He turns and gasps when he finds himself locked into her glare. "I'm sorry, she bit me, it just... it just happened."

"Why are you apologizing to the prisoner?" Tony asks. "Take her upstairs."

"I..." the man turns to where Quinn lies on the floor. She backs to the stairs and uses them to climb to her feet, never taking her eye from the man.

The kitchen door opens and Shelly glances in that direction long enough to see the man who'd taken Mr. Carlson step into the room. A bitter sort of relief washes over her; one less person to have to worry about.

"Come on, girlie," the goon says to Quinn.

Quinn raises two small fists. "Go with him, Quinn," Shelly says. "You won't be up there for very long and he won't be touching you anymore." The last she directs to the goon who looks from her to Tony.

"Yes, you will be touching her! Why wouldn't you be touching her?" Tony asks with a sigh.

"Well… it's just that… she said…"

"She is the prisoner," Tony says, he rubs at his temples. "I'm the one paying you, I have a gun full of bullets, why would you listen to her instead of me? Drag the girl up the stairs!"

The man picks Quinn up and throws her over his shoulder. He runs up the steps before anyone else can give him an order. Shelly curses under her breath as she watches them go. It is so much more difficult for her to control the situation when they're separated.

She turns to Tony. "This could have been so easy for you. If you'd just let them go when I told you, you'd have such a brighter future right now."

"Do you know what we are going to do with that little girl if you don't cooperate?" Tony asks.

Shelly smiles a knowing smile at him. "You aren't dealing with a mother who's never seen anything more violent than a Bugs Bunny cartoon. I know exactly what you will do with that girl regardless of whether or not I help you. As a matter of fact, I know that the only thing keeping her from being molested is that I haven't yet helped you."

She shrugs out of Larry's hands and he doesn't fight her. She takes a step toward Tony. "What you don't seem to fully grasp is that the only reason all of you are still standing is because you have that girl. The minute anything happens to her, you and your men are dead."

"You do have a way with words," Tony says.

"Oh, let's not play that game, we both know what I'm capable of."

"So, it's a stalemate is it?" Tony says.

"Mm hmm, but it's turning in my favor, you've already removed one of the hostages."

"I… what?" Tony says. Shelly nods to the goon standing next to the kitchen door. "What are you doing? I never ordered you to kill the old guy!"

"I didn't boss, he tried to punch me while I was searching

him and, I don't know, he must have had a heart attack or something."

Shelly smiles, a warrior to the end.

"Fuck," Tony sighs.

"It's not too late to let the girl go," Shelly says. "I will give you what you want."

"So, the one thing keeping you from killing me and my men, your own words, you want me to just let go of that."

"I do. I'd rather help you and spare her having to see any more of this," Shelly says.

"Well, that is commendable, but I have another idea." He looks to Larry and says, "Take her upstairs, put her in the room next to the girl's. I want her to hear the screams."

"This is a big mistake," Shelly says as Larry once more grabs her by the arms and guides her to the stairway. "What do you really think I'm going to do after you've tortured that girl?"

"Oh, I'm thinking it won't take too many of her precious tears until you are begging to cooperate."

"Huh," Shelly says, she chuckles a little and then it grows louder and louder until Tony flinches from it. At last she levels her deadly gaze at him and says, "I guess there are some things you really just can't learn from reading a file."

Tony stares back at her for as long as he can stand. In his defense, he makes it much longer than most. At last he cuts his eyes to Larry and says, "Get her out of my sight!"

CHAPTER TWENTY-THREE

"She's not here," Spacer says, looking around the restaurant parking lot. This is the rendezvous site Shelly insisted they agree upon on the first day of the vacay should a mission arise, and they get separated. Which reminds Spacer, he now owes her the something pretty of her choosing he'd bet her when he said they'd never need it.

"What does that mean?" Darren asks.

Spacer looks at the man and considers for a moment offering him a hopeful lie. Ultimately, he decides not to, he deserves to know what's going on. "It's not good," Spacer says.

"Quinn!" Sissy whispers, grabbing her husband's arm.

"When you say not good, tell me exactly what that means," Darren says.

Spacer shakes his head. "I don't know exactly. It could mean that Shelly was tailed and she's having to lose whomever is following her before she can meet up. It could mean the meeting place has been compromised, in which case we really shouldn't be here any longer than we have to."

"But it could mean other things, right?"

"It could."

"Could it mean that they are…" Sissy starts but her voice breaks as tears stream down her face.

"I don't think that's very likely," Spacer says. "If they're tying up loose ends then I'm one of them. If they have them then they'll want to use them as bait."

"Marvelous, I've always dreamed of being a loose end," Dr. Landsin says.

"You been an ass for as long as I've known you, may as well be an end too," Spacer says. He turns back to the Whitmans. "They want Landsin and me, Shelly knows where Landsin is, they aren't just going to kill her, then they'd have no way of finding him."

"But Quinn doesn't," Sissy says.

Now Spacer smiles a rueful smile, it's a look that does more to convince the Whitmans of his true nature than all of the guns, cars and gadgets combined. Scott steps behind his mother and clutches her dress.

"You don't really know us," Spacer says, "so I can see how this may be hard to understand. But Quinn is going to be the only thing keeping Shelly from tearing these people apart, literally, limb from limb."

"I believe you," Darren says.

"What do we do now?" Sissy asks.

"I need to leave a note for Shelly if she does show up. Then I get you all to a safe place…"

"We aren't going to Florida, not without my baby," Sissy says.

"No, I wouldn't think that you would," Spacer says. "But I do need to keep you guys out of harm's way while I go help Shelly. I can't be worrying about you and effectively fighting Mystery."

"That's his name? The mad man who may have my daughter?"   Sissy   asks.
"It is," Spacer says.

A kid rides by on a bicycle and starts placing flyers under the wiper blades of the parked cars.

"Hey, kid," Spacer yells, running up to him.

"Look, mister, it doesn't hurt the car, if you don't want it, just throw it away. Why you gotta hassle me?"

"I'm not hassling you, I need one of those." The kid hands him a flyer and he heads back to the restaurant. He stops, turns and says, "But don't you even think about putting one of these damned things on the Spyder over there."

"All right, god!" the kid says.

Spacer grabs a pen out of his glove box and scribbles a note on the back of the flyer. "I just need to hop inside for a minute, don't move," he says to the Whitmans and Landsin.

He runs inside the restaurant and spots the maître d'. It's a different guy.

"Do you have a reservation?"

"I don't, but I don't want a table," Spacer says.

"Well then, that works out perfectly as I would not be able to give you one."

"Yeah, you know what, be an ass on your own time, chief." Spacer holds the flyer out to him. "A woman may come in here, she's my wife, I need you to give this to her."

"I think you will find that many women come here," he says. "I don't imagine that they are all your wife."

"Wow, that whole, 'Be an ass later' thing just didn't sink in at all, did it?" Spacer says.

"I don't see how you intend for me to deliver a message to a woman I do not know."

"You'll have a hard time missing this lady, she tends to stand out."

"Yes, I'm sure to you she is the most ravishing creature who ever trod upon the Earth, but, if you'll forgive me, there's a slim chance that I won't share that opinion."

"Look, just take the damn flyer. If no woman walks in here that isn't the most ravishing creature who ever trod upon the Earth, then throw it away at the end of your shift. Why you gotta hassle me?"

"Very well," the maître d' says, reluctantly taking the note from Spacer.

"Thank you."

Spacer steps outside to find the Whitmans standing by his car looking at the windshield which has been plastered with flyers. "Seriously," Spacer says.

"We tried taking them off, but he snuck back up and put more on," Darren says. "Eventually we just gave up."

"Where is the little bastard?" Spacer asks, taking one of the flyers and balling it in his fist.

Darren points to the far end of the parking lot where the boys sits on his bike laughing.

Spacer throws the balled flyer at the kid, bouncing it off his eyeball. "Ahhhh," the kid yells, falling off his bike and grabbing his face.

"Sorry kid, you picked the wrong day to jump on my last nerve," Spacer says, pulling the rest of the flyers from his windshield and, seeing no trash bin handy, hopping in his car with them and popping them in his glove box.

"Well, are you coming?" he says to Dr. Landsin who

quickly climbs in next to him.

"Where are we headed?" Darren asks.

Spacer sighs, "Unfortunately, I'm running a little short on safe places. Shelly apparently has a great one, but she hasn't shared that with me. So, we're going to the only place I can think of at the moment."

"And where is that?"

"Um… better you just follow and find out when we get there," Spacer says.

"I'm beginning to dislike our time together," Darren says, walking to his van and climbing in behind the wheel.

CHAPTER TWENTY FOUR

Shelly pulls at the ropes around her wrists and ankles, they are sturdy and the knots are good. She can't say the same for Scott's little wooden rocker to which she is tied. She glares at the guard, the same one that had gone into the kitchen with the old guy, and he turns away from her.

She'd let them tie her up because there had been three of them. They'd left themselves open to an attack at least five different times each but there was never an opening she saw that wouldn't have left one of them enough time to alert the guy watching Quinn. She couldn't run the risk of having them hurt the girl as a form of retribution.

Now that she's bound they are comfortable enough to leave her alone with only one man. That, she has no doubt, she can handle. She just hopes there isn't a lot of sentimental value attached to the rocker.

She works her ankles around to the inside of the rocker legs and presses against them just to the chairs breaking point and she does the same with her wrists to the arms. She clears her throat and says to the guard, "You know, you can still save yourself a lot of pain by letting me go."

The guard laughs at her and says, "Lady, if you had any idea what Mystery would do to me if I did that you'd realize how stupid it sounds."

"Fella, if you had any idea the sorts of things I've done to people who didn't, you wouldn't have said that."

The guard swallows nervously but plasters a cocky smile on his face. "Is that so?"

"It is."

"Well, you sure talk big, but you're the one tied to the chair, not me."

Shelly pouches her lip out at the guard as if his words had made her feel just terrible. "Well, that's true," she says. "But I do know one thing you don't."

"What's   that?"

"I can't tell you," she says. Then whispering, "It's a secret."

"A secret? Well, you can trust me."

"Huh uh," she says, shaking her head.

He smiles at her. What the fuck is the deal with guys and adult women acting like children? She'd feel bad about setting back her gender if only it weren't so damned effective. "I won't tell nobody I promise."

"I can't."

"Sure you can."

Shelly thinks for a long moment before looking up at him, her grey eyes as innocent as a doe's. "I have to whisper."

"Sure thing, honey," the guard says, moving closer. For a brief moment Shelly feels some pity for Mystery, his men really are very stupid. "Now what's your secret, cutie?" the guard says, putting his ear right up to Shelly's lips.

"Chairs break," Shelly whispers, pushing one arm beyond its breaking point, snapping it loose from the frame and punching the blunt end of the arm into the guard's neck before he can yell an alarm.

As the guard staggers backward holding his throat with both hands and trying to yell but only croaking, Shelly breaks the chair legs and drops to the floor. She twists and kicks out with her right foot, sweeping the chair runner still tied to her ankle into the man's shin and sending him to the floor as well.

She jumps to her feet, rocker pieces hanging from every limb, and jumps on top of the man, slamming the wooden shards into his face and gut.

He opens his mouth in agony but the sound which should come is halted by his crushed windpipe. Shelly reaches under the man's jacket and pulls his gun from the holster. She curses when she realizes it isn't silenced. She won't be able to use that.

The man presses weakly against her and she punches him in the face. She's going to have to get a little dirty on this one. She grabs one of the broken rocker arms in both hands and plunges its broken post into the man's neck. The arterial blood explodes from him, a macabre Old Faithful and covers Shelly's face and tank top. She turns to avoid as much contact with her mouth and eyes as she can, but the damage is done.

Now there is a sound, but it is nothing like a voice, rather it is the dying gurgle of a man choking on his own blood. She pins him to the floor as he twitches, no fight now, just the muscles reacting to the random electrical signals sent out by a dying brain. But if he were to knock over a lamp or something else breakable, it could alert the other guy next door with Quinn.

At last the twitching subsides and Shelly pulls herself off of the body. She works quickly at the knots and untangles herself from the chair shards. She looks down at the man; his shirt where she'd lain was relatively clean. She rips it off of him and wipes her face as clean as she can, her hair will require a long shampoo but its natural blood red color should conceal the worst of it.

She stands and walks shakily across the room. She stops and sits for just a moment on the boy's bed. She doesn't like killing people that personally. She tries to reserve that for people who she really wants to suffer, when she wants to watch the life drain slowly from their eyes. Doing it with a guy who was just trying to make a dishonest buck, it bothers her more than she wants to admit.

"No!" she hears Quinn yell and she jumps to her feet. There will be plenty of time for self-pity later, she hopes. She releases the clip of the guard's pistol and examines it. It's full. She slides it back into place, chambers a round and tucks the gun into her waist band.

She walks to the bedroom door and opens it slowly to peer outside. The hallway is clear. Tony came with four men, she's just dropped that count to three.

Voices come from downstairs, Tony's eerily calm bass and Larry's weaker alto. At least two of them are downstairs. With luck a third will be as well. If they left one guy alone with Shelly they aren't going to be paranoid about Quinn. If not, Shelly's confident she can handle two of them and without putting Quinn in too much danger.

Pretty confident, anyway.

The girl screams again and Shelly steps quietly into the hallway. She keeps her back to the wall to avoid casting a shadow from the sunbeams streaming in through the windows at either end of the hallway. When she reaches the door to Quinn's room she grips the knob and it turns easily in her hand. They didn't bother to lock it.

"You know," Shelly hears the guy inside saying, "you really ought not to be playing with sharp things like this. You could hurt yourself."

"She found the steak knife in the jacket sleeve," Shelly whispers, smiling.

She risks a look. Quinn is standing in the middle of the room. She's not restrained. Only the one guard. Things are finally starting to cut her way. She pushes the door open completely, steps into the room and closes it silently behind her. The man turns at the sudden movement and Shelly sees a long, angry cut running across his face. Good for Quinn.

"What the hell?" the guy shouts. Quinn's knife is in his hand and he raises it quickly at Shelly.

Shelly steps to him, grabs his wrist and twists, shattering his it. This one does get off a scream of pain just before Shelly catches the knife falling from his ruined hand and swipes it across his throat, forever silencing him.

"Oh God!" Quinn screams, retching at the sight of the blood which has squirted across Shelly's face. This has not been a good day for her complexion.

Shelly reaches under the falling man's jacket and pulls his gun from its holster as it tumbles. That scream is going to draw some attention.

She raises both of her purloined pistols at the closed door and backs slowly toward Quinn.

"Mrs. Sharpe... Shelly, you just killed that man."

"Yes, dear, I did. I'll probably have to kill a few more in just a moment."

As if her words were a conjuring spell, the door bursts open and she fires four rounds, two into the chest of one of the goons but the two intended for Larry instead plunge into the plaster of the wall. Two guns at once has always been stupid.

Larry dives back into the hallway.

"Oh God," Quinn says again.

It's down to Larry and Tony, Shelly can end it all now, she

has no doubt. But Quinn is an unknown factor. How would she react in the middle of a fire fight? Shelly couldn't be sure and she couldn't risk it.

Larry sticks his gun in the doorway and fires three blind shots that land nowhere near either of them.

Shelly continues backing without taking her eyes from the door way. Her leg brushes against Quinn's nightstand and she stops. She conjures a mental picture of Quinn's room, there is a window behind and just to the left of her. She tucks one pistol into her waistband, picks up the nightstand without taking her eye from the doorway, takes a step to her left and throws it through the glass with a loud shatter.

Larry pops his head around the door and she fires a round, just missing his head. "Shit," she says as he ducks once more out of sight.

"Quinn, I need you to come here," Shelly says.

"Um... what do you need me to do?" Quinn asks, glancing nervously at the second gun in Shelly's waistband. "I don't really know how to use one of those."

"No, honey, I don't want you to shoot anyone," Shelly says. Quinn sighs in relief. "I just want you to try not to fall too fast."

"Huh?" Quinn says as Shelly pushes her through the shattered window and onto the slippery tiles of the porch over hang.

Quinn screams and scrambles to stop herself from sliding onto the ground.

Larry peaks into the room again and once more Shelly almost nails him. "Damn you're hard to shoot," she yells as he disappears again.

She jumps backward onto the roof doing a back somersault past the struggling Quinn. "Atta girl," she tells her as she flips backward off of the roof and lands in a crouch on the walkway. She stands and tucks both pistols into her pants.

"Okay, you can drop, Quinn," she yells and Quinn slides obediently off of the roof and into Shelly's awaiting arms.

Shelly quickly sets her on the walkway and says, "Get behind me."

Quinn ducks behind her as Shelly pulls the guns from her pants and fires once at Tony as he opens the door. He slams it again quickly and Shelly hears him yell, "She's getting away, where are you morons?"

"Quinn, dear," Shelly says. "I really have to keep my eye on the house just now, could you look behind us and tell me if my motorcycle is still parked where I left it?"

"Um, yeah, it's still there."

"Fantastic, do be a love and grab the back of my shirt and lead me to it whilst I shoot at the gentlemen trying to kill us."

"How can you joke right now?" Quinn asks, her voice a whisper.

"It keeps me calm and focused," Shelly tells her. "There's a very good chance that we don't survive without the jokes."

"Oh," Quinn says. "It that case I know a great one about talking muffins."

Shelly surprises herself by laughing out loud and drawing Larry's attention from the upstairs window. He points his gun at them but she gets a shot off first, dropping him. "Oh, damn, I meant to torture him for the pat down incident. Ah well," Shelly says. She breathes a sigh of relief, that was the last guard. Tony probably won't come after them himself. He seems actually capable of abstract thought enough to know what a bad idea that would be.

Then again, from what she'd heard about Mystery, he might prefer her quick bullet to whatever the magician would have up his sleeve for Tony when he found out about the screwup. She keeps her guns raised.

Quinn pulls on her shirt, leading them toward the bike..

"Okay, we're here," Quinn tells her when they reach the bike.

"Good, hop on."

"Shouldn't you get on first?"

"Why? You're going to be driving."

Quinn laughs nervously. "Me? Driving?"

"You're wearing the jacket," Shelly says with a grin.

"But I…"

"Didn't you ever drive Francis's bike?"

"Yeah, but this isn't Francis's bike and I never had a passenger."

"Look, I'm not going to lie, this thing has a lot more power than you're used to and it's quite a bit heavier, but the basic principles are the same. I know you can do this Quinn, and I simply can't. Not while keeping an eye on the house at any rate. Now climb on."

"Okay," Quinn says and Shelly hears her scramble on top of the bike. "I'm on."

"All right pick it up and kick up the stand." Shelly listens as Quinn follows her directions. "The key is in the jacket, start it up." The bike roars to life and Quinn yelps in surprise.

"Good girl," Shelly says, tucking the gun in her right hand into the back of her pants. "Now, I'm going to climb on behind you and, after I'm on, just take off slowly."

Without looking away for as much as a second, without lowering her gun an inch, Shelly climbs onto the bike and wraps her free arm around Quinn's waist. "Now go, honey," she whispers.

Quinn revs the engine twice before taking off in a slow, wobbling putt. They stagger a few times and Shelly is certain they are about to go over when Quinn opens the throttle and the two of them shoot away down the road.

Shelly waits until the house is well and truly out of sight before she tucks the second gun into her pants and wraps both arms around the girl's midsection.

"Do you want to switch?" Quinn yells back at her when she realizes Shelly is no longer watching the house.

"No reason for that, you're doing just fine," Shelly tells her.

CHAPTER TWENTY-FIVE

Tony zips the bag up over the old man's body, stopping at his face. It's locked into a grimace much like Tony imagines his corpse will one day wear given his position, temperament and lifestyle in general.

He zips the bag the rest of the way and stands.

He pulls a burner phone out of his pocket and dials as he heads toward the stairs. Mystery answers on the second ring. "Tell me," he says.

"She's riled," Tony says.

"Excellent," Mystery says. "How'd the boys do?"

"I mean, they got the job done," Tony says. "I very much doubt if they have any letters of acceptance from Mensa waiting for them back home."

"Any of them still left to check their mailboxes?"

"Oh, no, god no."

"You didn't expect me to send my best and brightest to be slaughtered, did you?"

Tony reaches the landing and turns toward the boy's room where Sharpe had been tied. "Not the brightest but maybe not the exact opposite of that."

"What can I say, Tony? The smart ones tend to recognize the abattoir."

"I suppose," Tony says, stepping into the room and examining the body. Even with the life he lives Tony hopes to never wind up looking like this. "We should probably stock up on men though."

"I think I might be able to gin up some local talent as well."

"Any idea of the caliber of talent?"

"My guess is they'll be more along the caliber of cannon fodder, but that'll be my problem."

"You're coming out?"

"If she's as riled as you say she is it seems like the perfect time."

Tony crouches to get a better look at the spike sticking out of the man's neck.

"Any civilian casualties?" Mystery asks.

"Huh?" Tony says. "Oh, yeah, old guy from next door. He was in the wrong place at the wrong time and his heart gave out."

"I see."

"Kind of a shame, I sort of liked the old geezer."

"Sorry to hear that. The price of doing business," Mystery says. "He have family?"

"Yeah, a wife. I took care of her. She's bagged up next to her husband. No family pictures in the house so there shouldn't be anyone asking the wrong kind of questions. I'll take care of both of them, leave the boys for the pros so they can start asking the right kinds of questions."

"Sounds like you've got this in hand. I'll be on the next flight out."

"Sure…" Tony takes a deep breath, lets it out slowly and says, "Boss."

"Yeah?"

"These spies…"

"Yeah?"

"Well…"

"Tony, I have a very full plate, I don't have time to drag this out of you."

"Okay, when they took down the machine we lost some guys, but they were all clean kills. What she did to these guys, particularly the guy I left guarding her, I wouldn't wish that on my third-grade teacher. And that bitch tried to teach me cursive and multiplication."

"Are you worried about me, Tony?"

"I'm just saying, if you wind up toe to toe with this lady, keep your guard up."

"You do know that death is the goal, right?"

"Yeah, but there's death…" looks once more at the body and then covers it with a sheet from the kid's bed, "and then there's death."

"I'll keep that in mind."

Mystery breaks the connection. Tony stands, snaps the phone in half and tosses it out the window. He looks one more time at the body, shudders and heads back toward the stairs.

CHAPTER TWENTY-SIX

"Okay," Spacer tells Darren when he comes to a stop outside the clubhouse. "You may not see it at first, but this is a pretty safe place for you and your family."

"Who in the hell is…" Pete yells, stepping into the parking lot. "Oh, Spacer man, it's you. Listen, brother, about Clint, I am so sorry. He is definitely out of the club."

"Good, he's a moron," Spacer says.

"Look, if there's a way I can make this up to you…"

"As a matter of fact, there is," Spacer says, nodding toward the Whitmans. "I just need you to keep an eye on these folks for a few hours."

"Um… we really ain't the sort for babysitting."

"Oh, that's okay, I'll just tell Shelly there are some things that you won't do to make it up to her."

"No, man, I didn't say that!" Pete says, quickly. "Look, I just, I don't really know how good I'll be at it, you know."

"Easiest thing in the world, keep them safe and try to keep them entertained."

"I'm not sure about this, hon," Sissy says as more of Pete's guys come out of the club house and look them up and down.

"Spacer, does this have anything to do with the girl from the other night?" Pete asks.

"The girl?" Darren asks.

"In a way," Spacer says.

"These are the bikers who took Quinn!" Darren yells.

"They're what?" Sissy asks, yelling to him across the parking lot.

Darren grabs Spacer by the arm. "Tell me the truth, did you have something to do with that the other night?"

"No!" Spacer says. "You know, outside of orchestrating the entire thing. Look, Darren, there's probably going to be even more stuff that really horrifies you and I'm just going to go ahead and pre-apologize for it, but what I need to know right now is that you, Pete, will keep them safe until I can get back with Shelly and Quinn."

"What about the old dude?" Pete asks, pointing at Dr.

Landsin as he walks up to them.

"Him, I need him alive, that's all I ask for. Outside of that, if you want to put him in a dress and chuck beer bottles at him to make him dance, go right ahead," Spacer says.

"Excuse me," Dr. Landsin says. "This is not the sort of treatment I expected when I sought you out. If this is the sort of thing I can expect I think that I will be on my way."

"The hell you will," Spacer says, grabbing him by the arm.

"I told you that arm was sore!" Landsin yells.

Spacer tosses him to Pete who hands him off to Rodrigo. "Make our guest comfortable."

Rodrigo pulls the struggling scientist into the club house. Pete looks to the rest of his guys. "Barry," he yells, "give the lady and the kids a tour... the nice tour."

"Oh..." Barry says, he looks at the needle-nose pliers in his hand, shrugs and jams them back into his pocket. "Would the two of you join me inside?"

Sissy looks to Darren. "It's all right, Sissy. At... at least I think it is."

She nods at him and follows Barry into the clubhouse. Pete nods at the rest of his boys and they all go inside the house. When he, Pete and Darren are the only ones remaining in the lot, Spacer says, "Pete, I've got to know that these people are going to be safe."

"I'll keep an eye on them."

"Do you have any more idiots I don't know about?"

"No, you know all of the idiots I have right now."

"More importantly, all of your idiots know me and what will happen to them if they piss me off, right?"

Pete nods, "Yeah, they know."

"Now, just hang on for one moment," Darren says. "Are my family and I being held here against our will like the doctor is?"

Pete looks to Spacer who scratches the back of his head and says, "Look, Darren, I'm not going to tell them not to let you leave if you insist but... honest to God, I hope that you will stay. If you're here I know where you are and how to check in with you, which reminds me..." Spacer digs into his pocket and pulls out a cell phone which he tosses to Pete. "Your phones are probably hot, the guy I'm hunting down may be listening in. If I need to talk to you, I'll call that phone I just gave you. If I want to be heard talking to you, I'll call the club house. If I call the club house, don't believe anything I tell you, understand?"

"Got it," Pete says. He nods at Darren, "So, what's the final verdict on them. Can they leave if they want too?"

"Yes, they aren't prisoners," Spacer says.

"I'm..." Pete says, turning to Darren. "I'm probably going to need to have you sign some form of waver though, should you choose to leave my establishment, relinquishing me from any responsibility as to your safety and general welfare."

"Okay, sure, if I leave I'll sign your waver," Darren says with a shrug.

"But the scientist stays, he's our bargaining chip. If it comes down to it, I will happily exchange him for Shelly and Quinn," Spacer says.

"Is that something we can do? Didn't you say the bad guy is building a machine to take over the world? If he has Dr. Landsin then we'll all be in danger."

"No, we won't," Spacer says.

"How can you say that for sure?"

Spacer stares at him for a moment. "Do you want me to tell you that or do you want to sleep tonight?"

"I think too much has been kept from me already, I want to know."

"Okay," Spacer says with a shrug. "You noticed how sore his arm is?" Darren nods. "When he was being debriefed by the agency I work with they put a chip in his arm. If he should be captured there would be a rescue attempt but, if that proved unsuccessful, they would activate the chip which would shoot enough adrenaline into his heart to explode it three or four times over."

"Dear God, this is our government doing this?"

"Part of it."

"How can you be sure?"

Spacer rolls up his sleeve and shows Darren the small,

white scar on his bicep. "I have one of my own."

"And you're just... just okay with that?"

Spacer shrugs, "Cost of..."

"Doing business, I know," Darren says. "I've heard unsavory people say that all my life. I hope you won't be offended if I tell you that I preferred you when your business was selling books."

"That is exactly why I tell people about that business and not the other," Spacer says.

"Okay," Pete says, "so the family can leave if they want to, but the scientist stays. Anything else I should know?"

Spacer shakes his head slowly. He turns to Darren and says, "If Shelly and Quinn are out there, I will find them, but, if you don't hear from me, you might want to consider going on down to Miami."

"You mean, without...?" Darren says.

Spacer nods. Darren's hands become fists and he turns his back on Spacer and walks into the club house.

here.

CHAPTER TWENTY-SEVEN

Pete steps inside the club house and slams the door behind him. Darren jumps at the sound but Scott jumps up from the table they're sitting at and runs over to him.

"Scott, don't bother the nice man!" Darren yells, grabbing for his son and missing.

"Nah, little man's okay," Pete says, kneeling down to Scott's level. "What can I do for you?"

"Is it okay if I play on your pool table?"

"You wanna play pool?" Pete looks up to the rest of his guys. "Hey boys, we got ourselves a Minnesota Fats here."

Darren stands and walks toward them cautiously.

"I'm not fat," Scott says.

Pete chuckles. "No, no I suppose you aren't. Sure, you can play. You can play…" he looks around the room until his eye falls on Kenny, gray haired with a long beard and pushing 350 pounds, maybe he looks enough like Santa to not freak the kid out any more than they might already be. "You can play Kenny over there."

Kenny looks up a little startled but when Scott turns to look at him he smiles broadly and waves. Okay, Santa typically has more than just the two teeth, but the kid smiles and waves back at him.

"Kenny, go dig up a couple of cues and, maybe, a chair he can stand on." Kenny nods and walks into the back room. Pete puts his hand gently on Scott's shoulders and leans in conspiratorially. "You go easy on Kenny, okay? He can't play for sh…" Pete stops when he realizes what he was just about to say to a young boy and tries his best to cover. "Shhhhhh-ooooom-ba-doodie."

Scott nods and says, "I'll go easy." He runs off to meet Kenny who just stepped back into the room with the equipment.

"You… you were really good with him just now," Darren says.

"Well," Pete says, pulling himself to his feet., "I've got a little one of my own at home."

"Oh? Really?"

"Yup, only she ain't so little any more. In a year or two she'll be as big as her old man."

"Oh," Darren says, looking around nervously. "She sounds lovely."

"She's the apple of my eye. I've got some pictures I'll show you in a sec but I've got to do this thing first."

"Thing?"

"Yeah," Pete says, stepping away and approaching Dr. Landsin who is sitting on a threadbare couch working his way through a bag of Doritos. He stops, towering above the scientist who looks up at him with a Dorito half-way to his mouth.

"May I help you?" Dr. Landsin says.

Pete motions Rodrigo and two of his other boys to join him. "I'm going to need you to stand up," Pete says.

"Why? Is this your favorite spot?" Dr. Landsin asks.

Pete nods to Rodrigo who pulls Dr. Landsin to his feet. The other two grab him and Rodrigo pats his hands roughly up and down the scientist's side.

"Is this entirely necessary?" Dr. Landsin asks.

"Got to make sure you aren't packing," Pete says.

"I notice the Brady Bunch isn't getting this treatment."

"First of all, that is two adults and one child. Brady Bunch is the best reference you could come up with? Really? Bunch?"

"Okay, the family from Webster."

"That was an interracial family! God you are bad at this."

"Well, who ever they remind you of, you aren't patting them down."

"They ain't being held against their will. They've got no reason to attack us." He nods to the clearly full pockets of the man's jacket. "Also, they ain't carrying heavy like you."

Rodrigo starts to pull items from the pocket as the sound of pool balls crashing together erupts from the table. "Awesome!" Scott says.

"Hey Pete, this kid's got chops. Did you hear that break?" Kenny yells.

"Sure did. Good job NC Skinny," Pete says without looking away. "What we got, Rod?"

Rodrigo looks through the cache. "Um, we got a pack of gum, wallet, keys, 'nother pack of gum, Chapstick, more gum…"

"What's with all the gum?" Pete asks.

Dr. Landsin shrugs. "People carry gum."

"No one carries this much gum," Pete says. He nods at Rodrigo. "What else."

"We got this," he says, holding up a squirt gun.

Pete takes it, sniffs it carefully, and looks at Dr. Landsin. "What's with the toy?"

"It's my nephew's. I forgot I had it," he says.

"How do I know it's not full of acid?" Pete asks.

"Because if it were, it and your hand would be melting now," Dr. Landsin says.

The sound of a click comes from the table and several of the guys gasp. "Holy shit, Pete, you shoulda seen this kid's bank shot."

"Little busy now, Ken," Pete says. "Oh, and ixnay on the itshay in front of the idkay."

"Orrysay," Kenny says.

Pete points the squirt gun at Dr. Landsin's face. "Well, you make a good point doc, but I think this might make a better one." He pulls the trigger and a stream of brown liquid sprays him in the face. Pete and Rodrigo lean in, examining him. He looks from one to the other, clearly uncomfortable but otherwise okay.

"Well, he ain't freaking out," Rodrigo says.

"Why is it brown?" Pete asks.

"My nephew likes to add food coloring. He thinks it looks like blood."

"It looks like diarrhea."

Dr. Landsin shrugs. "Kids are gross."

"What else?" Pete asks."

"We have a handkerchief with, yup, another pack of gum in it."

"What is with all the gum?" Pete yells.

197

"I just like gum," Dr. Landsin says.

"No one likes gum this much."

Dr. Landsin turns to Rodrigo and holds out his hand, "May I?"

"Huh?" Rodrigo says. Dr. Landsin nods to the handkerchief. "Oh, yeah," Rodrigo says, handing it to him.

"Are they at least different flavors?" Pete asks.

"The gum? No. All spearmint," Rodrigo says.

"Spearmint?" Pete asks.

"What's wrong with spearmint?" Dr. Landsin asks wiping the brown stuff off of his face with the hanky.

"What's wrong with…? I… I don't even know how to have this conversation." He turns to Rodrigo and says, "Is that all?"

"That's just the first pocket," Rodrigo says. "The left pocket is our bath and body pocket." He holds up various bottles and tubes. "You've got your cold creams, your mud mask, your little mesh bag of bath salts, some gloves, your ointments, lotions and various perfumes."

Pete cuts his eyes to the doctor and raises an eyebrow. "You turn over a Walgreens on your way here?"

"Running for one's life can be terribly stressful," Dr. Landsin says. "Forgive me if I take what few opportunities I have to pamper myself."

Pete sighs. "At least there wasn't any gum in that one."

"Oh, there were, like, seven packs. I just didn't want to mention them," Rodrigo says.

Pete turns on Dr. Landsin and jams his finger into the doctor's chest. "You have a problem, guy. You need to find yourself a group and take a dozen steps." Pete glares at him for a long moment before walking away.

Rodrigo shrugs at him. "He's not wrong."

Dr. Landsin reaches out for his things but Rodrigo drops them to the floor and walks away. Dr. Landsin sighs and starts to gather them up.

CHAPTER TWENTY-EIGHT

"Oh god!" Quinn says, pulling the bike to a stop on the side of the road. She puts her foot down to stop but she isn't used to the weight of the bike and the whole thing almost falls over until Shelly puts her own foot down as well.

"What's wrong?" Shelly asks.

"We forgot Mr. Carlson," Quinn says. "We have to go back."

"No, Quinn, we don't have to," Shelly says.

Quinn turns to look at her, her eyes are bright with tears but she doesn't allow them to fall. "He's dead, isn't he?" she says.

Shelly nods.

Quinn thinks for a moment. "You're sure? You aren't just assuming that he would have been killed by now since we left him there?"

"He was dead before they even took you up the stairs."

Quinn takes a deep breath and stills herself. "Did they torture him like they were going to do to me?"

"No, he fought with the man who was trying to pat him down for weapons and his heart failed him."

"He went down swinging? I think Mrs. Carlson will be happy to know that," Quinn says. She turns back around so that Shelly can't see her face. The rise and fall of her shoulders lets Shelly know that she's at last given up on holding back the tears. Shelly sits motionless and lets the girl work it out on her own.

After a few moments, Quinn says, "Mrs. Sharpe, yesterday I thought that it would be really cool to be you, but, um…"

"I don't blame you. Most days I don't want it either," Shelly says, hoping the girl doesn't hear the lie in her voice.

"I think I want to go back to my regular life now, Mrs. Sharpe, with my Mom and Dad."

"We'll get you back to it just as soon as we can, but first, I'm going to take you to a safe place."

"Okay," Quinn says, sliding off the bike and climbing on behind Shelly. "But, I don't think a can drive any more."

"I got it," Shelly says. Quinn starts to unzip the jacket but

Shelly stops her. "That's yours, you've earned it. Quinn nods and zips it again.

Shelly nods, guns the throttle and peels out onto the road.

CHAPTER TWENTY-NINE

Gerry rolls his eyes as his phone chimes for the third time that morning. He silences it and drops it back into his pocket.

"Somebody really wants to talk to you," Jim says.

"Well, somebody can really eat a dick," Gerry says, pinching a morsel from his half-eaten bran muffin and popping it in his mouth.

"Need a top off, Babe?" Sarah asks, sliding into the booth and kissing Jim hard on the mouth. She pulls back, holds up the coffee pot and says, "Now that you've been topped off, want some coffee?"

"Hell yeah," Jim says.

Sarah fills his cup and looks across at Gerry. "Want?"

"Nah."

"Just for the record, you were only being offered the coffee, not the top off."

"The record shall so reflect."

Jim looks from Sarah to Gerry and back. "You guys talk weird." Jim's phone rings. He pulls it out of his pocket and checks out the display. "Who the hell?"

"Lemme see," Gerry says, holding out his hand. Jim hands the phone over and Gerry glances at it. "Don't answer this," he says, tossing it back.

"This the dick eater?" Jim asks.

"Excuse me?" Sarah says.

"Wait, is this… him?"

"Yeah, you don't want to get in bed with this guy," Gerry says.

"I'd really like to be brought in on this," Sarah says.

"Yeah, easy for you to say, you already got yours."

"Who got whose?" Sarah says. She looks at Gerry, "What'd you get?"

Jim clicks answer and holds the phone up to his ear, "You got Jimbo," he says.

"Dammit, Jim!" Gerry mutters.

"Yes sir, you got me," Jim says, he looks at Gerry, smiles and says, "Sure is, sitting right here in front of me."

"Do not drag me in," Gerry says.

Jim takes the phone away from his ear and says, "He just says hello." He puts the phone back to his ear and says, "I'm sorry, what was that? Um… I reckon I could scrounge up some good fellers on little to no notice. How many you need?" Listens for a minute, whistles sharply and says, "That many? Wow."

"What does he need good fellers for?" Gerry asks.

"Who needs fellers?" Sarah says.

"I… I'm sorry, sir, there's just a whole lot of chatter around me," he glares and Gerry and Sarah. "Let me move to a quieter area so we can talk bidness." He motions to Sarah to scoot out of his way and, when she does, he slips out himself and walks to the men's room.

Sarah slides back in across from Gerry. "Okay, Ger, what the hell is going on with the boyfriend I haven't had long enough to get the stank of his last skank off him yet?"

Gerry shrugs. "I've got no idea what he's talking about but… well, remember that weird guy that bought me breakfast the other day?"

"Yeah."

"He had me do something for him, something I'm not completely proud I did."

"The… the dick eating?"

"Huh? No! God! That was just a figure of speech that got out of hand there."

"So, what did you do?" Sarah asks.

"I really don't want to say."

"You didn't hurt anybody, did you?" she asks. Gerry picks up his mug and takes a sip, cutting his eyes to the window. "You didn't, did you?" Gerry clears his throat and remains silent. "God dammit, Gerry! Who did you hurt and what kind of trouble are you getting Jim into right now?"

"What Jim does is not on me," Gerry says. "I tried to stop him, you saw me."

"You're disgusting," Sarah says.

Sarah jumps out of the booth and runs to the men's room. Without stopping she slams into the door and says, "Okay boys, zip 'em up or make your peace with it!"

"Dammit Sarah, you're not supposed to come in here!" Roger Ericson yells from the urinal. "Nick said he was going to talk to you about that."

"He did," Sarah says, walking past the urinals and looking underneath the stalls for feet.

"Well," Roger says.

"Roger, if a large man with a knife in his hand can't keep me from bursting in here what chance do you think you have with what you've got in your hand right now."

"Hey, no peeking!"

"Oh relax, I can't see anything, I'd need a high-powered microscope for that."

"I am so telling Nick about this."

Sarah stops at the only stall with feet sticking out beneath and hammers on the door. "All right, mister! You'd better have a good explanation for this!"

"Well," says a frail voice, "I'd like to say that it was just God's will but I think the more direct answer is that mine is no longer a young man's stomach and I should remember that before ordering the spicy omelet."

Sarah drops her hand and says, "Fa... Father Brown?"

"Indeed, my child. Will I be seeing you for mass this Sunday?"

"Yeah, yeah I'll be there."

"God bless you."

"Sarah?" Jim says from the last stall reserved for the handicap. "What the hell are you doing?"

Sarah walks down to the stall, "I'm trying to keep you from making a stupid mistake!" She sees the door is ajar and pushes it inward, "Now what the hell was that... OH GOD NO! Why?"

Sarah turns away and hides her eyes from Jim who is sitting pant-less on the toilet with his feet resting on the handicap rails on both sides of the stall like a modesty deprived woman in stirrups awaiting the gynecologist. "Jeeze Sara, privacy please."

"I thought you were on the phone!" she says, pulling the door closed.

"I am," Jim says. "So, anyway, you just let me know when you need 'em and I'll call in every favor I'm owed to get 'em over to you," he says into the phone. He listens for a minute and says, "All righty, I'll be here."

Sarah hears the beep of him cutting off the call and says, "I have several questions."

"Can they wait?"

"No! They are pressing."

"God, fine, what are they?" "First of all, what are you doing?" Sarah asks.

"What does it look like? I'm pooping."

"No, I've seen pooping, it does not look like that," Sarah says. "Why are your feet up on the rails?"

"I read on the internet it's good for the back."

"Well, that may be, but it is doing no favors for the front." "Is that all you needed?" Jim asks.

"No, I…"

There is a flush from a few stalls over and Father Brown steps out. He washes his hand and dabs them with a towel before stepping over to Sarah, patting her on the shoulder and saying, "It is through suffering that we attain grace, child."

"Thank you, Father," Sarah says. The priest pats her shoulder once more and then rests his hand on it. Sarah looks at the hand and says, "Your… your hand is still a little wet, Father."

"Oh! My apologies." Father Brown pats her once more and then walks out of the bathroom.

Sarah wipes at her shoulder and says, "What was with the phone call?"

"Ah, that was nothing, I just might have a chance to pick up a little side work."

"Side work doing what?" Sarah asks.

There's a flush from inside Jim's stall and a moment later he steps out and takes her hands in his. She looks down at his hands, then at the sink and at his hands again.

"Babe, don't you worry about me, I'm going to be just fine," Jim says.

"I would very much like to not worry about you," Sarah says. "Why don't you tell me the details of this side gig that I shouldn't worry about and then we can both not worry."

"Damn, hon," Jim says with a chuckle. "You really do talk weird." He pecks her on the lips and walks out of the bathroom.

Sarah walks to the sink and washes her hands.

"Finally, I thought you two would never shut up," Roger says from the urinals.

"Dammit Roger, were you there the whole time."

"You know I can't establish a stream when you're in here!" Roger says.

Sarah grabs a paper towel and heads to the door. "Establish away," she says, pushing through the door.

She steps into the dining room and looks at Gerry and Jim's booth. It's empty. She sighs and picks up the coffee pot from the table and walks back to the kitchen.

CHAPTER THIRTY

Spacer stares at the Whitman's home, police have strung tape all around it and are milling around, interviewing the gawking neighbors standing in their yards. Something big happened here and Shelly wasn't able to call in a cleanup team before the officials were alerted. Whether that was because she didn't have time or because she wasn't living he can't know. He takes in a long deep breath and notices without surprise how it shakes when he lets it out.

He feels the bulge of the cell phone in his pocket but resists the urge to whip it out and dial his wife's number. They are running silent now, they have to.

There are ambulances, five of them, but their lights aren't on. From his place parked down the block he has already seen three body bags loaded into them.

"Who's in the bags?" he asks when the passenger door to the Spyder is opened. He doesn't look away from the busy scene even as the PI drops into the seat next to him.

"I haven't been here too long, I saw a couple of guys, had the dumb look of hired muscle, but that's all I know."

Spacer nods.

"If it helps, I didn't see any spooks running around. If your girl had been one of the bodies I imagine there'd be a g-man or two."

"Not necessarily, we're freelance, there's enough distance between us and the CIA for them to deny any knowledge."

The PI shrugs. "What does this mean for the mission?"

"No CIA means Mystery is still out there. If he'd been a body, then they'd be all over that."

"So… the mission?"

"The mission is still on, the venue just changed."

"Any place I know?"

Spacer at last takes his eyes from the house and looks at the PI. "I'm not sure, I figured we'd finish this here, I left a note for Shelly directing her here."

"Well, we may not be able to count on her showing," the PI said, his voice matter of fact.

Spacer nods.

"So, you know another venue appropriate for a shoot-out?"

"Huh?" Spacer says.

"That's pretty much what this mission is, yeah? The O.K. Corral."

"Yeah," Spacer says, reaching across him and popping open the glove box. "And I know just the place." He hands one of the fliers he took from his windshield to The PI

"Wild West World?" The PI reads.

"It's a theme park opening in a couple of weeks... or so they think."

"Seems like just the thing folks would travel to the coast of North Carolina to visit." Spacer shrugs. "So, we're going to be delaying their opening, huh?"

"Oh yeah, there's going to be damages," Spacer says.

Spacer pushes open the batwing doors of the false saloon and saunters inside. He grins in spite of himself, scenes from every John Wayne movie he's ever seen flashing through his mind. Getting into the park had been no issue, there was no security as there wasn't yet anything to steal and all of the workmen had long since gone home for the day, apparently overtime was frowned upon in this day and age. One padlock held a chain on the gate but The PI had picked that with his pocket knife. Now the entire Wild West World is theirs to do with as they please.

Spacer drops his kit on a nearby table and pulls the hat from the head of an animatronic card player setup at a table in the corner, the one with the Ace of Spades protruding clearly from his left boot.

"You're taking the man's clothes?" The PI asks, stepping casually through the door as Spacer strips the robot of his duster.

"It's what he gets for cheating," Spacer says, pointing at the ace in the brim of the hat he's now wearing. He unbuckles the man's gun belt and cinches it around his waist, holsters dangling at his hip. He reaches into the bag and pulls a sheathed Katana blade which he loops over his head.

"You know what you're doing with that?"

"I'm not as good with it as Shelly but I hold my own."

The P.I. shrugs. "So, I'm guessing there's a plan," he says. "Apart from playing dress up."

"There's a plan of sorts," Spacer says, unzipping his bag and displaying his mobile arsenal. He pulls twin Colt .45 pistols and deposits them in the holsters. They sit awkwardly, the holsters were made for revolvers, and toy revolvers at that, but they work well enough and Spacer always did enjoy the drama of the job.

He gestures to the bag and says, "Help yourself."

"No thanks, I'm good," The PI says.

"Seriously, we're going up against some bad men here, you're going to want some fire power."

"If you don't tell me how to work, I won't tell you."

"You're my backup, make me feel better and take a gun."

The PI looks at his watch. "Daylight's wasting. We can sit here and bitch like a couple in the old folks home or you can let me go do what I have to do to get your back."

Spacer sighs. He hates to admit it, but he's right. There's a lot that needs to be done before they invite Mystery over, guns to stash around town, locating a good vantage point, to say nothing of the opening act, standing here arguing isn't getting any of that done.

"All right," Spacers says, "but hold on." He reaches into the bag and pulls an AK47 from inside it. He turns to a piano set up on a stage where yet another robot sits awaiting his chance to come to life and tickle the ivories. He fires a volley into the instrument until one leg falls out from under it and it crashes to the stage. He plucks the leg from the rubble and offers it to the PI. "Here, I know you know how to handle one of these."

"Yeah," the PI says, taking the heavy wood and hefting it, feeling its weight. "Yeah, this may work." He turns to walk out of the saloon, but Spacer stops him.

"Don't set up in the general store or the whore house near the entrance."

"I noticed the plastic explosives," the PI says. "I figured that's where you'd go with those." He walks out of the bar.

Spacer takes a deep breath and turns back to his bag. He notices a very slight tremor in his fingers as he digs out the charges. He hates to admit it, even silently to himself, but he's nervous. He's worked with the PI and found him to be remarkably capable, but he'd never done anything like this without Shelly at his back. All of the costumes, the jokes, the posturing, they weren't going to change the fact that he was severely handicapped on this one. His dad would say he was about to enter an ass kicking contest with one leg.

His hand brushes against cardboard and he looks to see a box of matches and pack of Coffin Nail cigarettes that had been left in the bag since he'd first infiltrated Pete's gang about a decade ago. He smiles at the idea that pops immediately into his head. Maybe a little more posturing could help.

He looks at the poker cheater and says aloud to it, "What size boot do you wear, feller?"

CHAPTER THIRTY-ONE

Tony steps back from the curb as the limo pulls up. The door opens remotely, and he steps inside. "I used to think that was fancy until I realized moms could do the same thing with their minivans," he says as Mystery presses the button to close it.

"Why must you strip me of all my joy?" Mystery says.

"What's the plan?" Tony asks.

"First we meet our men," Mystery says.

"And do we know what we're doing with our men once they've been found?"

"The spies will let us know when they are ready." Tony raises an eyebrow at him. Mystery sighs to himself. "Have I been wrong yet?"

"No, you've been maddeningly consistent," Tony says.

"You don't sound relieved."

"Well, I've been doing this sort of stuff for a while now and I've learned that people's number always eventually come up," Tony says. "I'm thinking you may be due."

Mystery smiles at him and leans back in his seat. He presses a button on the platform beside him and a panel slides back. There's a sound of machinery humming and a glass rises from the depths of the platform. Mystery grabs it and holds it out to Tony. "Do you know what this is?"

"It looks like ice cream," Tony says.

"Yes, to the uninformed eye, I suppose that it would, in fact, look like ice cream," Mystery says, with a nod. "In actuality, this is a hot fudge sundae with five kinds of ice cream, the obligatory heated chocolate, a marshmallow cream, pistachios and a cherry on top."

"So, it's ice cream," Tony says.

"Your flair for the dramatic truly underwhelms, Anthony." Tony shrugs. "Fine, it's ice cream," Mystery says. "More to the point, it is about to be the first ice cream I've ever eaten."

"You've never eaten ice cream before?" Tony asks.

Mystery shakes his head. "My father was, we'll say strict," he says with a sad smile. "I finally escaped him through the theater and then I was too concerned with keeping trim to consider it." His smile broadens, "If things go according to plan, I don't suppose the empty calories will really mean that much for me today."

Tony nods, considering. "In that case, bon appetite."

Mystery digs the spoon into the sundae and shovels it into his mouth. He takes a few moments, savoring it as his eyes scrunch together. At last he forces himself to swallow and looks at Tony. "That was not what I'd hoped for."

"They say never meet your heroes."

"Why do people enjoy this?"

"Most of them don't put five different kinds in the same bowl. Which flavors were they anyway."

"I don't know," Mystery says, rubbing his temple. "I just ordered the most popular. Is the piercing headache a regular occurrence?"

Tony shrugs. "Not all the time. It's called brain freeze."

Mystery relaxes and fixes his eye on Tony. "It happens frequently enough to have a name?"

"Yeah, I guess so."

Mystery sighs, puts the ice cream back on the platform and presses a button which retracts it once more into the depths. He pulls a napkin from a dispenser and wipes his fingers. "You may be wondering what that had to do with what we were talking about."

"Sure," Tony says.

"I was going to use it as metaphor for having one brief life to live and living it, at last, to it's very fullest. However, after suffering through that, I'm changing my response to, that was it, my number came up and we powered through. Should be smooth sailing from here on out."

The limo turns into the parking lot of a diner and Mystery says, "We're here, time to meet our men." He steps out of the car and Tony follows.

There is a congress of pickup trucks parked in no discernable pattern that Tony can see. The truck's owners mill around chatting, smoking and one of them is relieving himself in the bushes. "Dammit George, you want Nick seeing you doing that?"

"I ain't afraid of Nick."

Mystery approaches the man who reprimanded George, the leader he supposed. "Good morning," Mystery says.

The man starts and turns. Apparently, the arrival of the long black car had escaped his attention. "Oh, hi there, sir!" the man says. "Guys, get it together, this is him."

The men converge on Mystery and begin peppering him with questions, "What's this job you got?" "Never mind what, how much?" "Never mind how much, what's it pay?" "That's what how much means!" "I thought you wanted to know how much work." "Who would want to know that?" "I'd kind of like to know that."

"Jim," Mystery says to the powerless leader. "Perhaps you could introduce me."

"Sure," Jim says. He pats the arm of the man next to him, a guy around six and a half feet tall and several breakfast burritos beyond three hundred and fifty pounds, none of which were of muscle as he no doubt tried to make the ladies believe they were. "This big feller here is Chet. He's my righthand man. Kind of like your big boy over there." Jim points to Tony. The only thing keeping Tony from rolling his eyes is the fact that, if he did, Jim would know that he cared enough to listen.

"Who's the man watering the shrubbery?" Mystery asks.

"Dammit George," Jim yells at him. "I told you to cut that out. How much piss you got anyway?"

"I had two coffees and you know my prostate's been acting up!" George yells.

"That's George," Jim says. "We can leave him behind if you want."

"No, he'll serve my purposes," Mystery says. "All of these guys seem perfect."

"Fantastic," Jim says.

"Just what are these purposes we'll be serving, sir?" another man asks.

"He said he'd tell us when it was time, Randy!" Jim yells.

"I'd kind of like to know what I'm walking into, James!"

"What the hell are you afraid of?"

"You ever heard of human trafficking?"
"Oh, like anybody would want to human traffic you!"

"Gentlemen," Mystery says. "It's a fair question. I actually just need you all to stand and look very much like you do. I have some business interests in this town and there's a man who works with the government who'd like to get in my way."

"Fucking government," Chet says.

Mystery nods. "I just need him to see that I have strong local support. That's all."

"See, Randy," Jim says.

"You're offering us a lot of bread to pretend we like you," Randy says.

"It's a very important business interest."

"Don't worry, sir, we're there for you," Jim says.

"Fantastic. I'll get the meeting place very soon. For now, at ease."

Mystery turns to Tony, shrugs, and climbs back into the limo. Tony takes a last look at the men and follows him inside, at last allowing himself the eye roll he'd been holding back.

Spacer stands back and examines his work. The brothel and the general store on either side of the road are going to go up very quickly. He counts off fifty long paces away from the blast. It's probably not far enough but, any further and they won't be stopping right in the blast zone.

He looks around for the PI but sees nothing. Just as he should. He takes his phone out and dials the club house.

"Y-ello!" Pete says into the phone.

"Pete…" Spacer says.

"Spaceman!" Pete says. Doctor Landsin stops fishing in the bottom of the Doritos bag and listens intently. "You, uh, you know which number you called, right?" Pete says.

"You ever known me not to know which number I called, Pete?"

"I have not."

"Then there's your answer."

"Right on, Spaceman," Pete says. Dr. Landsin licks the

Dorito dust from his fingers as quickly as he can without drawing attention to himself. "So, what can I do you for?"

"We're camped out at the Wild West World until the heat blows off…"

"What the hell is the Wild West World?" Pete asks. Dr. Landsin gives up on cleaning his fingers and jams his hands into his pockets, pulling out the bath salts and squirt gun.

"It's the new amusement park opening at 364 North Maple just past the Starbucks with the weird topiary outside and before you get to the crumbling Kinkos, but that's not important right now. What is important is that nobody knows I'm here. Got it."

"Nobody knows you're at Wild West World, got it,' Pete says. "Stay frosty, Space." Pete hangs the phone up and turns to find the doctor pointing his squirt gun with some kind of pouch tied to its end directly at him. "The fuck?" Pete says.

"I'm afraid at least one other person knows where your Spaceman is now," Dr. Landsin says.

"I have to admit, it was actually subtler than I'd assumed," Mystery says, closing the audio file that the wiretap office sent him.

Tony nods. "I'll alert the men."

"I'm not sure what you're doing, Doc. But I'm finding it annoying," Pete says, taking a step toward him.

"You don't want to do that," Dr. Landsin says, fighting the urge to take a step backward. "I don't want to but I will fire… er… squirt if I have to."

"We've already established that your poop water is harmless," Pete says.

"That was before I attached the bath salts," Dr. Landsin says. "Once the solution in this gun passes through the salts and collects the extra sodium, it becomes a volatile substance capable of melting through… well, I haven't yet found something it wouldn't melt through."

Pete cuts his eyes to Rodrigo, "You buy it?"

Rodrigo shrugs. "Spacer don't trust him, neither do I. I

knew he was up to something with all of that garbage."

"What was all of the gum for?" Pete asks.

"The gum isn't part of this, I just like gum!" Dr. Landsin shouts.

Pete shakes his head. "I think you're bluffing."

"I can arrange a demonstration," Dr. Landsin says. He looks around and gestures to Scott and Kenny. "If you two could just…"

"Just what?" Kenny asks.

"Just, you know, scooch."

"Scooch?"

"Yes, just move to either side so that I can squirt the pool table."

"No, we're still playing!" Scott says.

"Don't worry, Little Man, he's just kidding."

"You call this kidding?" Dr. Landsin asks, squirting the table with a stream of purple fluid. It puddles and a stream flows toward the corner pocket.

"Pete, I told you that damn thing wasn't level," Rodrigo says.

"Fine, you were right," Pete says. "But the takeaway from this should probably be that the gun did jack-shit."

Pete takes another step toward Dr. Landsin who does step back this time. "It takes a moment for the full effect," Dr. Landsin says.

"Of course it does," Pete says, advancing.

"I don't want to shoot you, Pete, but I will!"

"I've been squirted before, the purple doesn't make it scary!" Pete says, reaching for him.

"You have to believe me I…" Dr. Landsin stops as smoke erupts from the pool table and the leg under the corner pocket melts, sending the table crashing to the floor.

Pete looks from the remains of the table, to the gun and finally at Dr. Landsin himself. "You weren't bluffing," Pete says.

"I was not," Dr. Landsin says. "Now please step back!"

Pete backs away from him. Scott stares down at the table and glares at Dr. Landsin. "I said we were still playing, jerk-head!" Scott runs over to the scientist and kicks him in the shin.

Dr. Landsin grabs him and holds the dripping gun half a foot from his head.

"Scott!" Sissy screams.

"All right! I have a few demands!" Dr. Landsin says.

The fleet of pickup trucks follow the limo through the open gate into Wild West World. Tony rolls his eyes as one of them side swipes the gate on the way in.

"Your eyes are getting quite a workout today," Mystery says.

"Didn't realize it was that noticeable."

"I don't think they've noticed," Mystery says. "If that matters."

"It doesn't."

"Remind me again of the McGuffin."

"Um," Tony says. "We're cleaning up the debacle over the machine, you know they know where the doc is and you want him back."

"Really? That's what we came up with?"

"It's kind of what they came up with, I just rolled with it," Tony says.

Mystery shrugs. "Well, that's an unsustainable illusion. But I suppose it should put the pieces in play which is really all I can ask for."

"Happy to help," Tony says.

The limo turns onto main street and the trucks follow. It comes to a stop several feet in front of the silhouette of a lone man standing with the sun to his back. "I knew I'd found the right people," Mystery says with a smile.

"Yeah, it's super dramatic, but I think the buildings full of explosives on either side of us are an even grander statement."

"I noticed that," Mystery says. "I'll need you to stay in the car until they go up."

Tony looks at the buildings and says, "Not that I'm not touched by the sentiment, but shouldn't you be the one staying in the blast proof car?"

"Can't work that way," Mystery says. "I've got an idea, but if it goes sideways I'm going to need you in one piece to help me finish this."

"You're the boss," Tony says. He shifts in his seat, clears his throat and says, "About getting out…"

"If you're about to say you're getting cold feet, Tony, you just couldn't have picked a worst time."

"No, I'll get out, but when the cameras show I'd really rather not be on them."

"Ah, yeah, I thought of that," Mystery says. He presses another button and a shelf protrudes with a baseball cap and dark glasses. He hands these to Tony who looks at them skeptically. "What?" Mystery says.

"Yankees?" Tony says.

Mystery shrugs. "I saw a hat and I grabbed it."

"You're talking to a ride or die Sox fan," Tony says.

Mystery tosses the hat to him and says, "This is your hat, wear it or don't."

"I guess I'll wear it. It'll be even more reason for me to remember to avoid the cameras."

Mystery glances at his watch. "Speaking of, the traffic copters will be another few minutes. We'll wait a bit."

"All right, man, we'll hear you out," Pete says.

"For the love of God, he's a child!" Darren yells. "If you want a hostage take me!"

Dr. Lansin looks at Darren and says, "Yeah, all right, I'll trade him for you."

"Really? Just like that?" Darren asks.

"Now that I've had a moment to step back and take a look at the situation, I realize that this is a level of villainy which I'm just not prepared to embody," Dr. Landsin says.

"Oh… well, thank you," Darren says. He looks at Scott and says, "All right, Son. Come and stand with your mother."

Scott takes a step but Dr. Landsin stops him with a firm hand on his shoulder. "I'm trying not to be a monster, I'm not trying to win sucker of the year. You come first."

"Of course," Darren says, he steps over to Dr. Landsin and

Landsin allows Scott to run over to Sissy.

"Okay, now that we've played musical hostages," Pete says, "what are your demands?"

"All I want is free passage out of here and a ride to a location to be divulged only to my hostage."

"Why divulged to me?" Darren asks.

"Because you'll be doing the driving."

"Ah, yes, that makes sense," Darren says.

"If I'm being honest, that was another reason I traded the kid for you," Dr. Landsin says. "But it was mostly the not being a monster thing."

"Yeah, we can't let you walk out of here with Spaceman's buddy," Pete says.

"Would you rather explain why you stayed here with what was left of Spaceman's buddy?" Dr. Landsin asks.

"I don't think you've got the stones to pull the trigger," Pete says. "You know, since you ain't a monster."

"I may not be bloodthirsty at heart, Peter," Dr. Landsin says. "But to my very core I am a coward and I fear the man I work for far more than I do the idea of melting the face of this man regardless of his innocence."

Pete takes a deep breath and backs up a step further. "Let him, boys," he says without taking his eyes from Dr. Landsin.

Dr. Landsin nudges Darren and they both walk slowly through the door and into Darren's minivan.

"All right," Darren says, turning the key and starting the engine. "Where is this undisclosed location?"

"Just one moment," Dr. Landsin says, turning on the van's GPS, clicking the home button and pointing to Darren's address. "Right there."

Mystery steps out of the limo and turns his back to the figure. He walks to the lead truck just as Jim is climbing out of the driver's seat. "That him?" Jim asks.

"Yeah, have your boys pull back a bit. I don't want to freak him out too soon."

"You sure?" Jim asks.

"I am," Mystery says. He nods at Chet who has crammed

himself into the cab of Jim's truck. "But I need to borrow your right hand for a moment."

"Huh?" Chet says.

"You want Chet?"

"Yes," Mystery says.

"Oh... okay," Jim says. He nods to Chet who pulls himself out of the cab.

"You need me, Mr... Sir-Boss-Sir?" Chet says.

"Let's walk, you and I," Mystery says. He turns and walks toward the figure making sure to keep Chet between himself and the wired building.

"Shit!" Pete says. "Shit-shit-sh..." he glances at Scott who is hanging on his every word. "Sugar."

"What's the plan?" Rodrigo asks.

Pete rubs his face while he thinks. Generally, his plans consist of three steps, 1. Be very large 2. Surround himself with equally large men with a common purpose 3. Do pretty much whatever he wants. Somehow, he does not think that plan is applicable. "Okay, we've got to work with what we've got here. Rodrigo, you think you can remember how to get to the Wassername's house?"

"Whitmans?" Sissy offers.

"Yeah, those names!" Pete agrees.

"Probably, you don't think they'd go there do you?"

Pete shrugs. "Probably not or I'd send more but it's all we got."

"What are you going to do?" Rodrigo asks.

"I..." Pete sighs, "I got to let Spaceman know about this." He looks around the clubhouse for a minute. "Anybody see what I did with that burner phone he gave me?"

Mystery stops walking while the armored car his still sitting firmly to his left and Chet stops next to him.

"Took ya long enough," the figure says. He strikes a match with his thumb and bends to light a cigarette and the small portion of his face which was not obscured by the sun backlighting him disappears behind the broad brim of his hat.

219

He blows a plume of smoke as he raises his head and says, "I thought your little tea party was never going to end."

"Good things are worth waiting for," Mystery says.

The figure nods and pulls something out of his belt. At first it looks to Mystery like a very thin rope but when the figure holds it up to the lit end of his cigarette Mystery realizes that it is actually a ridiculously long fuse to ignite the bombs.

"Hey boss," Chet says, looking at the explosives for the first time. "I think he's planning to…"

"He's bluffing," Mystery says. "Trying to keep me off guard before we talk business."

"How can you be sure?"

"Because if he lit that we could just cut it at any point along the mile of fuse he has and we'll be in no danger."

"Oh," Chet says. "Wow, the business world is nothing like I thought it was."

"I understand you have a little lost scientist," the figure says.

"That's what I'm told," Mystery says.

"Well, seems to me…" the figure begins but he's interrupted by the melodic sounds of John Bon Jovi telling everyone that he is wanted, dead or alive.

For a moment no one speaks until Mystery says, "Ring tone?"

"Yeah," the figure says.

"Do you need to get that?"

The figure sighs, "Probably." He drops the cigarette and crushes it beneath his boot. He reaches under his parka and pulls out a phone. When he puts it to his ear the hat pushes back and Mystery gets his first in person look at the face of the spy he's seen only in pictures up until this point. "What?" the spy says.

The spy listens and his face contorts, just for a moment, into a grimace of rage the reveals the true monster beneath the hero mask. Just as quickly he relaxes into the confidence he was wearing and says. "I got it." He ends the call.

He turns his attention back to Mystery. "You were never looking for Landsin, were you?"

Mystery shrugs. "I rarely look for that which isn't lost."

"He's been on your payroll this entire time?"

"He has."

"So… why are you here?" the spy asks.

Mystery shakes his head slowly. "We don't need to do this part."

"What you're saying is, you don't want to tell me why you chose to die today?"

Mystery smiles broadly and surprises even himself by chuckling a little. "I could not have put it better myself, Spacer Sharpe."

Spacer nods. "I supposed that is your prerogative," he says. "I hate that the phone call had to happen that way." He reaches under his parka to replace the phone. "You see, I was going for a sort of aesthetic here and I think we can all agree that's over now." He takes his hand out from under the parka and instead of a phone he's now holding a remote control. "So, I guess I'll just blow this thing the new-fashioned way."

Mystery ducks as Spacer presses the button. He doesn't see the pressure of the blast knock Spacer back five feet, he doesn't see the agony on Chet's face as shrapnel plunges into him, pin-cushioning his soft flesh and organs and pressing him into Mystery. In fact, the only thing he sees before shielding his eyes against the brilliance of the blast is the nose of the Channel 9 traffic copter approaching overhead.

CHAPTER THIRTY-TWO

"A new development just hours after a shootout on Waterfront Avenue there has just been an explosion in the yet to open theme park, Wild West World. WXII will stay on top..." "This just in, massive explosions in a new theme world, and no, they aren't a part of the act..." "Explosions rock the town of Bridges, NC..." "Possible terrorist activity?" "The Democrats have led us to this." "The Republicans are at it again."

"You don't honestly believe that I am going to take you and that... that weapon to my house," Darrens says.

"Yes, I do," Dr. Landsin says. "I think you'll take me there because I now know the address so I'll be going anyway and I think you'd rather be there to keep an eye on me when I do."

Darren sighs and turns the wheel to take the exit to his home. "But what could possibly be at MY house that would aid you in any way?"

"All will be revealed in time," Dr. Landsin says. He looks at the side view mirror but has little experience being tailed and therefore does not see Rodrigo four cars back and pacing after picking them up just two blocks from the club house.

Rodrigo actually has quite a bit of experience both tailing and being tailed but never at the same time and is concentrating so hard on doing the tailing that he does not see Clint's bike four cars back from him.

Clint had been sipping a beer through his wired jaw when he saw Rodrigo ride by alone. Those guys never went out without the buddy system. If he was going to get revenge for the way he was treated, it was now or never. He tossed the beer, ran out on the check and hopped on his bike.

Clint wouldn't have known a tail if it grew out of his ass but today, as in most days, nobody is chasing after Clint.

Mystery's vision is blurred but returning rapidly. His hearing on the other hand, that seems to be a thing of yesterday. Other than a very dull hum, he can hear nothing. He feels Chet's immense weight pressing against him and shoves, but it does no good. From the angle at which he is pinned he can't get the leverage to budge the big man.

Suddenly the weight is gone, and Mystery looks up to see Tony staring down at him wearing the glasses and the cap. His mouth is moving but lip reading is not a skill Mystery had time to master. Mystery pulls himself to his feet and looks toward the spot the spy was standing. He's gone. Preparing for the battle. Good, they need a moment to regroup as well.

Mystery looks toward the men they brought. They're shuffling nervously, some of them already in their trucks to retreat, the rest close to it. He turns back to Tony who is still talking. Probably the most words the man has ever used with him and he hasn't heard one of them.

"I'm okay," Mystery says. He's probably shouting judging from Tony's reaction. "Sorry, my ears are ringing a bit." He points to the men, "I need you to talk to them." Tony looks over to them, shocked. "They're freaked out right now, turning to scared. I need you to turn that to mad."

Tony's mouth moves again, knowing him he's saying something about how speeches really aren't his thing. "I was planning to do it myself, but the boom took more out of me than I expected. I really need a minute, and this has to be done now."

Spacer runs into the printing shop where families are meant to stop by and buy a souvenir wanted poster with dad's picture below the caption Wanted for Drunken Behavior or whatever makes them guffaw the most. He grabs the rifle from behind the press hand holds the scope to his eye. There's a note on it from the PI. "Nice boom boom but Alice Cooper ain't down for the count."

Spacer drops the note to the floor and climbs to the second window to set up.

"Yeah!" Jim says. The big guy isn't making a lot of sense, he's pretty much just giving speeches from old movies and Jim isn't sure what the business deal has to do with people never taking their freedom. But what he does know was that this business asshole just blew up the new amusement park before he could even check it out and Chet doesn't look too good and the big guy is handing out guns and that fucker is going to pay. "All right, fellas!" He yells, taking a Glock for himself. "Let's tear this jackass a new jackasshole!"

They run forward en mass but have to split to go around the battered limo. Jim goes right and stoops when he sees Chet. "Hey man, how bad is it?" He says. Chet says nothing, and Jim gently shakes him. He rolls over and Jim can see inside him, some organ that looks like a tentacle in a horror movie oozes out of his friend and settles in the dirt. Jim doesn't even realize the vomit is coming from him until it's already seeping into his friend's wounds. He turns away and wipes his mouth and then his eyes. "I won't let him get away with this," he says, reaching back to pat his friend. His hand lands in something soggy and he prays that it is his vomit.

"Oh my God!" Darren says, pulling up to his house and seeing the police tape stretched all around his property.

"All right, now very slowly, I need you to…" Dr. Landsin begins but stops when Darren bolts out of the van, rips through the tape and runs inside his home. Dr. Landsin sighs. Hostages are not as easy as modern television has led him to believe.

Dr. Landsin steps out of the van and walks up the steps of the porch. He glances inside but there are no signs of remaining police. Certainly, they would have Darren in their custody talking with him were they here.

He steps into the front room and his eye is drawn by the swinging door which leads to the kitchen. He walks toward it and presses it open slowly, Darren is nowhere to be seen. He must have glanced inside and then run somewhere else.

What IS there to be seen, however, is exactly the thing he'd hoped to find. On the far counter in a mess of flour bag, sugar, and various other baked good is a small phone in a pink case propped as if someone who didn't know how to bake had been watching a tutorial video.

Dr. Landsin crosses to the counter and scoops up the phone.

When he presses the home key to open it, it asks for his thumb print, or, to be more correct, the thumbprint of its owner who may or may not even be currently living. He curses to himself. He might be able to get around this, God knew the Scooter kid would be in it already reading her e-mails, but for him it might take a while.

He looks down at the counter and notices, in the middle of a pile of flour, one perfect finger print. He shrugs, pulls on a rubber glove from his pocket, presses his thumb into the print and then onto the phone.

It opens immediately. Dr. Landsin smiles. He'd have to remember that should he ever find himself in pretty much this exact position again. He couldn't really come up with any alternate situations in which this knowledge would be applicable.

"What are you doing?" Darren says, behind him.

He wheels, holding his squirt gun up on the man. "Only what I came here to do," he says. "Please don't try to stop me."

"Is that my daughter's phone?"

"Yes, I just need to send one Tweet from her account."

Darren stares at him for a moment, "How did you know that her phone would be here?"

"I wasn't sure what we would find here but this was the only teenage girl I knew about and I have a message that I need to go viral!"

The phone dings in Landsin's hand. Someone Quinn follows tweeted something that looks like cartoonish hieroglyphics.

"What are you trying to Tweet?"

"I need to send kids down to the amusement park where everything is going down." The phone dings again, another group of pictures.

"You're sacrificing children?" Darren asks.

"I'm not sacrificing anything. We just want dumb kids to Instagram this stuff so that everyone sees the big finale!"

Ding.

"You're turning dumb kids into war correspondents. They'll

225

be murdered!"

"I'm…" Ding "only…" ding "trying…" ding "Oh my God how do they put up with this? Is there not a moment's peace?"

"Let me see the phone," Darren says.

"What?"

"Just let me see it for a moment. If I don't give it back, you can always melt me with your juice stuff."

Dr. Landsin tosses the phone to him. "All right, but please give it back. I don't relish the idea of melting a fellow."

Darren scrolls through the phone for a moment and then looks at Dr. Landsin. "You're too late," he says.

"What?"

"The story's out. All of these Tweets are kids telling kids about the Wild West World thing." He tosses the phone back to Dr. Landsin who looks at the screen. "They did your job for you."

"How can you tell? Can you read these?"

"Not fluently but the preponderance of pistols and cowboy hats leads me to believe the cat is out of the bag." Darren shrugs. "You can try to write something in English if you want but they'll think you're a narc." He thinks for a moment and adds, "Or worse, a father."

"No," Dr. Landsin says, studying the screen. "Now that you point it out, I see what you mean."

"This is it," Jim says to himself as he presses his back to what is left of the town hall. The asshole who did Chet is staked out in the upper story of the print shop. All he has to do is run the half a block, break into the shop run up the stairs and plug him while he sits completely unaware. Sure, Cory just tried that, but that moron did not zig-zag.

Jim would have to be sure not to bring up the zig-zagging at Cory's service.

He readied himself, counted to three in his head and ran. "You got this," he told himself, making sure to zig. "You are the man," he said, zagging with all of his might. "Just keep up the…"

Something punches him in the chest hard enough to knock

him to the ground. A moment later there is the sound of a gun firing. Somebody must have hit him with something to keep him from getting shot. He should get out of the middle of the alley though, there could be another one coming.

He told his brain to tell his body to get up but there was a miscommunication at some point and he just kept lying there. He tried and failed again. A pain was starting to grow in his chest and it felt wet. What the hell did they hit him with?

He struggled to look at his chest and he saw a small fountain of blood bubbling from a hole where he was pretty sure his heart was. Son of a bitch, that's probably a bullet. Some asshole hit him with a bullet to keep him from getting shot. How dumb can you be?

"Sarah is going to laugh her balls off when she hears about this," Jim thinks aloud.

His vision starts to blur, and he closes his eyes. At least he thinks he does. But he can still see everything in the alley only now, for some reason, Sarah is here. "Babe, you can't be here," he says. "There's a nut with a gun."

"No there isn't," she says.

"No, Babe, swear to God, you got to get out of here."

"There's no man, Jim," Sarah says. She stoops and puts her hand on his heart. "It's just you and me." When she smiles at him, all of his pain flows away.

"God dammit!" Spacer yells, tossing aside the rifle. He'd suspected Mystery had hired some temp local help, but that guy proved it. He was a townie and pretty well known, well enough known that Spacer had seen him out and about.

"Fuck," Spacer says. A dozen guys that don't know their own asses he could have picked off from his nest without breaking a sweat. But not these guys. Ten to one they have no idea why they're even here or what they were going to do next. He's going non-lethal, he just hopes he lives to regret it.

He runs down the steps unholstering his twin colts and bursts onto the street firing everywhere but the hiding places the men had taken up that were so obvious in any other setting they'd be comical.

He'd never wasted ammo like this before, but it was doing it's job of keeping them out of ducking behind their barricades.

A light flashes to his left and he stops to see a girl who couldn't have been more that fifteen looking up from behind her phone. "The fuck?" Spacer says.

"God, sorry, I thought the flash was off," the teen says before running off to a different vantage point to film.

Spacer looks around the sidelines and sees dozens of young faces. "Holy God," he says.

The click of a rifle being cocked brings him back to the moment. He looks toward the sound, sees the barrel and instinctively sidesteps, raises his weapon and drops the shooter with one to the brain. He grimaces as the bullet the shooter got off tears through his right rotator cuff.

Another man stands, levels his own rifle and falls to the ground after taking a hit on the back of the head by a piano leg.

"You're a little late," Spacer says.

The PI shrugs. "I was dropping four others around the corner." He looks around and says, "Have you seen all the tweens with phones?"

"Yeah," Spacer says, wincing. "They helped me get this." He nods to the blood stain spreading over his sleeve.

"They're all over the place. This is way more publicity than a private dick needs, if you get my meaning."

"I get it, you're going to be a dick," Spacer says.

"I'm going to get out of here is what I'm going to do," he says. "I suggest you do the same. Cut our losses."

Spacer nods at him. "Yeah, just got a little more tidying up to do." The PI disappears into the whore house and Spacer does a little tidying math. There was five for the PI, he had four counting the big guy he got in the explosion. That leaves three of the hired muscle.

Spacer stumbles toward the saloon where he'd left his bag. He'd brought some medical stuff with him though what he can manage is limited.

He pushes through the batwings and finds his bag being

pilfered through by a gang of preteens. "Get the fuck out!" he yells.

They scamper like roaches and Spacer lurches to his bag. It's empty. "You took my rubbing alcohol?" he yells to no one. "You can get it at Walgreens for, like, sixty cents!"

He hobbles over to the bar hoping they were planning on mixing real hooch with fun-time sarsaparilla. He is not disappointed as he comes up with a new bottle of Johnny Walker Blue. "They take the Johnson and Johnson's and leave the Johnny Walker," he mutters to himself, pulling the cork out with his teeth. "God kids are dumb."

He takes a swig of the whiskey and then pours some on his shoulder. Tears stream from his eyes and he doesn't try to stop them. "Oh yeah, this is going to be surgery." He takes another bolt from the bottle and allows himself a minute to think. The kids didn't get any guns, at least not from the bag. Spacer knew this would be an easy target and never intended to use it. There were way too many entrances to hole up safely.

The only problem was, he'd dropped one gun when he was shot and fired the last bullet from the other gun into the shooter, so he also doesn't have a gun. The sound of a door slamming from the back echoes through the room. Clumsily, he works the sword from its scabbard with his left hand.

"So, what happens now?" Darren asks.

"My part in this is over," Dr. Landsin says. He gestures to the squirt gun. "I'm going to find a safe place to put this before it melts and takes whatever is surrounding it with it and disappear."

"And… I just…" Darren says.

"You do whatever. I have nothing to fear from you nor do my employers, so we wouldn't benefit from your death, if that's what you're driving at." Dr. Landsin unwraps a stick of gum and chews.

Darren nods at him.

"What the hell are you doing here?" a voice erupts from the porch?

Dr. Landsin looks at Darren who shrugs and they make their

way toward the commotion, Dr. Landsin and his squirt gun in the lead.

"Mmm hmm frrrlll nnn-nnn-nnn," another voice says.

"I don't speak lockjaw!" the first voice growls.

Dr. Landsin peers out onto the porch to see one of the biker thugs talking with another man who could be a biker thug except that he had extensive metal work apparently clamping his jaws together. Metal Mouth sees Dr. Landsin staring and lunges for the door.

The other biker tries to stop him but MM slams into the door before Dr. Landsin can latch it and he and Darren fall backward into the front room.

"Dammit Clint!" the biker yells.

Dr. Landsin tries to get up but Darren grabs him by the bicep. He turns to look at the man and sees a line of purple liquid streaked across his face. "Oh, good Christ!" Dr. Landsin says.

"Mother of God!" Rodrigo says, stepping into the front room and seeing Darren's face.

"What?" Clint says through his clenched teeth.

"Help me get him to a bath," Dr. Landsin yells, hooking an arm under Darren's armpit.

Rodrigo grabs the other side and the two hoist him up and carry him to the stairs.

"What?" Clint says.

"You just melted his fucking face, Dickhead!" Rodrigo yells. They disappear up the stairs and Clint watches them go. If his life has taught him anything it's when to cut and run. He notices the squirt gun lying where the doctor left it. Whatever was inside it seemed like something he might find useful. He grabs the gun, stashes it in the compartment beneath the saddle of his bike, and tears ass away from there.

"Bend over," Dr. Landsin says as they dump Darren into the tub of his master bath. "We need to mitigate we don't want that to flow anywhere else." He reaches up and turns on the shower, angling it toward the back of Darren's head as he crouches on all fours in the tub. "Just let the water do its work."

"Will this… save me?" Darren asks.

"To be honest, I have no idea how much damage has already been done," Dr. Landsin says.

"Doc, he needs an ambulance and I can't be involved in all of that," Rodrigo says.

Dr. Landsin nods and Rodrigo runs out of the room. "I…" Dr. Landsin says, his voice cracking. "I'm afraid I can't either." He takes a deep breath. "To the world I am a dead man and the next phase depends heavily upon the world continuing to think this." He stands and looks pityingly down at the trembling man. "I'll call for the ambulance before I go. But I'm afraid that's all I'll be able to do."

Darren nods and listens as the footsteps walk away. For a long time, he has no idea how long, he stays there, crouched in the shower, feeling no pain. Maybe he got into the shower quickly enough. There is the sound of the front door opening and Quinn calls out, "Mom, Dad, are you guys home?"

He smiles at the sound of the voice he thought he might never hear again. The tears fall from his eyes and he is ready to call out to her when the burning begins.

The man steps into the saloon, eyes wide and hands shaking. He stops when Spacer holds the blade of the sword just under his chin. "Drop it," Spacer says, and the sound of his gun clattering to the floor echoes around the empty room.

The man turns slowly and faces Spacer. "Please," he says. "I just want to go home to my wife. I didn't sign on for this."

Spacer glares at him. "Look, this is how we're going to play this…"

There's an explosion behind him and the man crumples to the floor, blood pooling out of the exit wound in the back of his head. Spacer turns. "Shelly?"

"I got your message. The maître' dee asked me to pass along his apologies for doubting you," she says, stowing her pistol in her shoulder holster.

"You didn't have to do that," Spacer says. "He was just a guy trying to get home."

"Yeah?" Shelly asks. She walks over to the body, flips it over with her foot and takes the derringer out of the back of his belt. "You're getting dull on me, Sharpe," she says, tossing him the tiny gun.

"It doesn't mean he was going to use it," Spacer says.

Shelly scoops the man's Glock up from where he dropped it, checks the magazine and offers it to Spacer. "You aren't great with a sword even when you can use your right hand, trade me."

Spacer lays the sword on the bar and works the sheath off his wounded shoulder. He puts that next to the blade and takes the gun from her. "I was trying to go non-lethal," he says.

"How much were you bleeding before making that call?" Shelly asks.

Spacer looks at his shoulder and then back at his wife. "All right, substantially less," he admits. "But that doesn't make it a bad idea necessarily."

Shelly grabs him and kisses him hard. He whimpers through the pain in his shoulder but doesn't try to stop her. At last she breaks the kiss and says, "Babe, you still haven't lost your faith in humanity and that's why I love you. For today though, we're through playing."

"There's two more hired guys, can we take them out my way?"

"Even if there were two more left I would not agree with that," Shelly says, patting him on the cheek.

"You've already taken them out."

"They prefer the term neutralized," Shelly says.

"I think they're a little beyond having preferences of any sort," Spacer says.

"They'd prefer it if they could," Shelly says. "Now I need your head in the game, we..." Shelly stops and points toward the door. Mystery stands there, perfectly still. They both raise their weapons and smoke erupts from his feet, hiding him instantly. They both fire a round into the smoke but it's obvious he isn't there.

They run through the door and look both ways, nothing. Shelly turns to Spacer, shrugs and says, "Fucker really is a magician."

A light flashes from across the road and the same fifteen year old stands there with her phone. "FML, what is with this flash?" she says.

Shelly takes the hat off of Spacer's head and frisbees it into the girl's face.

"Ow, hey, bitch!" the girl yells.

Shelly holds up her gun so that the girl can see it.

"Okay, use your words, you know? God!" the girl says, walking away.

"Who the hell invited the preschoolers?" Shelly asks.

"I thought the game was on." "It got preempted, there's some shit going on in a cowboy park on the NC coast." "Huh?" "Check it out, it's crazy."

Rachel steps into her apartment and drops the grocery bag onto the table. It had been a good day on the site but, as always, a good day with Habitat for Humanity means an evening of sore muscles for the helpers.

It's a kind of sore that Rachel looks forward to.

Ordinarily, she'd treat herself to a long, luxurious bath but she's been meaning to binge that Netflix thing where Stephen Spielberg's kids fight all of Stephen King's monsters or something like that. Everyone has been raving for months.

She reaches into her bag, pulls out her pinot grigio and digs a corkscrew and a spoon out of a drawer. She thinks for a moment about using a glass but, who is she kidding, there's not going to be anything to save and why dirty something that she doesn't need to. She takes the bottle, a carton of Starbucks ice cream and the utensils into the living room and flops onto the couch.

She turns on the tv and almost changes the input from the cable box to the roku when she realizes she's seeing news footage of something big with a lot of police presence. "Oh God, not another school shooting," she says.

But it isn't that, for one thing, it's most certainly not happening at a school. There's an actual fire and a mention of shots fired. So it's a shooting of some sort. Rachel cranks the volume in time to hear an announcer say, "And, yes, we now have confirmation of the reports that well-known Vegas magician Mystery is in some way involved."

"Oh my God," Rachel mutters as a picture of her former boss pops onto the screen. She opens the drawer of one of her end tables and takes out a thick envelope sensing that the opportune time may soon be upon her.

Mystery has to give Jim credit, God rest his soul. He and his boys had not only helped create enough of a story to keep the whirly birds flying above but they've bought him and Tony enough time to not only set up their last surprise for the spies but also to work out the intricacies of the park's underground tunnel system allowing him a last disappearance illusion. It wasn't necessary, but it is still nice.

He pulls himself up another rung and looks around, the spies still haven't seen him and he is almost to the top of the water tower.

He is also a little surprised at how quickly he's taken to his deafness. Focus has never been an issue for him but now, with the entire world shut out from him save that which he is seeing and touching, distraction is all but impossible. A small part of him grieves the fact that he will not have long to explore this new facet of existence.

At the last rung from the top, he turns and glares at the she-spy, willing her to look at him. If he were a lesser man he might assume that he's been granted telepathic abilities through the loss of one of his senses, but he is the fooler, not the fool. But for what ever reason, she turns toward him and they lock eyes.

"He's on the tower," Shelly says.

"Huh," Spacer says, following her stare. "He cornered himself without our chasing him? I'm surprised he didn't just paint, 'Really guys, I totally swear, this is not a trap,' right up on the tower."

"Let's do this," Shelly says, running toward the tower.

"Really?" Spacer says, hurrying to catch up. "You're just going to drop yourself right into his web? Weren't you just picking on me for going dull?"

Shelly shakes her head and increases her speed. It takes everything Spacer has to keep pace with her. "He thinks he's trapping us. He's never seen what the two of us can do together."

"I have…" Spacer says, gasping between words. "…a retort to that…" gasp, "but I'll have to give it to you later."

Shelly cuts around a corner with Spacer immediately on her heels. She bolts toward the ladder with Spacer right behind her. She flies sideways and slams into the large metal disc with Spacer only narrowly avoiding slamming right on top of her.

"Ow, God!" Spacers says, his shoulder screaming at him.

"What the hell?" Shelly says.

Spacer looks at the Glock now pinning the hand he was holding it in to the metal. "I think this is a magnet," he says, pulling his hand out from under the gun threating to crush every bone inside it. It pulls free at last. "A very powerful magnet."

"I guess he wants straight fisticuffs," Shelly says, worming out from under the sword. She drops to the ground weaponless. Spacer is still stuck to the magnet, squirming. "Come on, Babe, what are you packing under that poncho?"

"Wouldn't you like to know," Spacer says.

"I do know, I married it. But what else you got that's keeping you penned to the magnet."

"It's a big, honking belt buckle."

"Why are you wearing a big, honking belt buckle?"

"It fit the milieu."

"Well, take it off."

"That's what I'm trying to do! I'm working with one wing, remember?"

Shelly looks up at the water tower and then back at Spacer. "I got to go, whatever he's got planned for us up there he's just getting more and more time to perfect it."

"What? What about seeing what the two of us can do

together?" Spacer says.

"You'll catch up, then we'll kick his ass." Shelly jumps onto the ladder and climbs as if she'd been raised in the big top.

Finally, Spacer pops the buckle, unhooks it from his belt and slides to the ground. He looks up the ladder. Shelly's almost to the top already and he's going to be climbing one handed. He just hopes she can hold out until he gets there.

He pulls himself up onto the first rung and reaches up for the next when he is thrown backwards and lands five feet away from the ladder.

Shelly springs onto the foot and a half wide platform running the circumference of the tower. She looks around but there is no sign of the magician. She looks up just in time to jump out of the way of him dropping from the top of the reservoir.

Spacer looks up, instinctively holding up a hand to block the glare of the sun. He doesn't need to do this, the shadow of the man in front of him has completely blocked it out for him. It's the big guy who arrived in the limo with Mystery only now he is wearing ridiculous plastic shades and a Yankees cap. He was wondering when that guy was going to make an appearance.

"Can't let you go up there," the man says. "Private party."

"Well, you see, that's a problem because my wife is up there, and we never attend these sort of functions alone."

The guy shrugs. "You're not on the list."

Spacer glances at the magnet, their stuff is still stuck to it which means it is still on which means that this guy doesn't have any weapons either. No metal ones at any rate. More and more Spacer is growing to learn the advantage of a good piano leg.

"Well, I mean to go up there," Spacer says.

"I don't intend to allow that," the man says.

"Then I guess there's only one way of settling this," Spacer says.

The man cracks his knuckles. "You sure you're up to it? You aren't exactly in peak condition."

"You I could take with one functioning toe," Spacer says.

The man shrugs, "Gimme your best toe."

She's fast, as advertised, but Mystery has always been fast too. With some of his riskier illusions, his speed has been the only thing keeping him alive.

She drops her right shoulder just a fraction of an inch, she's going to throw a left. Mystery dodges the punch and wonders if his hearing self would ever have noticed that. She recovers from the miss and brings her right foot up in a roundhouse kick which would have taken his head had he not seen her cock her hip almost imperceptibly and readied himself for it.

He avoids the kick and while she's trying to steal a glance to see what's become of her partner, he strikes. She moves to block it but he makes enough contact to unbalance her both physically and mentally.

He smiles. He thought he might enjoy this part of the plan but had no idea he'd like it this much.

"Okay, I see you're familiar with that one too," the spy says, picking himself out of the dirt with his good left arm.

Tony sighs. He was okay with taking on one of them when he thought it would be a fair fight, but this feels more like kicking a puppy. His jaw does hurt a bit from the one square shot the guy got in but it doesn't warrant this level of pounding.

The spy turns on him, all of the humor he'd been using as a mask drops away and Tony sees his true opponent for the first time. "I'll be going up that ladder," the man says.

Tony nods at him, "We'll see," he says.

"Shit, he's good," Shelly thinks. "And where the hell is Spacer."

She throws two rights and a kick which he easily avoids. Is it possible that she's telegraphing in some way?

He throws a clumsy right and leaves himself wide open to a

punch which Shelly is more than happy to provide. He clutches his stomach and stumbles back to the rails just as a news copter flies over head.

"Why would he do that?" she says aloud. It hits her. "He's a showman, he's playing to the cameras."

She sees him flip over the rail and dives for him, catching his wrist and hooking her foot around one of the rail supports to keep him from dragging her over as well.

"I don't know what your plan is, but you aren't using me for a patsy," she hisses.

Mystery flicks his wrist and a deck of loose cards slides into his palm. "You really think this is a good time for gin rummy?" Shelly asks, straining against his weight."

Mystery shuffles the cards with one hand. He looks at her fingers, tight around his wrist, and says, "I haven't found a moment yet which wasn't enhanced by a good hand."

Spacer spits a wad of blood and most of a tooth onto the ground. He has to admit the big man has been a formidable opponent. Typically, when he takes a few lumps and learns someone's technique, they topple fairly easily. This guy has taken most of what Spacer has and is still on his feet. Without the ladder for support that might not be the case but on his feet is on his feet.

The big guy spits his own wad of gore and looks at Spacer through one broken lens of his plastic shades. The cap was lost under the tower several punches ago. "You're good," the man says. "Better than I suspected."

"You're not a slouch yourself."

"I suppose we're about to find out whether or not you get up that ladder."

"Looks that way," Spacer says.

"You think you could give me, like, one more minute?" the guy asks.

Spacer's shoulder screams it's vote for one more minute of rest, overruling any other instinct. "Yeah," he says at last. "We can do one more minute."

Shelly watches the man shuffle the cards around with one hand. She can't figure out why he would bring cards to a fight like this but more and more she doesn't really care. She just wants to watch the cards flow in and out of each other.

"Are your arms growing tired, Mrs. Sharpe?" Mystery asks her from a million miles away at the end of her arm.

"I could do this all day," she says, her voice sounds like she imagines it would sound if she could talk under water.

Mystery says nothing. He stops shuffling the cards and bends the deck so that it will shoot, all fifty-two cards, right into her face. She turns away from the onslaught but does not let go until she turns back to see the man holding a gun just inches from her face.

In the sudden shock she screams and releases him to plummet to his death in the full gaze of the news copters cameras.

"All right," Spacer says. "It's time we do this." He takes a step toward the man but Shelly's scream draws his attention to the top of the tower from which a figure is falling.

"No!" he screams but his scream is cut short when the man pounces on him and clamps two vice-like hands around his throat.

"Where is the gun?" Shelly screams as she watches the man fall with two obviously empty hands and no weapon plummeting with him. "I know there was a gun!"

She runs to the ladder and jumps onto it.

Spacer bats at the man's hands with his good left but it has no effect. He kicks backward limply but the man easily evades his kick. He looks up and sees his salvation sliding down the ladder with her feet on the outside railing, using it like a fireman does a pole.

She lands but without even seeing him she runs to the other side of the tower to where the body lies.

"She left me," Spacer thinks.

Shelly looks at the crumpled remains of Mystery. He's landed on the very edge of the magnet, practically breaking himself in half. It had to be a painful way to go. More importantly to her though, there is no gun. If it existed, it would be stuck to the magnet like theirs but only their arsenal is there. Her eyes had lied to her and, because of it, a man had died.

The darkness in Spacer's field of vision was almost complete. Soon he would pass out of consciousness and then out of life all together. And it would all happen just feet away from his partner.

The vice around his throat disappears and Spacer crumples to the ground. He watches the big man limp to where his hat lay on the ground. The man grabs it and plants it unceremoniously on his head. He walks back to Spacer and does his best to straighten his ripped and bloody sport coat. "I'm sorry to do that," he says. "It was a cheap shot and a fighter like you deserves better." He clears his throat, shrugs and says, "I just didn't have a lot left in the engine and I couldn't have you going up there until the plan was carried out."

Spacer stares at him but says nothing. He isn't sure he's capable of speech.

"Have a pleasant rest of your day," the man says. He turns and walks away.

Spacer watches him go and croaks as loudly as he can, "Yankees suck!"

Without turning the man holds up a fist in solidarity. "Preach!" he says, before disappearing around an outhouse.

Spacer pulls himself to his feet and hobbles over to Shelly.

"There wasn't a gun," she says, turning to face him. He looks into her face, the same face he coveted throughout high school, dreamed of throughout training and genuinely loved for the last five years and, for the first time in all those years, noticed some lines just at the corner of her eyes. How long had those been there?

Spacer puts an arm around his wife and they make their way

out of the park together.

In a small apartment in a Nevada town just outside of Vegas, a former magician's manager opens a thick envelope.

The shrill alarm of the IV machine screeches a foot or so from Quinn's head. She doesn't even notice. She's lost count of how many times she's heard it the past three weeks staying day in and day out in her comatose father's hospital room. The nurse will come in at some point and silence it.

She asks her mother to give her love to Scout and reminds them to be careful in that Miami sun and then closes her text app. She tosses her phone into her purse and forgets about it. She'll check it again in a day or so to see if her mom has sent her an update or if she's reconsidering the divorce. She doesn't hold out a lot of hope with regard to that.

Her father moans. He does that occasionally despite the fact that he hasn't been conscious since she found him in a pool of blood and shower water. She wonders how or even if he is healing, his bandages cover his face and make it impossible to know.

They've had some visitors over the past few weeks, the minister of the church in which they are technically members, a few CPA friends he used to get lunch with and several members of the press wanting to know if his injuries are in anyway related to the incident they've already named Cowboygate.

Quinn is very quick to suggest to those good folks just exactly what they are welcome to do with their questions and, should they be so inclined, they could chase the questions with the fucking microphones they keep shoving in her face.

The Sharpes have not been among the well-wishers, though the day after her dad was admitted an obnoxiously ostentatious flower arrangement was delivered to them anonymously. Quinn sent it away. It seemed in poor taste to send flowers to a man with no nose.

Between visitors Quinn keeps herself busy with her thoughts. There's a tv mounted near the ceiling which she keeps on almost around the clock for company, but she rarely watches anything on it. It's on right now but she doesn't know which channel.

But she doesn't mind. Lately she's found that she has quite a few thoughts to deal with and plenty of time to devote to the thinking.

Gerry counts to ten, slowly opens his car door and steps out. He's glad there's no one else in the parking lot. He zips his hoodie and jams his hands deeply into the pockets. He wants to put the hood up as well but he's aware that would just make him look stupid.

He walks slowly toward the diner door, looking intently at his shoes and nothing else until he steps up onto the stoop, reaches for the door and it doesn't open. He looks up at last to see Sarah standing just behind the glass door. She locks eyes with him, slowly shakes her head and flips the open sign to closed.

Gerry looks in the window. Maybe half a dozen diners are sitting in the booths and at the counter. Some happily shoving eggs into their faces, others glued to the drama playing out at the door.

Gerry nods at her, turns around and goes back to his car.

Sarah doesn't flip the sign back to open or unlock the door until his car has been out of sight for a full minute.

Rose glares at the guy with the wired jaw sitting at her bar sucking beer through a straw. She can't recall his name, just that, at one point, he was one of Pete's boys. For that reason alone, she'd served him. She'd hoped it'd be just the one and done but he is working on beer number four and has that settling in look about him.

She doesn't like the smell of him.

She sent her nephew out to see if he could find out this guy's standing with Pete's club. Assuming he is on the outs, she has another club she'll be happy to put him together with if he doesn't pay quietly and evacuate. It is currently sitting on a shelf just below her bar.

"Jeeze, Aunt Rose!" Teddy says, running in through the front door.

"Teddy! What's the word?" Rose calls.

"Huh? Oh, yeah," he glances briefly at metal mouth, "it's what we thought." Rose puts her meaty hand on the handle of the club, but Teddy stops her with his next question, "But what happened to the parking lot?"

She looks up at her nephew and raises an eyebrow. "How do you mean?"

"There's a big hole in it."

"What?" Rose walks out from behind her bar, most of the patrons, metal mouth included, fall in behind her.

She leads them outside and stops, gaping at the steaming pit that use to be her crip-spot. "The hell?" she says.

"My bike!" she hears from her, except that it's muffled, like maybe the speaker couldn't open his mouth.

She turns on metal mouth and says, "You were parked here?"

He lets out a string of muffled sounds that she can't make out and they both step up to the hole. They look in to see what could only be described as the melted remains of a Harley floating in a purple puddle of goo that was still eating its way through the very earth.

"MY BIKE!" metal mouth yells again.

"Yeah, and my parking lot," Rose says. Her voice is low, and she can see that it has had the desired effect. "What exactly were you carrying?"

Metal mouth shakes his head and feigns stupid. Probably the first time in his life that he's ever had to pretend. She slaps her hand on the back of his neck and digs her fingers in deep. "What say you and I step into my office and discuss just how it is that we make this right?"

Spacer flips a paper bag open with his left hand and sets it on the counter. He's getting good at that. Even after the surgery gives him back the use of his right arm he thinks he'll break it out from time to time as a sort of parlor trick.

"Whatever have you done to yourself?" Mrs. Brown asks. She's a regular of theirs. A woman easily into her eighties who comes in every Wednesday to peruse their horror section and she's always the first in line for tickets when they do a reading of Dracula in the theater in the back every Halloween.

"I don't know if you want to hear it," Spacer says with a wink. "It's a story filled with intrigue, risk and ingénues."

"Oh, that sounds right up my alley," she says with a small squeal of excitement.

Spacer shakes his head. "A fella has to maintain some degree of mys..." he stops himself when he realizes he'd almost said mystery. He clears his throat and says, "mystique."

"Oh, I can hardly stand it. At least give me a hint!"

"All right, it involves a canyon," Spacer says.

"On a moonless, foggy night?" Mrs. Brown asks.

"Sure."

Again, she squeals, this time clapping her hands as she does so.

Spacer picks up the copy of Nandy Ekle's One Murderous Week she'd just purchased and drops it into the waiting bag. "Now you make sure you aren't all alone in the house while you're reading this," he says.

"Oh, I can't wait to get my spine tingled," she says. "At my age that's almost the only tingle I ever get." Now it is she who tips Spacer a wink has she collects her bag and heads for the door.

Spacer grabs an umbrella and walks around the counter, meeting her before she can get outside. "Where are you parked, Mrs. Brown? I want to make sure you get there all right in this downpour."

"Such a gentleman," she says, holding the door open so that he can proceed her with the umbrella in his good left hand. "I'm just partway down the block."

Spacer settles her into her Mazda and nods goodbye. When he gets back into the shop he throws the bolt and says, "I'm calling it for today. No one else is going to be coming out in this."

"Sure," Shelly says. She's standing in front of the flat screen they typically use to promote the theater, but she's turned it to one of the news stations and is cranking the volume.

The shot is clearly one done by one of the kids on their

cellphones and it tracks Mystery's plummet to his death remarkably well. Whichever sociopath in the making shot it, their hand did not tremble, nor did they turn away. The footage cuts just before impact and they never show the man's mangled corpse. They were the news, they had their standards. Mangled corpses were what their website was for.

"Once again that is the Vegas stage magician Mystery falling to his demise at the conclusion of what is now known as Cowboygate," an anchor says as they cut back to her.

"But why was he there and who were the, pardon the pun, Mysterious shooters." Both anchors cackle at her wit and wisdom.

"Isn't it amazing, Brad, that not one single picture of the literally thousands taken got a clear shot of any of their faces? None of the video either!"

"Why do you think that is, Barbara?" Brad asks.

"I don't know!" Barbra says, throwing up her hands in defeat.

"Because, for its many flaws, The Agency is efficient in some areas," Shelly mutters.

"Well, one thing that we know for sure is that we'll all be talking about this for a very long time," Brad says, and Shelly kills the feed.

"Can I ask you something?" Spacer says.

"I guess."

"We won this one, right?"

"Huh?" Shelly says, turning to him.

"This... adventure, quest, mission, whatever you want to call it, did we win it?" Spacer says.

"Yeah, we won it."

"Are we sure?"

"We're alive, he isn't. Being the only one alive at the end is winning," Shelly says turning away from him.

"Yeah," Spacer says, tapping his fingers against his thigh. "I just wish I could get on board with that."

Rachel rings the doorbell and steps back. She remembers the last time she was here, that night when she got this damned envelope. She didn't know what to do with it then and she certainly doesn't now.

The door opens and the kid... what was his name? Jason! Jason stands in the doorway. "Oh hi!" Jason says. "Welcome to... well, your place, I guess."

"You knew about this?" Rachel asks.

Jason nods. "There's not a lot about Mystery I don't know." He thinks for a moment, shrugs and says, "Actually, at this point there is absolutely nothing I don't know about Mystery."

Rachel arches an eyebrow at him. She'd never fully understood his and Mystery's relationship, but she was certain that there was absolutely no one in the world that he would entrust with all of his secrets. Also, why was he speaking in the present tense. Was it possible that no one had told him AND that he'd missed the round the clock coverage for the last three weeks? Was she going to have to be the one to tell him? But, if he didn't know about Mystery then how would he know about her?

"Come on in," he says, standing to the side so that she can enter.

Rachel looks down at her bags which she'd set down just before ringing the bell. "Oh, right," Jason says. "Um, you can just drag them in here for now, I'll show you your room after."

"How chivalrous," Rachel mutters, hefting her bags and dropping them in the hall just inside the door. "Wait, after what?"

"Oh, I can't tell you that," Jason says. He starts off down the hallway and waves for her to follow.

She takes a few tentative steps, looking around and says, "It was much more crowded the last time I was here."

"Huh? Oh yeah, the heavies. We don't need them anymore, that was all phase one."

"Phase one of what?"

"Come on!"

Jason practically runs down the hall to Mystery's old office and lets himself inside.

Rachel steps in behind him and looks around. In a weird way it's claustrophobically filled with emptiness. "I've only been in here once before," she says. "And it was at his request."

"It's at his request now, too," Jason says.

"Hmm?" Rachel says, then looks at the envelope still in her hand. "Ah, yes, I suppose so."

"No," Jason says. "I mean, yeah, but, no."

"I'm sorry, I don't understand," Rachel says.

Jason waves her off with a flap of his hand. "It's cool, you will." He takes a deep breath and say, "Okay, before we go any further, I need to restate what was said in the envelope. You have full ownership of the business, the theater and the estate including the house and the grounds with the exception of these two rooms. These are by invitation only. Do you agree?"

"What two rooms? You mean the office and the bathroom?"

"Oh," Jason says, staring at the door to the bathroom. "Um... three rooms." He smiles sheepishly. "Okay, I guess the bathroom wasn't actually specified but, A: you'd have to come through the office anyway to get to it which would require permission and, B: you, just, you really don't want to go in there. I have... stuff in there, I don't think you..."

"Fine, thank you, I really don't want to hear the end of that sentence. I'll avoid that bathroom."

"Oh, good, I...I owe you on that."

"What's the other room beside the office and bathroom?"

"I need to hear you say that you agree to the terms."

"Fine, I agree, what's the room?"

"Yay!" Jason says. He digs in his pockets and produces a ring of keys. He unlocks the center drawer of Mystery's desk and slides it open. He selects a second key, slides back a false panel in the bottom of the drawer and sticks the key into a slot it reveals. When he turns this, a bookshelf slides away revealing a hidden room.

"Seriously? A bookcase?" Rachel says.

"Isn't it awesome?"

"At least there aren't bat poles."

"I wanted them but Mysetery said that the digging would take 'unnecessary time.'" He holds up his fingers in air quotes as he says this last.

He gestures to the room and says, "Ladies first."

"No, I'm very okay with rudeness this time," Rachel says.

Jason shrugs and walks into the room. Rachel follows closely behind him. It's frigid inside and there is a constant hum coming from what looks like rows and rows of server towers. "You spend a lot of time in here?" Rachel asks.

"Yeah, I…" he turns and sees her shivering. "Oh, shoot, I forget that a lot of people aren't used to it. Tell you what, I'll run and grab you a sweater or something but first I want to show you phase two."

"I thought this was phase two,' Rachel says.

Jason looks around at all of the computers. "Oh, well, kind of but not… ah heck, I can't say, you've just got to see!" He breaks away and runs the length of the room cutting right just before he hits the wall and disappearing behind a row of servers.

Rachel walks quickly after him, yelling to him, "Look, Jason, it's very nice of you to offer to get me a sweater but I really doubt that I'll be staying very long. Whatever this phase two is, I'm sure we'll be able to talk better about it…" she turns the corner and freezes in place.

"Hello, Rachel," a very familiar voice says.

"What?"

"Why, Rachel," Mystery says, taking her hand. "You look as if you've seen a ghost."

ACKNOWLEDGEMENTS

To anyone who has never read a book, it may come as a surprise that these things are not a one man show. In fact, a lot of hands went in to making this book that you are holding right now.[1] If you think there's a chance that you might be mentioned, you'll probably skim this portion at least looking for your name. For the rest of you, you've no doubt already tossed this book to your bookaroo[2] and are busily making jam for those you love. Which is a darned shame because the people mentioned herein are all responsible for the book that you just finished[3] and it seems a shame that you don't know them.

So, stick with me for a few more paragraphs and I'll do my best to make it worth your while.

First off, I must thank Suzanne Korb. Without her and Ink Hills this book would still be an unfinished word file on my hard drive. I'd written it for NaNoWriMo[4] and always thought that it might have potential but it was Suz who convinced me to dust it off, polish it up and give it that thing that all books need... the last couple of chapters.

I need to thank the family. I grew up in a home surrounded by

---

[1] I mean that literally. We only allowed these words to be printed on the finest materials and, as everyone knows, hand pulp makes for the best paper. There are a lot of folks named stubby now for your reading pleasure. But don't worry they were all bad. *If you're reading the E-book, twice as many.

[2] You're specially bred kangaroo who keeps your home library in her pouch which I'm so certain everyone already has that I'm questioning the need for this footnote.

[3] If you hated it, it was their fault entirely. Anything you liked, that was all me.

[4] Look it up. What? I got to do everything for you?

both books and madness[5]. My parents were never without a book and they showed me their value simply by reading. My brother and sisters are book lovers and insane, I learned a lot about personality from each of them. And now I have two nephews and a niece who are nothing but personality. I am learning every day.

I always have to thank my Ink Slingers. When you're being told you aren't what anyone in the industry is looking for day in and day out, the opportunity to have a group of people tell you they like your stuff and then help you to improve it is a God send. Although we haven't spoken for a while, I carry each of you with me every day.

I want to thank Kasey who jumped in and volunteered to help polish my little diamond in the rough.[6] I can't thank you enough for jumping in.

Lastly, I want to thank you, the reader.[7] These words only come to life when your eyes cross over them. Without you I would be screaming into the abyss.[8]

---

[5] The good kind of madness, not the people eating kind of madness.

[6] I did warn you I was a writer when we met.

[7] Ha! And you thought you weren't going to get a mention.

[8] This thank you goes triple for those of you who post a review. In case you're looking to up your thank you quotient.

ABOUT THE AUTHOR

Ryan Hunter is the kind of person who has a hard time taking the last piece of pizza even if he's alone in the house and he bought the pizza just for himself.

You probably wouldn't seek him out at a party but, if you bumped into him, he'd try to make some casual conversation. Whether or not you would enjoy the convo depends heavily upon your fondness for puns.

The good news though, is that he's channeled all of this madness into some very interesting characters who, against all odds, come across as terribly likable.

He started his writing career in his teens hammering out scripts for a local community theater. Later, when he began writing fiction, his early theatrical work stayed with him and he wrote many dialogue heavy books, including Mr. & Ms. a novel written entirely in dialogue. His work also includes Werehouse, Ted & Stuff and his series of short stories available only in e-book form called After Sahara.

Ryan lives in Hayesville, North Carolina, he is still involved in his community theater and in his spare time he very much enjoys drinking wine and holding lengthy debates with his dog Hope.

One day he plans to win one of those debates.

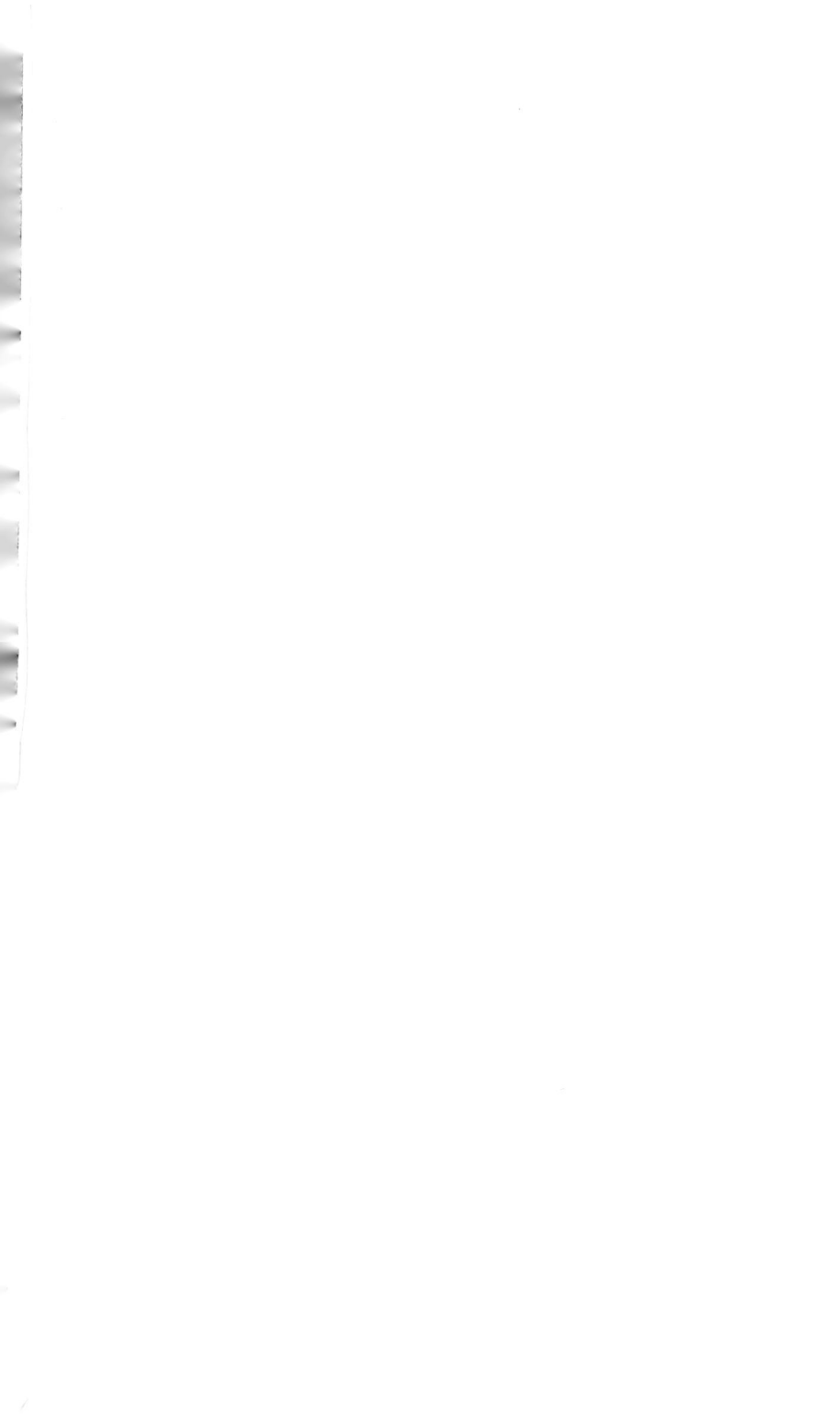

Printed in Great
Britain
by Amazon